Life
&
Death

by

Céleste Perrino-Walker

Farenorth Press
Toussaint, Vermont Series: Book 1

Farenorth Press
P.O. Box 1005
Rutland, VT 05701

Amazing Grace, lyrics by John Newton 1779 (Public Domain)
http://memory.loc.gov/diglib/ihas/html/grace/grace-timeline.html

La Bastringue, traditional, https://thesession.org/tunes/3052

O Come, O Come Emmanuel, Latin, c. 12th century; Ancient Antiphons (Latin), versified in 18th century
http://www.hymnary.org/text/o_come_o_come_emmanuel_and_ransom

Except for God, of course, all characters, names, corporations, institutions, organizations, events, or locales in this novel are a product of the author's overworked imagination or, if real, used fictitiously. Any resemblance to real people, places, or things, living or dead, is a product of yours.

worldwide. www.zondervan.com The "NIV" and "New International Version" are trademarks registered in the United States Patent and Trademark Office by Biblica, Inc.™
First Edition

Cover Design by Wicked Book Covers, www.wickedbookcovers.com

ISBN-10: 0-9908361-5-0
ISBN-13: 978-0-9908361-5-5

For

F

Because best friends come and go, but a sister is forever.
Toi et moi, ça ne change pas.

And for all the women (the many I know and the many I don't know) who
have lost their spouses too soon.

And for French-Canadians on both sides of the Québec border for being
passionate about your heritage, particularly your language.
Je me souviens.

"Fiction reveals truth that reality obscures."
—Ralph Waldo Emerson

"Bíonn dhá insint ar scéal agus dhá leagan déag ar amhrán."
(There are two versions to a story and twelve arrangements to a song.)

Wait! Don't skip this part. Seriously.
Important information ahead.

Usually when foreign words are written, they are italicized to indicate their foreign origin. I didn't do that when I wrote the French in this book because I felt that it made a distinction between the two languages that doesn't exist in reality where this story takes place. I wanted the language to flow seamlessly between English and French the same way Franglais (that unique dance between French and English that takes place on the border of Québec and the United States) does in real life. Because I'm also a pragmatist and know what it feels like to be reading a book and come across foreign words I don't understand with no explanation, I've also included a section at the end with translations for all the French I used and a pronunciation guide so it will all be in one place, but I footnoted it as well for your reading convenience.

The "Toussaint, Vermont" books all take place in the fictional town of Toussaint, Vermont, which lies so close to the shores of Lake Champlain and the border of Canada that if it was closer to either it would fall in or need to change citizenship. While the physical place does exist as a position on the map and my childhood home is there, the fictional place lives only in my imagination. I was a child with a rich inner life, and it's where I grew up.

There is no Native American tribe called Bieneki. It was created so as not to offend any particular tribe by the creation of various fictitious aspects ascribed to them. For more information about other real or imagined elements, see the "Acknowledgments" at the end.

This book is the first in my Toussaint, Vermont series. As planned, each will feature a separate character you will have met in a previous book, though they will all take place in the same town, and you'll bump into many characters with whom you're already familiar. Recipes from this book (and other Farenorth Press books) will be available in the fun *Farenorth Press Community Cookbook Project* compiled by Marise, assisted by Emerson, and coming out soon. If you are signed up for my Reader's Group (cperrinowalker.com/readers-group-signup.html), you'll receive a complimentary copy as a "thank you for your interest in my work" perk as soon as (or maybe even before) it's released to the general public.

Speaking of which, if you like this book (or my work in general) and want to know when my new releases are coming out, as well as be automatically entered in any drawings I hold for freebies and goodies, sign up for my Reader's Group on any page of my website (cperrinowalker.com) or click the link above. I only send out news every couple of months when I'm about to release a new book, and I strive to send you the "there is too much to explain; let me sum up" version. I don't have time to clutter up your Inbox with chatter, or I wouldn't get any books written.

Now, with no further ado, you may proceed.

Chapter One

No one was surprised it happened, or so they claimed. I heard old Angelique[1] Marten, who had lived in Toussaint,[2] Vermont, all her life and ran the small town grocery, said she was only surprised it hadn't happened sooner. The way that trailer park was situated, with those mobile homes lined up like bowling pins only yards from a long stretch of highway, it was just a matter of time till some fool got sleepy at the wheel. The miracle of it was that out of ten mobile homes he only took out half of one. And a dog house. The dog wasn't in it at the time.

Everyone agreed it could have been worse, with the exception of Theresa and Mimi Bang. They lost husband and father respectively when that eighteen-wheeler left the road doing a cool 70 mph, according to police, and flattened the right half of their trailer where Michael Bang was asleep after working a double shift at the battery plant. Thinking of Theresa and Mimi left my stomach knotted like a fist in my belly. I knew exactly how they were feeling right now.

I read about the tragedy in the *Northern County Reporter*, a very tiny local rag that was very much a one-man operation, but I had already heard the whole story from at least a dozen people, all with more details than the *Reporter* provided, its columns crowded with things like the Lake Champlain ice pool, the fast-breaking maple sugar report, and county fair squabbles. I folded the paper and laid it down on the worn Formica table next to my coffee, wondering what songs I'd be asked to play at the funeral; I was the unofficial pianist at the little community church where the funeral would be held. Theresa Bang, the dead man's widow, had already approached me; she'd even offered to pay. I refused the money, but hoped that none of the songs would be the same as those I'd played for Danny's service. Even now that would be difficult.

Unconsciously my fingers drummed the tabletop as I ran through a difficult passage of music in my mind. Fortunately the funeral songs wouldn't require much practice. There wasn't a lot of time left over these days. The Canada geese were returning. Spring was on the way. Lambing would start soon.

---

[1] An-juh-leek
[2] Too-sont

The ice on Lake Champlain was preparing to break up, which was a big deal around these parts; Angelique had an ice pool going. While I took a mild interest in it because of the local hype, mostly relieved when it was over, I refused to join. Ever since that lake had claimed my husband Danny's life in a ski-dooing accident a few years before, I'd lived beside it with grudging reluctance.

One of Danny's dogs pushed its nose into my leg demanding attention. I looked down into its bright face. There were two of them, both Border Collies. They were like disreputable mops of hair covering bundles of energy. The littlest one, Gyp (short for Gypsy), pushed me again and looked at the door. I knew what he wanted. It was time for their walk.

"Okay, okay, you win." I swirled my coffee around in the mug but decided it was too cold to finish and tossed the remains down the drain. Setting the empty mug in the sink, I pulled my jacket off a peg by the door. The duct tape on the elbows of the down parka was starting to look tacky, but I still couldn't see any reason to get a new one. Not even when my mother-in-law made disparaging comments comparing me to a street person. Especially, I admitted, when my mother-in-law made disparaging comments comparing me to a street person.

"Come on, you mutts." The door creaked open with a rusty squeal. It needed a shot of something. I made a mental note to check Danny's stuff in the garage and see if I could figure out what. The dogs bolted out into the sunshine, barking wildly. Racing ahead, they crested the hill and disappeared. I buried my hands in deep pockets and hunched my shoulders against the cold. My loosely tied Sorels slapped the half frozen ground. As soon as it warmed up a little mud season would really kick in. Then our daily walks would be like slogging through setting concrete and the dogs would be coated in mud when we returned. I was really looking forward to that. Yeah.

Danny had given the dogs plenty of exercise when he'd been alive, had bought them sheep for dog toys, in fact. He reveled in sheep dog trials and was incredibly proud that he'd trained them himself. I had taken almost no notice of either sheep or dogs until after he was gone.

In the end, caring for them had gotten me through. The shearer, booked before Danny's accident, showed up on schedule, and suddenly I had bags of fleece to contend with. Once that was processed, I was up to my ears in skeins of yarn, and my best friend Marise[3] suggested I start knitting as therapy.

It was remarkably effective. The steady click of the needles, the satisfying shape of a project. I knit, knit, knit day and night. Most of the people I knew had something I'd knit during that dark time. Then the knitting had turned into a cottage industry and slowly the sheep began to interest me for their fiber and not just their ability to be herded by the dogs.

A few clouds, high up, crawled across the sky. As I came over the top of the hill, the view suddenly fell away. On the left, the hill ran down to the shore of Lake Champlain, still iced over. The lake ventured inland at this spot in a secluded cove, like a sheltered half dollar. For reasons no one could remember, it was called Shipyard Bay. One lone fishing shanty, abandoned, was half sunken into a melted patch of ice. Closer to shore the official ice pool Christmas tree, kindly donated by the ambulance squad after Christmas, was propped up in the ice. It listed hard to the west waiting for breakup.

The ice went on as far as the eye could see, interrupted only by a spit of land out by Gander Bay, stretching like a finger pointing east. To the north was Canada, the border somewhere out there on the frozen water. Below me a dirt road followed the shore. This led into the town of Toussaint, what there was of it. Basically, it amounted to a combination gas station/store, a very small post office, and a non-denominational church. There were a few other home-based businesses: Alberta's Clip and Curl, Guy's (that's "ghee" not "guy") Saw and Blade Sharpening, and Rosaire's Bait and Tackle, places like that.

The biggest attraction, by far, was the Champlain Inn. This was a sprawling resort that covered a vast portion of the shores on this section of the lake. Tourists were drawn by the proximity to the lake as well as the abundance of amenities. Tennis courts, a pool, bike and paddleboat rentals, hiking trails, Olympic-size swimming pool, stables, and dinner theatre at their own five-star restaurant were only a few of the perks. Guests could stay at the luxurious hotel or rent one of the quaint guest cottages along the shore. Honest. That's what the brochures said, but it was true. All the cottages were quaint.

There was also an entire building and massive playground area devoted to children as well as armies of local boys and girls whose summer job it was to babysit for the Inn. For those who really wanted to get away, you could stay

[3]Mah-rih-se

there for a week and almost never see your children, unless you wanted to. The winter population here was a mere hundred or so souls, but in summer, it swelled to six hundred plus or minus.

I strode down the road to Toussaint, glancing back for the dogs. They were at the shore nosing at who knew what. "Gyp! Dash! That'll do!" Both heads came up in an instant, and they streaked toward me, hardly touching the ground they ran so hard.

Small cottages lined the road. Some were vacant for the winter. These were second homes and tourist rentals. In others, there were signs of life. Beside one the washing rocked stiffly in the morning breeze. It was frozen solid. Angelique Marten lived there with her ancient father. I would have known by the laundry even if I hadn't been in the warm kitchen on occasion to drink tea and play checkers with Mr. Marten. The old man's tattered, red, flannel union suits marched woodenly on the line beside his daughter's flowered housedresses, Wrangler jeans, and checkered wool shirts. The first she wore at home, the others when she worked at the store.

"Emerson? Em is that you?" a thin voice called uncertainly from a house to the right. A woman's hand sticking out of a window waved a dishtowel. "Em?"

"It's me. I'm coming." I quickened my steps, and the dogs followed hard on my heels. Catching the screen door, I herded them ahead of me with my boot. They scrambled over the doorjamb and into the dark kitchen, sniffing in all the corners and sweeping up crumbs from beneath the table with their quick, pink tongues. Marise Gaudet was my best friend. We played in the same band, The Kitchen Music Band—rather Marise played her fiddle and I plucked determinedly on my banjo and usually sang when the song had words. We wiled away many tedious winter evenings playing music, baking, or just sitting at her kitchen table drinking bottomless cups of tea and yakking.

I heard the window come down hard. Marise's footsteps were sure and even as she entered the kitchen. Her long, curly, blonde hair was captured loosely with a tortoiseshell barrette. She wore a hand-knit sweater (I know because I knitted it) and faded jeans. She smiled warmly. Only her eyes, with their vacant stare, gave her away, though not always.

Marise was blind, had been since she'd taken a fall while hiking the Long Trail, a rugged footpath that stretched from Vermont's southern border to its northern one. But she was the most independent, stubborn blind person I'd ever met. She wasn't in denial about being blind, of course, but she did rather prefer that she wasn't defined by her blindness, which made her a bit touchy about it. She didn't want to be thought of as "Marise, that nice blind woman." She wanted people to think of her first and let her blindness be an afterthought.

We'd been friends forever, but not close friends until after Danny's death, when I was trying to figure out what to do with his sheep. Marise was a fiber artist. She'd been one before she'd lost her sight, and she saw no reason to stop just because she was blind. Besides, fiber was very tactile, and she already had the skill.

I suppose it was a credit to her that she didn't play up her blindness to increase sales. She didn't need to anyway; her creations were beautiful. We had begun to collaborate on projects: I provided the raw materials and Marise transformed them into beautiful works of art. In the process, she'd taught me how to knit, crochet, spin, and felt which had slowly begun to heal the open wound that was my heart.

"Hey, Hon. Did you need something?" I asked.

"I'm so glad it was you. I heard the dogs." She blushed. "I think the toilet is jammed. I wondered, could you look for me?"

"Sure. I haven't had an offer like that in years."

Marise laughed. "I prayed for someone tall, dark, and handsome. But I got you."

"So you'll settle for short, dark, and devastatingly beautiful?" I peeked into the bathroom and flipped on a light. Chopin, Marise's guide dog, was sprawled out beside the tub. I skirted the big, black Labrador Retriever to reach the toilet. When I removed the cover on the tank and jiggled the flush lever, I noticed the chain had come undone. "Here's your problem. The chain is off. I'll have it fixed in no time."

Marise had followed me. "Is he in your way?" She snapped her fingers at the dog. He woke with a start just as Dash darted in, licked his face, and scooted out. He rose good-naturedly to his feet and ambled out of the bathroom. "I'm worried about him," Marise confided. "He's getting old. I think he's going a bit deaf. He'll be eleven in two months. We've got an evaluation soon, and I'm afraid they'll retire him."

"Will you get a new dog?" I replaced the toilet cover and washed my hands.

Marise shrugged. "I don't know. I guess it depends if one is available. And with the summer season coming up, I don't have the time to take off to train with a new dog until fall. You wouldn't believe all the stuff they expect us to learn and teach this year." She groaned. Marise was the principal violinist as well as a violin teacher for the Champlain Summer Music Festival which was held at the Inn and drew a crop of talented young musicians each year. "Sometimes I want to throw my violin across the room. What got into them? Why are they so ambitious suddenly?"

"I dunno, but I'm glad it's not me." I dried my hands on the only towel I could find and followed Marise back to the kitchen, hoping she wouldn't trip on my dogs. "Between work and fiber prep I haven't had much time for anything else, and pretty soon I'll be up to my eyeballs in lambs."

"Lambs," Marise said wistfully. "Don't you love that time of year?"

I laughed. "Absolutely."

"Would you like to have a cup of tea?"

I considered the offer. It was tempting to spend a leisurely morning chatting and avoiding work, which this morning included cleaning the barn. Then I remembered my early piano lesson. "I would, but I'll have to take a rain check. I have to give a lesson at eight thirty."

"Thanks for fixing my toilet."

"No problem. If I run into the Prince Charming you were praying for, I'll head him in this direction."

Tripping over the dogs, I made my exit. The early morning breeze had become a bitter wind whipping off the lake, wrapping icy fingers around my neck, and burning my cheeks. The dogs raced on, and I stepped up the pace eager to reach the comfort of Angelique's store.

The dogs beat me there and panted on the step, whining and scratching on the door. I let them in and followed gratefully. The store was empty except for Angelique hunched over a newspaper at the counter. A woodstove pumped out heat in the corner. A wall of food dryers busily churning out Angelique's famous beef jerky hummed in the background with a comforting whir and perfumed the air. Canned goods were crowded together on shelves shoulder-to-shoulder with fishing tackle, old-fashioned beauty products that were nearly antiques, every conceivable type of ammo, and gizmos of all sorts. Angelique often bragged that if she didn't have it, they didn't make it, and nobody needed it.

"What's doing?" she said when she looked up from the *Reporter*. She didn't wait for a reply. "Don't know what's wrong with them down there. This is the third week in a row they got my ad wrong. Does it take a rocket scientist to spell jerky right, I ask you? This week I'm selling jiky. Last week I urged folks to come try my new batch of Peppercorn Jeerky. And the time before that I was praised for my world famous jerry. I'm going to call that blame, no-account Jeff Daniels later today and give him a piece of my mind." She looked pleased with the prospect. She gnawed a chunk of her troublesome jerky and actually smiled, showing all three good front teeth while doing it.

It was no secret that Angelique had been sweet on Jeff Daniels since there were in school together so many long years before that no one really remembered the exact dates. The mere thought that he might return her feelings after all this time would be utterly laughable if it weren't for how often her ads were mistyped. Jeff was meticulous. A private investigator would be hard put to find a single typo in the rest of the paper.

It wasn't too many years ago that Annette Garbeaux ran an ad thanking St. Jude for blessings bestowed when her husband was declared cancer-free after a grueling regime of chemo. Every word was letter perfect. Not two weeks later when Albert Garbeaux dropped dead of a heart attack, his obituary was so misspelled folks wondered if Jeff hadn't fallen on the keyboard. Anyone who wanted a copy for his or her scrapbook had to cut it out of the *St. Croix Herald.* Theirs was pristine.

Some people, including me, suspected there were other, more devious, subconscious reasons for the errors. Either Jeff purposely misspelled the words hoping for a reaction from the offended party, or the poor man became so flustered when typing words for someone with whom he was smitten that he suddenly became all thumbs.

I opened the jar on the counter and pulled out three sticks of jerky. The dogs looked at me expectantly, and I threw each of them a piece and bit off a section of the third. "How's the kitty for the ice pool?"

Angelique sniffed. "Tolerable. It'd be higher if people weren't so picky about their choices. Most of the good spots are taken, and they don't want to throw away good money on a long shot. Better a long shot than no shot, I tell them." She shrugged. "We'll get there. Won't be long now, neither."

"Couldn't tell that today," I said cheerfully. I put some money on the counter, waved to Angelique, and headed out. I was going to be late for work if I didn't step on it. If there was one thing I hated, it was running late. Behind me Angelique grunted goodbye and returned to her paper.

Ducking my head against the cold, I ran into something that shouldn't have been there. I looked up, a bit dazed. He was tall, dark, and handsome. I nearly laughed in his face.

"Excuse me," I blurted out. "I wasn't looking." His features were vaguely familiar. His car, parked by the gas pump, didn't help place him. It was a forest green Ford Explorer and shone even in the weak sunlight. It had Quebéc plates. It was too early for a tourist; the Canadians didn't usually start their southerly migration until summer. He must be on his way to Montréal.

His smile didn't quite reach his eyes. He stepped aside. "No problem."

I hurried by and chuckled to myself. Too bad I couldn't stop by Marise's house and share the joke over a hot cup of tea. Maybe I'd have time to call later. It was too funny to keep to myself. But by lunchtime, something had happened that drove all thoughts of the handsome stranger right out of my mind.

Chapter Two

I took a break just before lunch after giving three lessons and hastily cleaning the barn stalls where I kept the sheep. They were all out now on their pasture for the afternoon with a pile of fresh hay. I had a couple hours before the after-school kids showed up for their piano lessons. There would be just enough time to sort through some yarn I'd made and get it ready to deliver to the yarn shop in St. Croix. But before I could get started the phone rang. Annoyed, I pushed up from the table and grabbed it on the third ring.

"Hello?"

"Mrs. Giroux?[4] This is Trudy Livingston, the principal at Toussaint High. I'm afraid I have some bad news. Your daughter Adrienne broke her wrist in gym today. Please don't worry. She's fine. An ambulance is transporting her to the hospital to have it set. If you'd like, I can pick you up and drive you over. I'm headed there myself."

My mouth hung open. Addy had broken her wrist? My Addy? Immediately, strong, protective, maternal feelings surged through me. Never mind that Addy was seventeen years old and so independent it was more like having a roommate than a daughter in the house.

"Mrs. Giroux?" Trudy Livingston sounded worried. "Honestly, she's fine. She was joking with the ambulance attendants."

That sounded like Addy. "I'm sorry. It's just such a shock. I was trying to figure out what to do. I'll have to make some phone calls. I have lessons to cancel."

"Shall I pick you up then?"

"No. No, thank you. I'll drive myself. I wouldn't want to make you wait for me."

"It's no trouble," Trudy insisted.

I wavered. "Well—no, really, thanks."

Trudy was all business again. "In that case, I guess I'll see you there."

St. Croix[5] was too small for a city, too large for a town. It had the nearest hospital and lay twenty minutes south of Toussaint. Fortunately, there was a highway where the speed limit had been increased to 65 mph. I never glanced at the speedometer, but thinking back on it I'm quite sure I exceeded it.

---

[4] Jir-oo
[5] Sahnt Crwah

I made the drive, from driveway to parking space, in fifteen minutes. In my decrepit truck, that was impressive. Mentally I covered years in those miles. Feelings I'd been trying to stifle came roaring over me. How is it that something so important can bury itself in your subconscious and work its way out when you have the least amount of emotional strength to deal with it? These were old feelings, the ones that had followed Danny's death. They marched like soldiers: frustration, helplessness, inadequacy, loneliness, and uselessness. Fear settled on top of them all like a heavy blanket.

I had tried to tell myself that this was how life was. People needed you; then they didn't. Children only needed you for about eighteen years, and then they didn't. They became people in their own right, responsible for themselves. It felt like a long time since Addy had needed me. Next year she'd be a senior, then she'd graduate, then she'd be gone.

For awhile, after Danny . . . we had needed each other. But still, Addy recovered first. Addy got on with her life. Addy needed me no longer. In time, I dried my tears and followed. After that there had been an emptiness inside. Danny didn't need me. Addy didn't need me. Uselessness was hard to live with.

"What good is life when no one needs you?" I had complained in exasperation once to Reverend LaPierre, who also happened to be my brother Marcel, shortly after Danny had died. Before Marise and I had become close, he was the only one I'd ever confided in, about anything. I wanted to feel needed again. What should I do about that?

Marcel, I could never quite get used to calling him Reverend, wasn't what you'd call an intellectual. He had begun life a farmer's son and grown up to be a farmer himself. He'd never, to my knowledge, spouted lyrical nonsense to placate or impress. I wasn't sure he was capable of it. He just spoke from his heart, which was simple, earthy, practical, and usually surprised me since the things I remembered most from childhood tended to be the times he'd tormented me with frogs or put gum in my hair.

"Needed?" Marcel had asked. Then he'd brought me out to the barn and shown me the sheep. "Here you go."

I had stared blankly at the sheep. "I don't know anything about them. They were Danny's."

"But," Marcel had said simply, "Danny isn't here to take care of them. They need you."

And so they had. In taking care of them, something broken inside me had slowly healed as well. It still hurt, and its fragility was breathtaking. Almost anything could set me back, start the grieving process all over again. But I'd learned to live with it the way you'd learn to cope with a weakness in your body.

I had a vague sense that there was a better way, an easier way, but for the life of me, I couldn't figure out what it was. I suspected it had something to do with God, at least, that's what Marcel and Marise kept telling me, but we weren't on speaking terms just at the moment. I blamed him just as much as Lake Champlain for taking Danny away from me. If he'd wanted to help me, not breaking my heart would have been a good start.

I found Addy sitting comfortably on an exam table in the emergency room. Looking at my daughter, I saw a younger reflection of myself. Addy's shoulder-length, mahogany brown hair was pulled back into a short ponytail. If she had been standing, we would be eye to eye. We had the same athletic build, with mine being more curvy and mature. The most striking difference was in the eyes. Addy had inherited Danny's hazel eyes which changed color from green to blue depending on what she was wearing. Mine were brown, nearly black.

Addy was cradling her newly cast arm and chatting animatedly with a tall, stylish woman dressed in an expensive suit and elegantly coiffed. She had the kind of complexion people described as "cream" and a gloriously abundant cascade of wavy red hair about which Celtic poets liked to wax eloquent. I raked my fingers quickly through my own tousled hair and smiled nervously.

"Hi, Hon."

"Mom!" Addy could have been hosting a tea. Somehow she made the cast look like a fashion accessory. "Mom, you know my principal, don't you? Miss Livingston?"

The elegant stranger turned to me with an enthusiastic smile. I guessed we were about the same age. Maybe this woman was a little younger. The name rang bells, of course; it was on all the paperwork Addy brought home. But since she wasn't the kind of kid who forced me into uncomfortable tête-à-têtes with the principal to discuss behavioral problems, we'd never actually met.

Suddenly it hit me. "Did we go to school together? I remember a Brian Livingston. I think he was in my class."

Trudy Livingston smiled. "My older brother. I was two years behind you. Funny isn't it? I don't think I could name five people in his graduating class. And here we all live in the same area."

I had to agree with her. I barely remembered five people in my graduating class, either. High school was a vague blur filled mostly with the alternating angst and joy of dating Danny. College memories were a little clearer only because we had been married by then. But it was odd. Though we had finally been together, married, most of my memories weren't of Danny but of work, recitals, college, and exhaustion.

I forced myself to smile and ask Trudy about her brother. I barely remembered him. "How is Brian?"

"Fine, fine. Sick of the 'Dr. Livingston I presume' jokes." Trudy laughed indulgently.

"Doctor?"

"Ph.D. It doesn't stop the jokes though. You know college kids. They've got to find something humorous in everything."

"So he's teaching then?"

"Yes, at the University of Vermont."

"Mom?" Addy interrupted. "Did you hear how I got hurt?"

"I'm sorry," Trudy Livingston apologized. "Here we're talking about ancient history, and the two of you must want to talk about why we're here in the first place. How insensitive of me."

She became brisk. "Adrienne, you're in capable hands now, so I'll take myself off. If you decide to stay home for a few days, just call my secretary." She wagged a warning finger. "And stay away from that balance beam, okay?"

Addy nodded. "Thank you, Miss Livingston."

"Yes, thank you," I added.

Trudy Livingston rested her hand briefly on my arm. "It was good to meet you. I'll give Brian your regards."

"Yes, please do."

Trudy smiled warmly and was gone. Her high heels tapped quickly down the hall.

I turned my attention to Addy. "Okay." I sat in a nearby chair, stuffing my coat and purse behind me. Pulling the chair closer, I leaned forward. "How did you do it?"

Addy's eyes shone. She loved to tell an interesting story. "You know how we've been doing gymnastics in gym? Today we had our testing. We had to do a short routine on our choice of the areas: floor, balance beam, parallel bars, or horse.

"I chose the floor and the horse. I had made up a pretty good routine for the floor, I thought. But when I finished my routine, Mrs. Barnes said I still had to do one routine. I reminded her that I had vaulted over the horse. She said she didn't remember. She was probably gossiping with the other girls while I was doing it. She's so chatty sometimes I wonder if she pays any attention to us at all. Anyway, she said the horse had been put away, and why didn't I jump onto the balance beam and do a simple routine.

"I don't like the balance beam, but I had practiced it and felt capable of doing something simple." Addy wrinkled her nose and paused for dramatic effect. "I would have been okay, probably, if I hadn't tried a round-off up there. I didn't even come close to nailing it. I went down like a ton of bricks. It could have been impressive because I did land on my feet. But my balance was so off that I bounced to one side and plowed my hand into the mat." She motioned to her left wrist. "You probably know the rest."

"Poor Addy," I offered sympathetically, though my daughter certainly didn't look in need of sympathy.

Addy threw back her head and laughed. "Why poor? Honestly, Mom, it wasn't that bad. I was the center of attention. I don't think there's been that much excitement in school since we had the bomb threat."

Apparently she was right, too. The next day she insisted on going to school. I begged, cajoled, wheedled, but nothing made her waver. She said she wouldn't miss it for the world. She returned with a cast so covered with signatures and funny drawings it was impossible to tell its original color.

I debated whether or not to try to contact my parents. They were on a Caribbean cruise. In the end, I decided against it. The news would only upset them and spoil their trip. I did place a quick call to Danny's parents to let them know what had happened to their granddaughter.

They were glad I had called and were politely concerned. They asked me to be sure and tell them if I needed anything and to give Addy their love. I knew they wouldn't even send a get well card. I wondered sometimes if they would be more involved if Danny hadn't died. It was something I would never know.

Life barely skipped a beat. Addy didn't need much help. She got along pretty well even with only one hand. I felt a little deflated, but before I had time to worry more about it, I had to play piano for Michael Bang's funeral.

Theresa had not chosen any of the songs I'd played for Danny's service, and I was relieved. It was an eclectic mix, to be sure. Either Theresa must be, or Michael had been, a great movie buff. The list of tunes Theresa had requested included the theme to Schindler's List, The Titanic song, My Heart Will Go On, as well as, for reasons I could not fathom, Pachelbel's Canon.

"It's so peaceful," Theresa had said.

Still, I wondered which one of them liked it, and where they might have heard it. They didn't seem the type of family that listened to much classical music. *Ah, well,* I thought. *Looks can be deceiving. What do I know?*

The morning dawned clear and sunny, warm and fickle as spring. I tucked the piano music under my arm and headed into Toussaint to the little non-denominational church. Theresa asked that the funeral service be part of the regular service, and Marcel had agreed. After all, the Bang family had always attended services there. He couldn't see much sense holding two separate services for the very same congregation.

The little white church was a solid, functional, plain building. It had white clapboard sides and a narrow steeple containing a modest bell which was almost never rung for any occasion. It stood centered on a well manicured green like the address on a letter. It was the only building in town to have any lawn at all, a fact that Angelique Marten had been heard to complain about loud and long. Every Green-up Day the local Girl Scout troop planted flowers along its crumbling stone foundation and walkway border. Today, despite the warmth in the air, not even a crocus bloomed to brighten things up.

As I climbed the stairs to the entrance of the church, I noticed a bicycle half hidden in the shrubbery. My hand gripped the big iron doorknob, and I heard music from within. Immediately, I wondered if I'd gotten the time wrong. A glance at my watch confirmed that I was exactly on time. Next I wondered if Theresa had changed her mind and asked someone else to play because the song filtering out of the church was the Titanic theme. It was being played in a completely unorthodox way, but the tune was unmistakable.

I eased the door open and slipped inside. The rows of old-fashioned, austere wooden benches were empty. A space in front of the center aisle had been cleared to make room for the long black casket, which would arrive with the hearse. The piano was to the left of the lectern, half turned to face the congregation. Behind it, I could make out the top of a Kool-aid dyed red head. Playing whole-heartedly, totally oblivious to her surroundings was Mimi Bang, the dead man's daughter.

My throat tightened. I turned to leave, but the music stopped abruptly.

"I didn't hurt nothing," Mimi exclaimed. She jumped up and scrubbed tears out of her eyes. "I just wanted to play it for him one last time. On a real piano, I mean. I only ever learned it on an electric keyboard we've got at home." She paused and amended, "Had. It was destroyed in the wreck."

Mimi Bang was tall. The top of my head was on level with her chin. Yet, the girl couldn't be more than fourteen. Her arms and legs were endless and her torso angular and awkward. Her brown eyes were too big for her face, her lips full and pouty when she wasn't on the defensive.

I finally located my voice. "It sounded lovely, Mary Margaret." I stumbled a little over the girl's Christian name. "Won't you keep playing?"

"Nah," Mimi said, though she looked back with longing at the piano. "It was nice being able to play on a real piano though. It sure sounded pretty. An electric keyboard is so . . ."

"Limiting?" I supplied.

"That's it! Limiting. I've taught myself to play most anything I hear on the radio," she boasted. "Want to hear?" she slid back onto the piano bench and began to play Bach's Air on the G String, then broke off and entered an unusual version of Presto from Vivaldi's Four Seasons. "I listen to public radio all the time," she said, not pausing. She finished her performance with a few bars of Pachelbel's Canon, and I began to suspect how it had appeared on my playlist.

Mimi stood up reluctantly. "Did you want to practice?"

I nodded. "Just for a few minutes. Then I need to play while people come in and find seats."

"Can I watch you? I'll be real quiet."

I smiled at the girl. "Sure, go ahead."

Mimi sat down in a front pew, angled enough that she could scrutinize my every movement. You would have thought she had scored a premium seat at Carnegie Hall to look at her. I tried not to let Mimi see how uncomfortable I felt under such close scrutiny. It was understandable at a concert, but a bit unnerving at a funeral. I warmed up for a few minutes, then began to play.

"Hey, can you play Jesu, Joy of Man's Desiring?" Mimi asked excitedly.

I nodded and transitioned into Mimi's request without skipping a beat. I ventured a look at the girl halfway through the piece and nearly lost my concentration. Mimi was enraptured. Her face shone. Her eyes were huge and dreamy in her face. Her lips were parted slightly, her mouth almost gaping.

I finished and waited in silence. It seemed almost disrespectful to play anything else until Mimi came back to herself. Slowly her eyes focused, a look of wonder and admiration infusing her face.

"Sheep May Safely Graze?" she suggested hopefully.

I nodded and began to play. Before I finished, people started filing into the church. I continued to play, switching to the songs Theresa had chosen. At one point I noticed Addy come in and take a seat with Angelique.

The service went smoothly. Theresa Bang remained stoic, if not dry-eyed. She wasn't a tall woman, but her erect posture made her seem so. Her brown eyes were red-rimmed. Only because I knew her family did I know that Theresa and her deceased husband were Bieneki Indians.

The Bieneki tribe had been consumed by white society such a long time before that it was no longer possible to tell them apart by physical characteristics alone. Some surnames were dead giveaways, but for the most part you had to know. Even then, most Bienekis thought nothing of marrying outside the tribe, and so Toussaint and the surrounding areas were full of people who were completely ignorant of the Bieneki blood in their own background.

It was the more cultural Bienekis who suffered the most. They were victims of racial prejudice and the butt of local jokes. Many lived well beneath the poverty level and struggled with alarmingly high rates of alcoholism and drug abuse, not only as teenagers, but into adulthood as well.

I knew that Theresa Bang worked as a waitress at a diner in St. Croix. I wondered what would happen to mother and daughter now that they no longer had Michael's income to rely on. Insurance, no doubt, would take care of the trailer. But who would take care of Theresa and Mimi?

My thoughts were interrupted when the pallbearers lifted the casket, and I had to play the song Mimi had been playing when I entered the church, My Heart Will Go On, the theme from the movie Titanic. I could feel Mimi's eyes riveted on me as I began to play. When I finished the introduction, I was startled as Mimi stood and began to sing in a quavering voice. I recovered myself and gradually Mimi's voice grew stronger until it was really quite lovely.

When the song ended, there was utter silence followed quickly by hearty clapping. Theresa Bang dabbed her eyes with a wadded up tissue and squeezed Mimi's hand. Mimi smiled shyly, ducked her head, and dropped back into her seat. Slowly, the applause died down, and the congregation began to file out after the casket.

I continued to play until the last person had exited. Then I picked up my coat and followed. I found Addy at the grave site where Marcel—Reverend LaPierre today—was saying a short prayer that would dismiss them all. I reached out and put my hand on Addy's shoulder.

"Mom," Addy asked, when Marcel was finished. "Can we go into St. Croix and visit Mémère LaPierre?"[6]

I nodded, knowing that the solemnity and finality of death had affected Addy as it had me. Regardless what happened after death, there would always be pain and sorrow for those left behind. Most of the time you could get away with thinking life would go on forever. But not at a funeral.

"Sure, honey. It's been far too long. She'll be happy to see us, I bet." If I had only known how happy, I might have postponed the visit yet again.

---

[6] Meh-may La-pea-air

Chapter Three

Nicolette[7] LaPierre was more than happy; she was ecstatic. My grandmother's joy made me feel like a heel for not making an effort to visit more often.

"Look who's here!" Mémère exclaimed. She leaned forward in her wheelchair reaching for us, pulling us close.

"Hello, Mémère," I bent down to brush a kiss against the old lady's soft, warm cheek.

"Bonjour, Grand Mémère,"[8] Addy said, showing off her French.

"Ah, Adrienne, très bon,"[9] Mémère clapped her hands with glee. "Ça va?"[10]

"Ça va mal,"[11] Addy replied, raising her arm to display her cast. "No, really, I'm fine, but my wrist has been better."

"Come, come, you must sit down and tell me all about it, but first let me catch you up on all de news. Did you hear dat dere Alphonse LaMotte[12] runned off?"

I wondered if "run" was a word you could really use describing Alphonse. During one visit he had greeted me in the lobby of the nursing home as he began to head back to his room. A half hour later he had passed by my mémère's room, not a hundred yards from where he started.

"He went outside, him, to see his son to de car den wandered off. He was missing for tree hours! He should never have been in de parking lot in de first place, him. His son should never have let him out. The lecture he got for dat blistered his ears, I can tell you, me. I was on my way to my painting class dat afternoon and was passing outside Mrs. Preston's office, just passing mind you, when she was talking to him. Dere was even a policeman in dere wid dem so young Mr. LaMotte would know how serious it was."

"He knew all right," Mémère nodded smugly "He sure knew it was serious, him. I never seen no one so red as dat man when he come out of dat office. No sirree, I have not."

---

[7] Nick-o-LET

[8] Bonjour Grand Mémère (grahnd mey-may) – Hello, Great Grandmother

[9] Very good

[10] How are you?

[11] I'm (bad) terrible.

[12] Al-fons La-mot

She paused for a breath, but no one had a chance to say anything before she rushed on. "An dat crazy Laura Burnsley, you know what she did, her?" Mémère lowered her voice. Laura Burnsley was her roommate, now seated in a chair by the window but so deaf she was incapable of understanding a word to or about her unless it was spoken in a roar.

"Beverly de nurse, her, she come in to give Laura dat medicine she takes, and Laura, her, she can't swallow dem pills, you know? So Beverly, her, she puts dem in applesauce. Well, dat Laura, she chews and chews." Mémère paused to give us a quick demonstration, moving her jaw up and down furiously.

"When she get done, her, Beverly say, 'Laura, you swallowed dem pills?' and Laura, her, she says, 'Yes. Nothing left but dese little seeds.' An she sticks her tongue out and dere's dem blessed pills sitting right dere on de tip of her tongue!" Mémère laughed soundlessly and slapped her thigh. "Beverly, her, she was fit to be tied."

In the pause following our laughter, I heard an old woman cry, "Madame, Madame, j'ai besoin vous!"[13]

Mémère snorted. "Dere she goes again, her. Always hollering. Night or day, makes no nevermind to her. How she expect us to sleep, I ask you, me?" She glared at us fiercely for a moment as if it was our fault. Then she gasped in mock horror. "You can't believe what happened to me de utter night. I could feel someone staring at me, you know? I don't sleep well, me. And I looks up and dere she is, dat crazy lady. She starts hollering how she needs me. I rung for de nurse, quick, and dey come and take her away." She shivered dramatically. "Scared me like to death."

"Mémère, I . . ." But Mémère cut me off.

"Dat Alphonse is such a rascal, why de utter day he . . ."

"Girls? Girls?" An old man tottered into the room holding his hospital gown up under his chin like a napkin. He was completely naked from the waist down, a catheter bag strapped to one bony leg. "Girls?"

Addy and I gaped at him, but not Mémère. "Get out of here!" she shrieked. "Bertram! Bertram!" Picking up items from her bedside table she began throwing them at him feebly.

In all the commotion, before I recovered my wits enough to even rise from my chair, a large man in a scrub suit came in the room.

---

[13] Madame, Madame, I need you!

"Mr. Bolio, what are you doing down here frightening these nice ladies?" he drawled, hooking an arm easily under the scrawny man's elbow. "You need to go back to your room now." He steered Mr. Bolio around, gently tugging the hospital gown out of his grasp and making him decent once again.

"Beverly was going to give me my medicine and empty my bag," Mr. Bolio grumbled querulously.

"Yes, I know. She had an emergency," we heard Bertram reply as the two of them moved further down the hall. "I'll help you, okay? How's that?"

Mémère smoothed her housedress over her ample lap. "Nothing but a nuisance, dat one dere," she said primly. "Wanders around here, him, all de time hollering for dem nurses like dey got time for nothing else but run here for him, run dere for him. Dey ought to tie him to de bed."

"Grand Mémère!" Addy said, shocked.

I laughed. "Oh, you love it, Mémère," I teased. "Wasn't it exciting to be rescued by that handsome young man?"

Mémère preened. "He is handsome, isn't he, dat one? Me, I wisht I was terty or forty years younger."

"Only thirty or forty?" Addy asked, doing some quick math.

"Why not?" Mémère demanded. "I was plenty beautiful at forty-five for any man, wasn't I Emerson? She knows, her. You tell Adrienne how beautiful I was, me."

I nodded. "You're still beautiful, Mémère."

The old woman accepted the compliment with a modest incline of her blue-haired head. "Say, did I tell you what dat Beverly done last week?"

I shook my head, but tuned out my grandmother's chatter. Spending time with Mémère made me feel like I'd put my head in a blender. It had always been that way. Richard and Nicolette LaPierre were my father's parents. Richard, a hard-working contractor, had been the quietest of men. That was as it should be, most people agreed; Nicolette talked enough for both of them.

There had been a saying in Marquette,[14] the next town over from Toussaint, when the LaPierres lived there: "The fastest way to spread news was to telephone, telegraph, or tell Nicolette." It wasn't that she was a malicious gossip. She was just bored. Paired with her natural curiosity, the two produced a combination lethal to her neighbors. Living right in the heart

---

[14] Mar-ket

of Marquette as she did, it was an easy matter to keep track of all the goings-on.

It was impossible to have a secret in Marquette in those days. There were whispers, though they were never confirmed, that a great many people breathed a heavy sigh of relief the day Mémère went to live at Winterhaven Nursing Home in St. Croix. It wasn't long before relief was thin on the ground at the nursing home, however. Every detail of life, every spoken word, she relayed enthusiastically to whomever was willing to listen. On one memorable occasion she had even been instrumental in the firing of a nurse's aide she disliked.

Annette Gadbois[15] considered her work to be the most disgusting job she had ever performed. In front of the nurses, she went about her duties in surly silence. When she was alone with patients, it was a different matter. In secret, she kept up a constant barrage of angry, derogatory words. After one such session, during which even the nearly insensible Laura Burnsley began to weep, Mémère had threatened to tell Mrs. Preston, the director, and get Annette fired.

"You just go ahead, you old bat," Annette had sneered, according to Mémère. "Nobody's going to believe an old fool like you."

That sort of threat might have cowed the other patients, but it didn't have quite the same effect on Mémère. Annette would have been safer wearing a red dress and dancing the hokey-pokey in front of an angry bull. Oh, but Mémère had bided her time, though, until one night when Beverly and Annette were working the night shift all alone.

Mémère had told Beverly her plan. Beverly was to tell Annette she was going to the restroom, but sneak into Mémère's room and hide in the bathroom. Then Mémère would ring her call bell, and Beverly would be a witness to what happened. Beverly was skeptical, but Mémère was one of her pets, so she did it.

She later admitted she'd never seen anything like it. Annette had come into the room swearing. It went downhill from there. Before it was all over, Annette had thrown a glass of water in Mémère's face, and Mémère had slapped Annette's. Beverly had emerged ashen and tight-lipped from the bathroom nearly shocking Annette into an early grave.

That was the end of Annette, who was let go by the director the very next morning before her shift had even ended. Mémère was a hero. Her wagging

---

[15] Gad-bwah

tongue was forgotten in the gladness and relief that swept through the nursing home. Some patients gave her cherished mementos they had kept when they broke up housekeeping. Some paid homage with stale cookies hoarded from the stash their relatives delivered. All were grateful for a time. Those were the glory days. They soon ended and life got on much the same as before.

When I tuned in again, my grandmother had finally stopped talking and Addy was recounting her accident. It was obvious where she received her storytelling ability from. Mémère listened gleefully, her face alive with excitement.

"My, but you had some adventure, you." Her eyes twinkled merrily. "Dat reminds me of de time dat . . ."

"Mémère? I'm sorry, but we really should be going." My head was pounding.

"So soon? Aw, dat's a shame. Come back anytime, won't you? I didn't tell you half my stories, me." She returned our hugs and waved as we left. "I'll save de rest for next time."

"Have a nice day," said Mr. Bolio. He was dressed now in baggy clothes and seated in the lobby.

"We will," Addy assured him. "Wasn't that fun, Mom?" she asked when we were outside.

I looked at her and laughed. "A real trip."

It wasn't until I was having tea with Marise later that I began to see the humor of it all. I took a sip of scalding tea. "She's been like that my whole life. I used to dread it when Maman and Papa dragged us there for dinner on Saturday nights. Every Saturday night I was growing up, practically. She never stopped talking. About everyone. I shudder to think what she's told people about me."

Marise smiled. "It could have been worse."

"How could it have been worse?"

Marise's slim shoulder lifted. "She could have been an ax murderer."

The thought of my little grandmother chasing anyone down with something sharper than her tongue made me laugh out loud. "Okay, it could have been worse."

"She *is* amusing."

"Yes," I nodded. "That's true. She can't seem to help herself."

"Your grandmother is not what's bothering you."

I sighed deeply. Of all Marise's senses that had overdeveloped to compensate for her blindness, intuition seemed to be the strongest. She was rarely wrong. "No. That's not what's bothering me. I mean, it does bother me, but I'm used to it. I'm, well, when Addy got hurt the other day I started thinking about the fact that she's not going to be with me much longer. I don't want to be . . . alone." I forced out the last word even though I realized Marise was in the same boat.

"Addy's so independent, what if she leaves and doesn't ever come back? It's just my luck that the one child I have has been independent from birth. She was never a snuggler. She walked sooner than other babies. Other kids would cling to their parents and cry if they had to be left with someone. Not Addy. She was more than happy to spend time with anyone. Even when Danny . . . she didn't even need me then. Not for long anyway." I fiddled with the handle of my mug. My chest felt tight, and I was afraid I'd start to cry. This was ridiculous. Marise reached her hand out and took one of mine, squeezing it. And then I did cry, blast it all.

While I was dabbing at my eyes and trying to collect myself, Chopin lurched to his feet and whined, looking at the door. "He needs to go out," Marise said, starting to rise.

"No, let me get him." I stood up. "It's nice to be needed. Even if it's only by a Labrador."

Marise chuckled and sank back into her chair. "Okay, then. Just let him out and tell him to get busy. He knows what to do."

Gyp and Dash pushed past the Lab and squeezed out the door before him when I opened it. They raced around the fenced-in yard barking at the wind. I stepped out on the stoop and wrapped my sweater closer around myself. My elbows poked through holes in the sleeves, and I could really feel the cold air on them. The temperature had dropped and water that had collected in the mud and on the leftover snow had frozen, making the landscape a treacherous, slippery expanse. The Border Collies skidded back and forth, looking for the best places to mark their territory while Chopin lumbered to his favorite spot.

On his way back the old dog got frisky. With a low woof he made a dash after Gyp, but he had less purchase on the ice, and he went down hard. He tried to get up, but his legs splayed every which way. Finally he stopped struggling and looked at me with dignified appeal.

"Stay put," I told him. "I'm coming." The ice was slick, and I skidded a few times myself before I reached Chopin. Meanwhile both of my dogs had decided he was down there to play, and they were making dashes at him to worry his ears and pull his tail.

"Go on." I shooed them away and put both arms around the big dog to haul him to his feet. He stood unsteadily and together we slid and skated to the door. "It's murder out there," I told Marise when we were all safely inside. "I'll run over in the morning with a bag of sand and do something about your walk, or we'll find you and Chopin frozen to death in a heap on the ice."

"The ice on the lake isn't ever going to go out at this rate." Marise put her mug in the sink and began to fill it to wash up her dinner dishes. "Unless we get a sudden thaw, I threw my five dollars after foolishness, as my father used to say."

"He was quite right," I said, feeling a certain sense of self-righteousness. I took up a dishtowel and began to wipe the rinsed dishes. "You should know better than to bet on that stupid thing in the first place. I'm pretty sure Angelique has it rigged anyway." Despite being blind, Marise landed a quick flick of the towel on my shoulder before I could duck.

"What are you doing?" Marise demanded.

I kept wiping the clean dishes and putting them in the cupboards. "I'm helping. What do you think I'm doing?"

"I can do it myself," Marise said mulishly.

"I know that. But I like to feel needed. Remember?"

Marise laughed. "Oh, all right. Just this once. If it'll make you feel better."

"Sure." I helped with the dishes and other chores whenever I came over and hard as I tried, I was never able to make Marise understand I would have done it in any case, or more particularly, even if Marise hadn't been blind, which was what she suspected. It was just something I liked to do. "Are we going to play some music or did you want to skip it tonight?"

"Of course we're going to play. Unlike some people I know, I've learned a few of the new songs we found. Just try to keep up with me."

"Ha! I may surprise you. I've been practicing quite a bit myself since no one needs me to do anything for them." Marise picked up her fiddle and began tuning the strings while I tidied up the kitchen.

"Is Marcel coming tonight?" Marise asked.

"No, he had a church thing." My brother Marcel was the third member of our band and played the uilleann pipes. Besides Marise's fiddle and my banjo, Marise and I took turns playing the bodhran, an Irish drum. The piano was my primary instrument, but it didn't figure prominently in traditional music with the exception of Cape Breton, which featured driving chordal rhythms, but we didn't play much of that. They tried to talk me into playing accordion, and I might have considered it, but when I had tried, I found the instrument too heavy for me. My second instrument was the banjo, and I could hold my own in our little threesome.

Occasionally, I sang. Sometimes I sang in French the songs we'd learned growing up. Other times I sang in Gaelic traditional songs that we'd come to love. Marcel had a beautiful voice and often sang with me.

Marise started playing A Stor Mo Chroi, a beautiful Irish tune. As the first few strains of the music flowed into the room, I felt myself going with them. This was one of my favorite times, when it was just me and Marise, playing the music, singing, the dogs listening. The light was soft and dim. Sheet music would have been too hard to read, but we didn't need it. The music poured out of our souls and into the night.

I knew I put more feeling into these practice sessions than I ever did at a concert; no matter how hard I tried, it was just never the same. On a good night, when everything was perfect, the strings of my banjo vibrated beneath my fingers like they were alive.

As I walked home later, humming, the sun was just sinking into the lake, leaving ribbons of pink and orange in the sky. I pulled my sweater closer against the cold breeze and walked briskly along. I was a little surprised to see Mrs. McCarty at her cottage, every light blazing, the front door open to the elements, and all her linens hanging on the line for an airing. Mrs. McCarty herself was standing on the front porch beating the dust out of a braided scatter rug. She looked up for a moment and caught my eye.

"Hello, Emerson," she called. "Good news!"

"Oh? What's your news?" I stopped and leaned on the front picket fence.

"Got a renter." Her eyes twinkled. I knew she and Mr. McCarty relied on their cottage for income, and she'd had a few bad experiences in the past with college kids trashing the place. "A nice steady man this time. Taking the cottage for the whole summer he is."

"That's wonderful!"

"Dr. Bachand's son, Seán," she elaborated, as if eager to prove his trustworthiness. "'Bout your age, isn't he?"

Seán Bachand[16] was indeed my age. Had been in my class, in fact, though I didn't really know him. He'd been a tall, studious kid with huge glasses, unruly, brown, curly hair, and had been more than a bit shy. We had never

---

[16] Shawn Bah-shan

talked much. With all the references to old classmates lately I was beginning to feel like I was at a high school reunion. "Yes, he was in my class at school. Can't say as I know him though."

Mrs. McCarty puffed up slightly with importance. "No? Well, Dr. Bachand tells me he's a big shot doctor himself up in Montréal. But he might be looking for a change of pace, so he's taking some time off, a leave of absence he called it. He'll be moving in any day now."

"Is that so? Maybe the big city isn't all it's cracked up to be," I suggested.

"Maybe not," she agreed. "Maybe not." She inhaled deeply and looked out over the lake. "Would be hard to beat this though, wouldn't it?"

"It would indeed, Mrs. McCarty, it would indeed."

She turned back to her rug beating with a vengeance, and I continued on my way home, whistling up the dogs and not giving another thought to Dr. Bachand's nerdy son. Had I realized at that moment just what his presence in my little town was soon going to mean, I might have drilled Mrs. McCarty for everything she knew about him.

Chapter Four

Anyone who hoped for a speedy resolution to the ice pool question had a rude awakening the next morning when we woke to find two feet of snow on the ground. I had to shovel a path just so Addy could make it down to the end of the driveway to catch the bus.

"I knew it; I just knew it," cackled Angelique later when I stopped in for some cans of soup and a newspaper. "I knew it was going to be late this year. I have my money on the end of March. You just mark my words."

I was about to concede she was probably right when the tall, dark, and handsome stranger I'd run into days before pushed open the door to a tinkling of bells and radiated his beauty our way. His dark brown hair wasn't exactly curly, it just curved exactly right around his face. His eyes were a striking blue we could see even at that distance, and his cheekbones were works of art. Even I felt a little lurch in the pit of my stomach, but I think Angelique nearly fell off her stool.

"The gas pump doesn't seem to be working," the guy said, jerking his thumb over his shoulder in the direction of the pumps outside.

"Oh, I know just what it is," Angelique simpered, hurrying around the counter and hustling the guy back outside to the pump where she could do her magic and bask in his megawatt smile for thanks. By the time she came back inside, she knew everything about him. Or so she said.

"Can you believe it?" she huffed the minute she'd gotten back to her stool and slid her bottom onto the edge. "That's Doctor Bachand's boy. The middle one." She narrowed her eyes at me. "You must know him; you're about the same age."

"There were several Bachand kids, Angelique," I replied. In fact, there were seven Bachand kids. But in my gut, I knew which one it had to be. The—formerly—nerdy one. The famous Montréal doctor. The one who was renting Mrs. McCarty's cottage. It had to be Seán Bachand. "Was it Seán maybe?"

She snapped her fingers. "That's it exactly! He's renting a cottage up here from Lois McCarty. Staying with his folks at the moment while Lois gets the place ready. Taking a break from doctoring's what he said. Don't know as it's a bad idea at that." She held up a ten dollar bill triumphantly. "He even contributed to the ice pool."

That I could hardly credit. "How would he know which date to pick?"

Her nose inclined several inches. "He left it to my discretion."

I grinned. "So what date are you giving him?"

She grinned back. "March fourteenth at nine a.m."

"You sly boots," I said with admiration, picking up my paper, tossing the soup cans into my bag, and heading out the door. I couldn't help chuckling at her deviousness. I was sure that particular time on March 14 hadn't been taken, Angelique was that honest. But it didn't matter. We'd pass it about the time the dogs and I got back home, and the ice wasn't going to melt that fast; Seán Bachand was not going to win the ice pool this year.

Addy called around lunchtime to ask if it was okay if she stayed over at her friend's house that night since they were going to be up late studying. I agreed, reluctantly, though I didn't let Addy know that. She said she'd stop by in the morning for breakfast and fresh clothes. The evening was going to be dull without her to talk to. Just me, the dogs, and my spinning wheel it looked like.

I had to take a skein off the bobbin before I could start that night. Then while I was at it, I soaked it in hot water to set the twist, so it was late before I finally got my fiber picked out and sat down to start spinning. Not long after I settled down to the rhythm of the wheel, a knock on the door startled me. The person huddled close to the door when I opened it startled me even more.

"Uh, hi, I'm Seán Bachand. I don't know if you remember me? I wondered if I might borrow some eggs?" He edged toward the warmth emanating from the kitchen behind me. He didn't even have a coat on.

"What? I . . ."

"I'm sorry to barge in on you like this," he apologized. "But I only just moved in. Mrs. McCarty said she would stock the fridge with essentials, but she forgot the eggs, and it's hard to make an omelet without them."

"Oh, are you staying at the McCarty's camp already?"

"I just moved in this afternoon. I was actually staying with my folks for a couple days while she got it ready for me. I could have driven into Marquette and borrowed the eggs from my mother, but I thought it would be quicker to come here. I saw your light on."

I suddenly realized he was shivering and that I was keeping him standing on the doorstep like a census taker. "I'm so sorry! Please come in. I'll get the eggs. How many would you like?"

"Six, if you can spare them." He stamped his feet on the stoop and stepped gratefully into the house, rubbing his hands together and trying to warm them with his breath. Gyp and Dash came over to check him out, found him benign, and returned to their baskets by the fireplace. I wrapped the eggs carefully in a dishtowel and placed them in a wire basket I kept on the counter for fruit.

"They should be safe in here," I told him. Eying his shivering, I asked, "Would you like some mulled cider before you brave the cold again?"

He flashed me a grateful smile. "That sounds wonderful. Yes, I'd love some."

I poured some cider in a pan and dropped in a bundle of spices I kept on hand for mulling. "You know, you could catch your death running around dressed like that at this time of year. It wouldn't be very good advertisement." I hid a smile at my own joke.

"I underestimated the windchill factor," he explained sheepishly. "So Mrs. McCarty gave me the lowdown on all the locals this afternoon when I moved in." I had to admire the way he adroitly changed the subject. "She said you were in my class, but she only told me your married name. Emerson Giroux, is it? I remember Danny Giroux, high school soccer star."

I felt a stab of pain go through me, but after all this time, I was pretty good at hiding it, and I didn't think he noticed. "Yes, Danny was my husband."

"Was?"

I took a deep breath. "Snowmobile accident. He went though the ice on the lake."

"Oh, I'm sorry to hear that." It was the kind of automatic response you give anyone, but the troubled look in his eyes made me believe that he really meant it.

"It was a couple of years ago," I said softly. "We had—have—a daughter, Adrienne." I laughed a minute as a strange thought hit me. "She's as old as I was when we went to school together."

A thin smile crossed his lips. "Seems hard to believe that," he murmured. "I remember you a little. You don't look any different than when we were in school."

I couldn't catch the snort in time, and it burst out as a derisive chuckle. "Yeah, I bet."

He had the decency to look embarrassed. "No, I'm serious," he protested. "I feel every bit my age, but you . . . you look like you could have graduated yesterday."

I gave him an amused and skeptical look. "Are you sure you don't need glasses?"

"I'm sure. So what was it?"

"What was what?"

"Your maiden name? I can't remember it."

"Oh, that. It was LaPierre."

I watched him process this, trying, as I had when I was told he would be back in town, to eek out every little thing he could remember about me back then. From the look on his face it wasn't much. "Emerson's not much of a French name," he said finally.

"No," I agreed. "But my dad fancied himself a poet, and Emerson was his favorite." I moved the cider, which had scented the kitchen nicely, off the stove and used a ladle to fill a mug for each of us. "My Mom had already taken her turn when she named my brother. Marcel," I supplied before he could ask. "Would you like to sit down for a minute?"

He grinned, showing off sexy smile lines around his eyes. "I thought you'd never ask." He wandered into my living room as I searched for a tray to carry the mugs and some chocolate cookies Addy had made. I heard him give a little exclamation of surprise.

"What have we here?"

By the time I reached the living room, he was camped out on the sofa strapping on Marcel's uilleann pipes, which he usually left behind at my house or Marise's, wherever we had practiced last. I almost dropped the tray.

"Do you play?" It was a stupid question, but I was so shocked I didn't know what else to say. Most people couldn't pronounce the name of the instrument much less play it.

His laugh was so rich and full that I was embarrassed to find I was eager to say something else remarkably stupid just to hear it again. "I'm not a professional or anything, but I play a little. We had kitchen cèilidh[17] in my house practically every Saturday night when I was growing up. We played a bunch of instruments, my brothers and sisters and I. Mum sang. Dad fiddled. We were pretty musical. Is it okay if I give them a whirl? It's been awhile."

"Sure, yeah, fine." I looked at him in awe. I could hardly believe that growing up in the same town, loving the same thing, our worlds hadn't

---

[17] Cèilidhs (Irish/Scottish) and tunks (French-Canadian) were gatherings of music, song, and dance often held in someone's farmhouse kitchen.

collided. I would never have suspected the nerdy doctor's son of having a hidden musical soul. But then, I guess he had never suspected it of me, either. My hands were shaking as I put the tray down.

"Let's play something. What do you know?" He looked at me expectantly. "That is your banjo isn't it?"

I nodded, not trusting my voice. "I'm not much good though, which is why I sing. The piano is my real instrument." Still, my hands reached for the banjo, automatically tuning up, tightening the strings. "Do you know Swallowtail Jig?"

In reply, he began to play. Fast. I hadn't worked with the tune for awhile, and I had to concentrate to keep up with him. When we finished, I was breathless and dazzled. "You play more than just a little," I said accusingly. "You're really good."

He shook his head. "You wouldn't say that if you could have heard me play back in high school. I've lost a lot. But it's a bit like riding a bicycle. Most of it comes back."

"My brother Marcel, my friend Marise, and I have a small band. We play for contra dances, and sometimes we do little concerts."

He looked a bit regretfully at the pipes, and I had the impression he thought he might be wearing out his welcome, so I said quickly, "Play another? What else do you know?" I was rewarded when his eyes lit up.

"How about Angeline the Baker?" he suggested and off we went.

I was so absorbed in the music that I didn't even notice the time passing. We traded tunes and talked about music, and when I finally became aware of my surroundings again, it was like surfacing from a wonderful dream to face reality. The cider in our mugs was gone, and it was ten o'clock. It dawned on me all of a sudden that he'd come to borrow eggs for his supper, and now it was late.

"I'm sorry, I forgot all about the reason you came over in the first place. You never got to have your omelet."

He grinned. "Don't apologize. This is the most fun I've had in years."

It occurred to me then that I had the two things needed to make an omelet, the stove and the eggs. "You must be starving. If you'd like, I'll make that omelet for you here."

He looked like a kid granted reprieve from a distasteful task. "Would you? I'd love that."

"I would." I set my banjo in its stand and went into the kitchen with the dirty mugs. Seán continued to play in the living room, and it was relaxing to listen to him. It reminded me of the times when Marcel used to play at home while I was at the kitchen table doing my homework when we were kids.

I grated some seriously sharp cheddar cheese and threw that into the omelet just before the eggs had finished cooking. The entire thing slid out of the pan onto one of my blue willow plates and steamed gently as I carried it out to the living room for him.

Seán set the pipes aside and reached for the plate. He closed his eyes and inhaled. "Oh, wow, that smells wonderful. But where's yours?"

"I'm fine," I said with a dismissive wave.

"I insist," he protested and something about the way he said it made me believe he could be stubborn when he felt like it. "I don't want to eat alone. Go get another fork and join me."

I hesitated for a second. The smell was making me hungry. "Okay, sure." When I came back from the kitchen, he was still waiting, fork poised over the plate. "Well don't stand on ceremony," I said. "Dig in."

He grinned wickedly and did. "I was starving," he said around a mouthful. "I think I forgot to eat lunch."

I took a forkful of eggs myself. "You should have said something. I wouldn't have forced you to play music for . . . what's it been? Two hours? Did we really play that long?"

"It has. And you didn't force me. If you'll recall, I was the one who started playing."

"Oh, yeah. You're right. So it's your own fault you're starving. Can I get you anything else? I have a whole kitchen full of food."

He shook his head. "No, this is perfect. So," he said around a mouthful of eggs, "you said you sing. Will you sing something for me?"

"Sure." An unexpected request like that when I'd first started singing would have made me hyperventilate. Growing up, it was Marcel who had been touted as having the angelic voice, and he did. But for some reason this music preferred a more organic voice, like mine. Beauty was not in perfection but in character, and my voice had plenty of character.

I considered my options for a second before deciding on Ailein Duinn, a beautiful, haunting song I'd learned at a festival once; it was a woman's lament for her love who had drowned at sea. It had particular meaning for me because of Danny, and I think my own yearning translated through the Gaelic words which people never understood, but always thought were beautiful.

I closed my eyes so I could concentrate, and when I finished and opened them, I knew that the wonderful, unexpected evening we'd just spent was over. But it felt right, like the last notes of a tune drifting out the window on a silky summer night, or the laughter of friends fading as everyone parted ways after a night of music making.

Seán's face was ravished with pain, and his voice choked. "I haven't heard anyone speak Gaelic since my grandmother passed away."

I started to say I was sorry if I'd struck a nerve, but he wasn't finished.

"Sad, isn't it? Not the song, I mean. Life, death . . . for so many years people came to me, hopeless people, expecting me to cure them, to save their lives. And many of them I could save. The losses were always a tragedy, of course. But in the middle of life and death, I fancied myself on life's side." He cleared his throat. "Then one day it was me, and there was no one to go to, no one to offer hope."

I was afraid to ask, but the silence stretched on so long that it grew uncomfortable. "Are you saying . . ."

He grinned wryly at the irony. "The brain surgeon has an inoperable tumor."

"So you . . ."

"Came home to die?" he finished for me, then shook his head. "I've spent my whole life saving other people's lives. I didn't have a family. I didn't have much of a life at all. I put it all off because my job was important. I thought the rest was something I'd get to one day when I had time. Well, time's up." He paused and then he looked me straight in the eyes. "I've come home to live."

He stood up. "I guess I'd better be getting back. I turned the heat up before I left. Maybe it'll have warmed up enough that I won't be able to see my breath now."

My laugh was hollow, but I tried. "Don't count on it. I'm not so sure that cottage was meant to be lived in year-round."

I followed him to the door. When he opened it, a blast of cold air hit us, and I remembered he didn't have a coat. "Wait, here, take this." I handed him my ragged jacket with the duct-taped elbows which had been Danny's so it would fit him. I felt a lump in my throat as he pushed his arms into the sleeves and stood there on my doorstep wearing my jacket—Danny's jacket.

"Thanks so much for everything," I began. "For the music, it was wonderful . . ." My voice trailed off. How do you say, "I'm so sorry you're dying?" I couldn't find the words.

He smiled and his face softened. In the moonlight the sure knowledge of his fate seemed etched in the sadness of his eyes. Before I could finish he leaned down and kissed me gently on the cheek. "Thank *you*," he said. "Good night."

I stood there like an idiot, consumed with sadness until the chill forced me inside. My mind was whirling so badly that I couldn't go to bed, but there was nothing to stay up for. So I did something I hadn't done since I was a kid facing some traumatic situation or other. I dug though the linen closet in the bathroom until I found my childhood quilt, one that Mémère LaPierre had quilted for me. It was worn out and faded with holes and threadbare patches in the hand-pieced maple leaf squares, but it was comforting to me. I took it out to the living room, inhaling the sharp scent from the lavender I kept in the linen closet to keep the blankets fresh.

Wrapping the quilt around me, I curled up on the couch, feeling guilty for being grateful that Addy wasn't there so I wouldn't have to explain why I was snuggled up trying to come to terms with life and death yet again.

No, I didn't have to explain it to anyone. That would come the next morning. Because I forgot to set my alarm clock, so of course I overslept.

Chapter Five

The dogs' whining should have woken me up, but I was in one of the sleepy stupors that sometimes come over me in the mornings. It was the kind of morning when I could have slept in till noon like I used to do when I was a teenager and my mother had to drag me kicking and screaming into the day. I was having a lovely dream that I couldn't really articulate, but "Kesh Jig" was on repeat in my head. That didn't wake me, either. What woke me was Addy's insistent shaking of my shoulder and pistol-shot questions.

"Mom? Are you sick? Why are you sleeping out here on the couch? What's been going on? Why is the sink full of dirty dishes? Why haven't you let the dogs out? Don't you have to feed the sheep?"

That last bit jolted me because I did, indeed, have to feed the sheep. But I was deep under, and as I floundered toward actual consciousness, I started answering her questions before my brain had fully engaged. "Seán Bachand was here last night, and we played music. I let the dogs out late so they're fine." They weren't, as evidenced by Gyp whining and scratching at the door.

Addy stood there with her hands on her hips and a look of disapproval on her face. "Who was here? I thought you were practicing with Marise and Uncle Marcel last night."

I pushed myself up and brushed the hair out of my eyes. Little bells were going off in my head. Too much information, they rang. "Uh, no, Uncle Marcel had a church thing and Marise is visiting her parents. I wasn't even planning to play last night; I was spinning. But Seán stopped by for eggs, and it turns out he can play the uilleann pipes."

Addy looked skeptical. "He can play the pipes?"

I laughed a little, fully aware that it sounded weak and nervous. "Yeah, I was amazed, too. But it's true. And he's really good. Better than Marcel, but don't tell him I said that. Marcel, I mean," I amended.

"Oh, don't worry," Addy said grimly. "I won't."

I was spared any further recriminations by a knock on the door. "Get that, please," I croaked. "I have to get dressed. And let the dogs out, too." Wrapping the quilt around me, I bolted for my bedroom.

There wasn't time for much, so I pulled on a pair of jeans and a sweater that I'd worn the day before. I ran the brush quickly though my hair and pulled it back into a ponytail. No time for makeup. I grimaced at my reflection in the mirror. Ten years ago maybe I could have pulled off a look like that, but no longer. I looked washed out and—curse the thought—old. I fumbled in my cosmetics drawer for some lipstick.

Not great, but better. I stuck my tongue out at my reflection and turned my back on it. What was that song Stan Rogers sang about the mirror telling lies? I wished mine would.

Chores, projects, and a couple piano lessons paraded through my day like floats, and I didn't have much time to worry about Addy, though when she got home from school I did notice her brooding presence a couple times. I almost wished she'd had sports to play or somewhere else to go. I didn't have time to talk to her until supper, and by then she had switched from brooding to distant.

"So are you gonna tell me what's up?" I asked as nonchalantly as I could when we sat down to dinner at the kitchen table with sandwiches and grapes.

She leveled a look at me that would have done Danny proud. It was his aggrieved look. The one he used when he thought an injustice had been done him. "I just don't think it's right, that's all," she said a bit stiffly.

The way to handle the aggrieved look was with patience and by listening. I knew this because I'd dealt with it many times with Danny. "What isn't right?" I prompted, to show I'd been listening.

"You know," she gestured vaguely toward the living room where we kept the instruments. "Having some guy over here when you're all alone. Do you even know him?"

I tried to remember that this was my daughter. That all the values I'd instilled in her were sure to make her concerned for my reputation and that it was only natural. I even made a mental note that this conversation was probably more about the threat of the possibility of replacing Danny/Daddy than it was really about me or that I'd played music in my own living room with a man. Gasp. Alone.

"Actually, I do know Dr. Bachand." Even to my own ears I could hear the formality creep into my voice. I was distancing myself from the situation, and I didn't even have anything to hide! "We went to school together. He grew up here, in fact. So yes, I've known him for many years. I just didn't know him well. And we're grown-ups, Addy. We were playing music. Nothing more."

Addy chewed on her lip. I could tell my answer wasn't completely satisfying. "I just don't like it."

"I'm sorry," I said. And that was pretty much it.

After supper I pulled on my gloves and a thick sweater, missing my jacket acutely, and made my way out to the barn. It was an old converted dairy barn, long and low. Inside, because Danny hadn't cared so much where the sheep lived as about their function as dog toys, nothing had been changed much. The sheep were able to mill around inside between the old iron cow stanchions. The gutters, which made the flooring a bit treacherous in the dark, had long since filled in with straw from the deep bedding form of livestock management I espoused. I hadn't really been inclined to change anything, but I had added some lambing pens and hay feeders. For the most part the sheep had free access to the barn from the adjacent pasture.

Today they were congregated just inside staring out at the snow. They had ventured out a little and made some paths through the snow, but sheep are funny animals. They tend to stick close to home when the weather is bad.

Of all the kinds of sheep Danny could have acquired for the dogs, I thought it was practically a miracle that he'd gotten exactly what I would have chosen myself once I'd gotten interested in the fiber aspect of it. The funny thing was he had never really liked this breed—Bluefaced Leicesters. He complained that they were ugly and their beautiful curly coats were just a nuisance to him because he never bothered to put coats on them, and invariably, they'd get covered in hay and burdocks.

I, on the other hand, loved them. I loved their soft wool, and I thought their beautiful bluish faces and sleek Roman noses made them look like swans. They had a grace you didn't usually associate with sheep.

They also had the sort of attitude that reminded me of aging matrons who dressed a bit outlandishly and carried handbags, not purses, mind you. Who wore straw hats and used aprons when they baked. They were practical; they never took a shortcut when they didn't have to, and didn't indulge in the leaping and cavorting shenanigans I'd seen other sheep perform. They could also be a bit bossy, which made them challenging for the dogs.

I checked the ewes I'd put in the lambing pens who were due any minute practically, but nothing. No sign of lambs. I gave them fresh water, more hay, and rubbed the sleek proud faces of the friendly ones while they chewed their cuds contemplatively and hopefully concentrated on having those lambs soon.

By the time I finished with the sheep, Addy was thick into a research paper for school, listening to her iPod while she flipped through a book from the library. I decided to tackle the rest of the driveway. I'd shoveled a walking path but if I ever hoped to get my truck out of the driveway I needed to clear out some more snow.

My driveway was long. It wasn't a simple matter to shovel it, but it was a great point of honor. Danny had always shoveled. My parents had always shoveled. I had no doubt that my relatives, traced as far back as France, had shoveled. I didn't really mind shoveling. This time I had left it for too long. I should have shoveled the day it snowed instead of waiting. By now the sun had melted it enough that the snow was heavy and dense and came off in chunks the size of cinder blocks.

By the light of the rising moon and the house lights, it was very peaceful. I settled down to the quiet rhythm of it all, trying to forget how much my arms hurt, trying to ignore the howling of my back. Suddenly I picked up a movement out of the corner of my eye. Someone was coming cross-lots over the snow. I straightened gingerly. It was Seán Bachand on snowshoes.

He waved and paused. "What are you doing?"

I studied him a minute and decided he wasn't trying to be funny. "Shoveling."

He grinned. "I mean, why?"

Why? Pride added inches to my stature. I felt my back unkink as I grew taller. "Why? Because I'm a Vermonter," I replied with what I fancied was a hint of regal grandeur. Clearly he had been out of the state too long.

"Why don't you hire a plow?"

Why, indeed. "Because I'm a Vermonter!" I called back with a laugh. As I renewed my attack on the snow his faint chuckle floated back to me.

By the time I finished it was a wonder I could even lift my banjo out of the case, but lift it I did. It was that or suffer the wrath of Marise who was determined that we practice so we could play a concert soon. Marcel was there, too, for a change. I'd had to lug his pipes from my house along with my banjo and other assorted musical clobber.

As I puffed into the kitchen trying not to bang any of the instruments on the doorjamb, I shot Marcel a dirty look. "You could have stopped by and given me a hand," I said pointedly.

He smiled languidly (almost everything about Marcel was languid.) "I could have. But you didn't ask."

I wanted to wring his neck, a feeling I remembered fondly from years of growing up with him. "Here," I said, passing his pipes off to him. "By the way, I met someone who plays uilleann pipes."

Marcel looked skeptical, but Marise nearly dropped the violin she was taking out of the case.

"You met someone who plays the pipes?" asked Marcel, missing the point.

"You met someone?" asked Marise, who nailed the point, a fact I dearly wished I could lord over Marcel, but I didn't want to draw too much undue attention to it. "A guy someone?" Marise pressed.

"Yes, a guy someone, as it turns out," I said as casually as I could, knowing that no matter what I said or how I said it, Marise would have me paired off before the end of the evening. And there was no way I was going to blurt out that he was dying just to set her straight. "Someone I went to school with, in fact."

Marcel narrowed his eyes at me. "Someone we went to school with? Not Dr. Bachand's son, the one everyone's talking about. The famous doctor from Montréal."

"The very same, actually," I said, not meeting his eyes.

"And how did you happen to know that he plays the pipes?"

"He dropped by to borrow some eggs last night. He saw your pipes, and we played for awhile."

It was fortunate that Marise was blind because if she could have been granted the use of her eyes, even for a moment, the look she would have given me would have killed me outright. As it was, I squirmed uncomfortably in my chair and pretended to be having a lot of trouble with one of my strings. "Emerson," she said quietly, too quietly. "Why don't you come over for tea tomorrow, yeah?"

"Sure, Marise, yeah, no problem." But I knew I was being summoned. The trouble was that I wasn't sure if it was really my place to tell Marise Seán's story.

Marcel grinned wickedly and sang, "Emerson's in trouble."

"Oh, shut up, Reverend," I snapped, suddenly wishing I hadn't said anything. To change the subject, I quickly asked, "Why didn't we ever have a kitchen cèilidh anyway?"

"We called them tunks," Marcel corrected.

"Tunks?" Marise asked. "What's a tunk?"

"That's the French-Canadian version of the Irish cèilidh. They're get-togethers the old folks used to have," Marcel said, giving me a funny look, as if questioning why I'd bring up such an odd subject. "Because everyone was so spread out and they didn't have much time for socializing with all the farm chores, they'd get lonely. So every now and then, they'd have a kitchen tunk in someone's house and play music, sing, and dance. They'd push the furniture up against the walls. Sometimes the musicians would sit on chairs on top of the table. Over time a lot of them died out; the musicians got old and the younger people didn't learn the music, so there was no one to carry it on. I went to a cèilidh once, though."

"Did you?" I perked up in spite of myself. "Where did you get to do that?"

"At the Bachand's." Marcel's face was placid, but his eyes were laughing at me. I could feel a blush creep up my face.

"Why didn't I go?" I demanded irritably.

"Because you weren't dating any of them. I happened to be going out with Sorcha Bachand at the time. If I remember right, Dr. Bachand is Bieneki, but his wife is Irish." His eyes looked a little dreamy. "Very musical family, that. Knew how to have a good time."

That explained it. If I could have remedied one thing in my past with a well-placed wish, I would have wished heartily at that moment to have been Seán Bachand's girlfriend in high school. "Well, why didn't we have any ourselves, then?"

Marcel sighed deeply. "They used to. I dunno why they stopped, but I remember Maman talking about the ones she went to as a kid. There were some pretty strong personalities according to her. Like Uncle Pacifique and Uncle Louis-Philippe. Remember them?"

I remembered them, but only as old men sitting on the fringe of the room at family get-togethers. They spoke no English at all. "Yeah, but I didn't even know they played instruments."

"Oh, they played all right, before our time though. I guess they were always trying to outplay each other. Maman said that once Uncle Louis-Philippe got so sick of Uncle Pacifique showing off that he 'accidentally' kicked his chair out from under him. Sent Uncle Pacifique flying, and put a big scratch in his guitar. Wounded his pride more than his instrument though."

Marise snorted a laugh. "Maybe I'll try that sometime when you're showing off," she told Marcel smugly.

"You're too genteel," he said calmly, not taking the bait. Honestly, the way the three of us got along we were more like siblings than friends. I waited patiently for the two of them to stop bickering.

"Okay, time to get to work. What are we doing first?" Always the taskmaster, Marise bowed a few random chords. "Well?"

"Hector the Hero," Marcel responded, without looking up from his pipes. We always started that one slowly, but by the end were ripping right along. It was one of my favorite pieces. Marise and I played while Marcel harmonized on the pipes, weaving in and around like he was playing tag with us. Once we were warmed up, we played some faster songs: Spootiskerry, Red-haired Boy, Swallowtail Jig, Reel du Mentir.

To catch our breath, we followed that up with one of the most haunting songs I knew: Port na bPúcaí. The story behind the song was that fishermen from the Blasket Islands heard the songs of whales and tried to recreate it with music. But a more fanciful version of the story was that they heard the songs of selkies[18], those mythical creatures of the sea, and the song was their music. Considering the incredible, haunting beauty of the song it seemed appropriate to have a completely improbable and mystical explanation.

"Emerson?" I got the distinct impression that Marcel and Marise had been talking awhile because Marcel was looking at me with concern, and Marise's head was cocked as though she might be able to intuit my thoughts through waves in the air.

"Sorry. What?"

"Practice tomorrow night? So we can have a gig soon. What do you think?"

"Oh yeah, sure, definitely. Are we going to do a food drive again?"

"I think we should," Marise said. "I heard donations are down this year, and I'm sure the foodbank could use the food."

"Okay, great. So I'll see you both tomorrow? Marcel, want me to take your pipes to my place?" In the back of my mind, I'll admit I hoped Seán would drop by again. It would be convenient to have the pipes there, ready and waiting.

"No, that's okay. You've got enough stuff to cart around. Leave them here. I'll be back tomorrow night anyway."

I started to say it was no trouble, but Marise cut me off. "You'll come by tomorrow morning for a chat, right?"

---

[18] Mythological creatures said to live as seals in the water and shed their skins to become humans on land.

It wasn't really a question, but I pretended it was. "Sure, we can have tea. My first lesson is late tomorrow morning. I'll stop by early after I go to the store. I'll bring my banjo, and we can practice some more."

Marcel had darted out and driven off before I could think to ask him for a ride, so I closed Marise's door behind me and started the short trudge home. The air coming off the lake was brisk, but the sun had melted some of the snow off during the day. Still, the white blanket made everything look pretty. It wasn't really late, maybe nine o'clock. I was surprised to see all the outside lights blazing at the McCarty's place and a bundled figure outside, snow flying.

I stopped next to the gate, switching the banjo case to my other hand to give my arm a break. Seán looked up for a moment.

"What are you doing?"

"Shoveling!" he grinned. "Like a real Vermonter."

"I'm impressed," I said admiringly. "Your roots are starting to show."

He leaned on the shovel and took in the sight of me burdened with my instrument. "Want to come in?"

I considered the offer. It was tempting. "I'd better not," I said reluctantly. "Addy'll wonder where I am. She wasn't exactly thrilled when she found out we'd played music together last night." The minute the words were out of my mouth I could have slit my wrists. Why, why, why did I say that?

A look of concern and puzzlement crossed Seán's face. "Why's that?"

Any response was too complicated to contemplate. "I'm sorry," I said quickly, "I've really got to run. This banjo is heavy and I'm late. I need to get home."

"Want some help carrying it?" he asked, making a move to put his shovel down.

"No, no, I'm fine. Thanks anyway. I'll talk to you later." I was already moving down the road, wishing I hadn't stopped, wishing life wasn't so cruel.

Somehow, learning that Seán was dying had spiraled me down toward the abyss I'd so recently made some progress crawling out of. I just didn't like dancing on the edge like this. But I enjoyed his company, thought he was a nice guy. It seemed stupid to avoid being friends with him because I knew how it was going to end and also stupid to miss out on the fun we could have playing music together while he was here and alive.

By the time I made it through my front door, I was almost in tears. I shoved the heavy door shut behind me and submitted to the attention of the dogs, who came to bark at me and sniff my boots and wag all over as they greeted me. I set the banjo down and squatted so the dogs could reach my face, which they licked. I hugged them to me, and they wriggled all over, happy for the affection.

Addy was curled up on the couch. She looked up from the book she was reading. "How'd it go?"

"Fine, just fine. We made it through most of the songs we want to do for the gig."

"You set a concert date?"

"Yes," I replied automatically, then realized what I was saying. "I mean, no, but we will."

Addy looked at me with some concern. "Are you all right?"

"Fine, I'm fine. I'm just tired. I think I'll go to bed."

"But it's only nine." Addy glanced at the clock as if to assure herself that she wasn't going out of her mind.

"I know. But, I'm tired. See you in the morning." I gave her a kiss on the cheek and tried not to notice her bewildered look as I fled for the comfort of my own bedroom and relief from prying eyes. I felt stupid and petty and confused.

I fell down on my bed fully clothed, grabbed the edge of the quilt and rolled over so it was covering me. My forehead felt hot, and I wondered if I was getting sick. But being sick was the last thing I had time for. Tomorrow I had a tough job ahead of me. I had to face Marise and decide whether or not to let her in on Seán's future.

Chapter Six

Wednesday morning dawned cold and clear. No lessons; I had the whole day to myself. I skipped my morning cup of coffee because I knew Marise would offer me tea when I reached her house. Grabbing my banjo, I shooed the dogs out ahead of me, and stepped into the crisp morning.

My breath made little puffs in the frosty air as I walked, hunched into one of Addy's jackets, an old, puffy, down one that made me look like a giant blue marshmallow. I kept my eyes trained on the frozen ground as I made my way past the McCarty's place and then Marise's. I didn't breathe a real sigh of relief until I pushed open the door of Angelique's store and, in very short order, found out I should have waited a smidge longer to be relieved.

Seán was leaning against the counter chatting up Angelique who looked as though the sun itself had descended on her humble establishment and was illuminating it from within. She twinkled—I swear it was true—twinkled up at him and laughed coquettishly at something he'd just said. I may as well have been a bill collector for all she noticed me.

The dogs did their dust mop routine, wriggling their small bodies under shelving units and around corners in their hunt for morsels of food that might have been dropped, emerging dust covered and happy. They parked themselves on their hairy hindquarters at Seán's feet and without breaking stride in recounting the finer points of making a top-notch cappuccino he reached into the beef jerky jar and threw them each a stick as if it was our everyday routine. I wasn't sure whether to be irritated or impressed.

I cleared my throat, and Angelique tore her attention from Seán, glowering sourly at me. "Yeah?"

"My paper?" Honestly . . . I'd been coming to her store every morning for at least twenty years for a paper and miscellaneous other items; what did she think I wanted? She slapped the paper down on the counter grudgingly and rang it up for me with the jerky.

"I'll get that," Seán said quickly, reaching into his pocket for his wallet.

"I've got it. Thanks." I tossed my money onto the counter quickly before he could rally, snatched my paper, and beat a hasty retreat.

I wasn't halfway across the parking lot before I heard his footsteps pounding the asphalt behind me. I squared my shoulders inside the cushy jacket and steeled myself for the encounter. For reasons I understood but resented, I was irritated with him and with myself: him because he was dying and me for letting that fact affect me.

Danny had been gone for almost four years now. When would I let go of that? When could I face death in the face and not flinch? I mean, come on. We all have to die; some sooner, some later. It was a fact of life, the very first fact, the one that became reality the moment we drew our initial breath.

"Hey, wait up," he called, catching up and falling into step with me. "Have I done something to offend you? Whatever it is, I'm sorry."

A sidelong glance confirmed that he did indeed have a worried and contrite expression on his face. I sighed. "It's nothing. I'm a little out of sorts lately, that's all."

He seemed relieved at that and continued to keep pace with me, his hands shoved into the pockets of his jacket—a nice down parka and not the shabby jacket of Danny's that I'd loaned him. He was staring a bit pensively at my banjo case. "Going to play some music?" he asked wistfully.

"Just a little practicing. With Marise. That's all."

The silence hung over us with all the weight of Mount Mansfield. The pressure mounted and I was no match for it. I wasn't any good at this kind of thing. "Would you, er, like to join us?" The words were hardly out of my mouth when a big grin split his face.

"I'd love to!" he said. "Thanks for asking."

"I think Marcel left his pipes at Marise's."

He shook his head and gestured toward his house. "The rest of my stuff came yesterday, so my own pipes are here now. We can swing by my house and pick them up."

I sighed, knowing I was getting further and further in trouble with Marise, but unable to help myself. Part of me was writhing with the knowledge that Marise was going to kill me for short circuiting our talk this morning because she could hardly get any juicy details out of me with the object of discussion sitting right there. But the larger part was incredibly excited that unexpectedly I would have the opportunity to play music with Seán again. I was a little frightened to find out if our last experience was a trick of my imagination or something that could be replicated.

"I'm sorry about the mess," Seán was saying as he turned the key in the lock and pushed the door open. "I haven't had a chance to go through all the boxes yet."

I wasn't sure exactly how he defined "mess," but it was pretty clear that our definitions weren't the same. There were maybe five boxes stacked neatly against the wall. The rest of the cottage was spotless. A few dishes were drying in the rack on the counter, but otherwise you'd never even know Mrs. McCarty had rented the place. I shut the door quickly, blocking the dogs from following us in, and barked a hasty, "Lie down!"

I'd never been in their cottage before. It was charming. It made me feel immediately nostalgic for my childhood home and growing up. Even though it was still cold outside, the cottage made you remember sunny summer days when you tracked beach sand onto the floors and hung on tire swings eating Popsicles. Partly it had to do with the way the old place was constructed; the McCarty's hadn't done much to update it and stay with the times. The appliances were old models that still functioned, and I was pretty sure Mrs. McCarty herself had braided the cheerful rugs that lay scattered on the floor.

In fact, evidence of her handiwork was everywhere from the typical granny square afghan on the sofa, each square a burst of color surrounded by a black border, to the quaint curtains made of original (I was willing to bet) feedsacks from the 1930s. It was a place that remained frozen in time. In a better time, if you asked me. I didn't realize Seán was standing quietly holding his instrument case watching me take it all in until my eyes finished their tour of the living room/kitchen and came to rest, a little dazed, on him.

"It's pretty special, isn't it?" he asked quietly, seeming to understand what was going through my head.

I didn't trust myself to speak, so I just nodded.

"I'm ready," he said, indicating the door with a jerk of his head. "Shall we go?"

I cleared my throat, still not trusting that I could utter a sound without croaking. "Yeah, sure."

I waited on the doorstep as he carefully locked the door behind him. "You lock the door, huh?" I asked.

He looked a bit shocked. "You don't?"

I shrugged. "Not many people do in the winter. I think partly it's because of the old custom of leaving cabins unlocked in places where there's severe weather so if anyone needed shelter they could get warm, eat, and have a place to stay out of the cold until they could move on. That's probably what the old-timers would tell you. Some of them never lock their doors, even in the summer. The rest of us aren't quite so trusting. A lot of people come through here in the summer. Most of them are okay, but sometimes the teens get into trouble. Never anything major, just some vandalism when they've had a bit too much to drink. The border's so close it would probably make sense for us to lock up year round."

"What's the border got to do with it?"

"Well, sometimes people cross illegally. My great uncle Pacifique once found a man sleeping in the bed of his pickup truck. He scared him off with a shovel, but then afterward felt sorry for him and drove down the road to give him a thermos of coffee and a bag of sandwiches. Turns out the guy had crossed the border during the night without bothering to inform the border patrol because he was wanted in Canada for armed robbery. Nice enough fellow, according to Uncle Pacifique, but he started locking his doors after that."

We had arrived at Marise's, and I knocked before it occurred to me that maybe I should warn him not to make a big deal about Marise being blind, to treat her like anyone else. "By the way, I should tell you that Marise is . . ."

The door flew open before I could finish. Marise was smiling, but I knew her well, and it wasn't a good smile at all. "Marise is what?" she said, overly cheerful.

"My best friend," I finished lamely. "Seán, this is my best friend, Marise Gaudet. Marise, this is Seán Bachand, the famous Montréal doctor you've been hearing about." Seán had the grace to look abashed.

"Just Seán will do," he said. "I'm running away from the famous part and the Montréal part."

"So nice to meet you," Marise said, shooting me what was meant to be a withering glance, but giving him a real smile. "I've heard so much about you. Are you playing with us this morning? Emerson says you're a great uilleann pipe player. Can I take your instrument or would you prefer to carry it yourself?"

How? How did she know he had an instrument? I could never figure out how she did little party tricks like that, and she would never tell me. "Maybe I'm just pretending to be blind," she sometimes joked.

"No, I've got it, thanks. I'll just go take it out of the case and let it breathe a little. Where do you want me?"

"Straight through to the living room. And don't mind the dog. He's getting a bit hard of hearing." Seán hadn't even made it out of the kitchen before she turned on me and hissed, "Qu-est que tu fait?"[19]

"Me?" I squeaked, "I didn't do anything. He followed me here."

---

[19] What are you doing?

"I just bet," she said acidly. "Like a lost puppy, I suppose. Now we can't talk about *anything*."

I breathed a sigh of relief, but hid it by saying, "That's okay. We'll talk later. You'll love playing music with him. He's excellent. I promise."

"He'd better be," she growled, still perturbed. "I've been looking forward to this chat all morning. I have very few pleasures in my life, you know," she said with a saintly air that I knew was a crock, "especially since I lost the ice pool last night." Which explained everything as far as I was concerned.

I grinned. "Aw, pauvre petite chouette,[20]" I murmured with insincere sympathy.

When we walked into the living room, we found Chopin sprawled out on the rug with Gyp and Dash curled up tight against him as though he were a furnace. Seán was strapping on his pipes and pretending that he hadn't overheard our entire conversation. I felt my face flame and buried it behind my hair as I busied myself getting my banjo out.

By the look on Marise's face, I knew that had she been a sighted person she would have had a wicked glint in her eye, and I cringed. She was going to put him through his paces. I lost all hope that this would be a nice repeat of the other night and flexed my fingers a few times to get loosened up. We were in for it now.

"So Seán," she said innocently. "Why don't we start with something easy. Do you know Red-Haired Boy and Devil's Dream?"

I groaned inwardly. That was one of our faster sets. Yup, we were in for it now.

"I think so. It's been awhile. Why don't you set the pace?"

Marise grinned and picked up her fiddle and bow. "Okay. Ready? On three."

She counted out and blew right into the piece, which I expected so I followed her easily. Seán, on the other hand, faltered at the beginning, but quickly caught up. I could see the look of consternation on Marise's face, but by the time we were on to Devil's Dream it had changed to admiration. I was relieved and satisfied to find that I hadn't tricked up my impressions of the night we'd played together. He really was that good, and playing with him was both a challenge and a thrill.

Marise led us from one song directly into another until by the time she finally stopped and rolled her shoulders to ease the tension, we'd been playing

---

[20] Term of endearment. Literally: poor little cabbage.

for hours. I was nearly ready to drop. I glared but knowing the effect was lost on her, I had to satisfy myself with a small jab. "What's the deal? Are you planning to try out for speed fiddle and forgot to mention it?"

Marise laughed my comment off and said sweetly, "Hey, I told you to practice."

"Yeah," I grouched. "But you didn't say anything about playing at hyperspeed."

To his credit, Seán ignored our friendly bickering. He stretched and glanced at his watch and then did a double take. "Is that the time? Noon already? Seems like we've only been playing a few minutes."

I never wore a watch, but Marise, being Marise, had a clock on the wall behind him. "Lunchtime already. You're right. Seems like we just started."

Seán started packing up his pipes in a rush. "I have to run. I'm meeting someone for lunch."

"It was great fun playing with you," Marise said, setting her fiddle aside and rising to see him to the door. I knew better than to offer to do that myself, but I stood up to follow them into the kitchen. Out of politeness she added, "You'll have to come play with us again sometime."

"I'd love that," Seán said with so much enthusiasm that Marise visibly started. "I can't tell you how much I'd love that. I miss playing and my family is so spread out now they don't play like we used to when I was growing up. I'm finding out just how long twenty-four hours are when you don't have a job to fill them."

"Uh, sure." Marise, generous to a fault, recovered her poise quickly. "You're always welcome to play with us. Maybe you should think about joining us for a gig if you're going to be around all summer."

Seán's face clouded. "I'm not sure I will, but maybe. We'll see how things work out." I saw him catch sight of Marise's Bible which lay open on the counter, and a quizzical line formed between his eyebrows as he stared at it. I nearly shoved my fist in my mouth to keep from laughing.

Marise's Bible was in Braille, but entire passages were highlighted, the highlighter being capped and resting innocently on the table next to her tea cup. I knew that look on his face because I'd felt it on my own countless times. *Is she crazy or am I?* That was the thought going through his mind. He shook his head, as if to clear it, and turned his attention back to Marise.

"Thanks again. I'd love to do this another time whenever it's convenient."

"You're more than welcome," Marise replied, having no idea what had just transpired.

Seán looked over Marise's shoulder and caught my eye. "See you?"

I flushed, but tried to infuse my voice with the proper mix of nonchalance and friendliness to convey willingness, but not too much willingness. "Sure, yeah. After all, you know where I live," I joked. Seán grinned and gave a little wave as he strode hurriedly down the walkway.

Marise closed the door gently, and then turned to me and hissed, "You. Now. Spill."

I sat down at the kitchen table while she swept up her tea cup and an empty plate, rinsed them, and placed them in the sink. Then she began filling the teapot with water, but she was turned in my direction. I played with the highlighter, thumping it on the table first on one end and then the other. "Well?" she finally said in exasperation.

"What?" I shot back defensively. "There's nothing to tell really."

Marise rolled her eyes. She rolled her eyes at me! "Come on, Emerson. You like him. I can tell you do by the sound of your voice when you talk to him."

"I don't," I said stubbornly. *Not like that*, I wanted to add.

"Do." Her smile was smug.

"I don't," I snapped peevishly. "And even if I did it wouldn't matter. He's dying." As soon as the words were out of my mouth I could've bitten off my own tongue. Blast that woman! I was still trying to decide if I was going to tell her that.

All the life drained out of her face, and she clutched the countertop for support. "Oh, Em. Is he really?" The playfulness was gone. "I'm sorry. I didn't know. What of?"

"Inoperable brain tumor," I heaved a miserable sigh. "He said."

"And you can't stop thinking about Danny," she observed, her perceptiveness beaming in like a laser. She moved the kettle to the stove and sat down at the table.

"And I can't stop thinking about Danny." The grief hit me like a tsunami, the one I'd been bracing myself for since Seán had told me he was dying. My misery must have been palpable because she sank into a chair and reached across the table taking one of my hands. And suddenly it didn't seem as important to hide the truth from her as it did to admit it out loud.

"You didn't know him, ya know? He was all that. He really was." As long as I'd known Marise we'd never really talked about Danny. We'd talked about sheep. We'd talked about fiber. We'd talked about art. We'd talked about Addy and the town and music. But I'd never told her about Danny. In fact, I'd never spoken to anyone about Danny and the hole he'd left in my life when he died. Not anyone.

"He never forgot my birthday or our anniversary or anything, although he wasn't the type to plot romantic getaways or elaborate date nights. Nothing like that. But he'd do little things. He'd bring me a huge bouquets of daisies because he knew how much I loved them. And he'd get me these surprise gifts, all the stuff a man's man would never think of: lingerie, perfume, jewelry. And he had great taste.

"Not that he was what you'd call a romantic," I added swiftly, not wanting to give her the wrong impression. How easy it was to remember the past with rose-colored glasses. "I mean, in a lot of ways he was a total guy. He had refrigerator blindness like they all do; couldn't see the ketchup if it flew off the top shelf and clocked him on the head. He was an awful slob, and he could be gone all day playing with those friends of his and the dogs and sheep and not even realize I was missing him and that I would have liked to spend the day with him.

"But he was a one-woman guy. I never even caught him looking crossways at another woman. His eyes would light up when I came into a room. And I slept in his arms, literally; he held me all night long, like he was afraid to let go. I always knew I was the center of his universe, and I really was. I miss that," I sniffed.

The teapot whistled and Marise let go of my hand to go get it. My hand felt suddenly cold.

"He sounds like a great guy," Marise said softly, dropping two teabags into mugs and filling them expertly with the boiling water.

I sighed. "He was."

"So why don't you ever talk about him?"

I sighed. "I guess the short answer is because it hurts too much. Still. And that's true; it does. Although it's a bit of a relief at the same time to talk about him; almost brings him back a little. But really I think it's because there's no one to talk to about him who knew him, who can appreciate the memories. I guess that's really why I've locked them inside, like jewels in a vault." I smiled wryly at the image.

"I didn't have any friends, you know . . . before you," I amended. "I've always been a bit of a loner. Danny, on the other hand, had lots of them."

Marise set our mugs on the table. She wrapped her long slender fingers around her mug. I pulled mine close but didn't take a sip.

"I was supposed to be with him that day, you know," I said softly. "The day he went out snowmobiling on the lake. It was practically midnight, and they had a bonfire going on the lake. But we'd had a fight, and I wouldn't go down so he went alone, him and a bunch of the other guys and some of their wives. They weren't drinking or anything, they weren't really into that, but they started racing each other up and down the lake to see who was fastest.

"Danny went past the marker they'd set up, and he hit a patch of ice that wasn't frozen. The guys said they saw him, like a shadow because there was a full moon, and then nothing. He was gone. By the time they got there it was too late. He'd slipped under the ice. The police found him a week later." We were both quiet for a few minutes, and I was startled to find that although I was still sad the deep, sucking force of the grief had faded without my knowledge. Or consent.

"Anyway," I said brightly, a little too brightly perhaps, "that's really got nothing to do with Seán."

"You like him," she said, but I knew that she knew that I knew she was following my lead and trying to change the subject so I played along.

"Yenta," I snapped unconvincingly. "Anyway, even if he wasn't dying and I did like him and was even slightly interested in men again, I don't know him very well. He could be a raving lunatic. Or arrogant. Or selfish. Or just a total loser."

"Maybe," she conceded and leaned forward with anticipation. "So tell me what he looks like." She took a tentative sip of her tea. "He sounds cute. And tall."

I couldn't help it; I laughed. "You're a terrible friend," I informed her.

"I know. Now tell me."

"He's tallish," I said, grudgingly, though because I was short, "tall" was a relative thing. "Somewhere around six feet. I haven't measured him."

Marise snorted.

"He's got dark hair and his eyes are this incredible shade of blue. Very striking."

"Of course they are." Marise sipped her tea. "Hair?"

"Dark brown, almost black, kinda long. Not super curly any more like when we were in school, just these big, loose curls . . . Actually," I said thoughtfully, blowing on my steaming tea, "if he had a gold hoop earring in one ear and a rapier strapped to his side, he'd put you in mind of a really

52

dashing pirate. But somehow I get the feeling he's come by the look dishonestly. Like he's let himself go native in a sort of rebellion of his former life. Suits him though. I can't really imagine him all trimmed and groomed meticulously."

"No," Marise murmured softly, and I knew she was trying to conjure him up in her mind. I laughed.

"You're the one who needs a guy," I laughed.

"Of course I do," she admitted shamelessly. "But there's no rush."

As it turned out there was. Only it had nothing to do with men: hers, mine, or anyone else's.

Chapter Seven

I spent the rest of the day with Marise. While she did some weaving, I baked muffins and rolls for her breadbox. We whiled away the time companionably listening to a new CD she'd bought of French-Canadian tunes and found that we agreed on three that we absolutely had to add to our repertoire. After consuming gallons of tea and at least two of the freshly baked muffins, I sloshed happily home, though I did feel a twinge of disappointment when I passed the McCarty cottage and the driveway was empty. I wondered briefly where Seán had gone off to in such a rush, but pushed the thought out of my mind. After all, it was none of my business, was it?

My foot hadn't even landed on the driveway when I caught sight of Addy, no coat, no hat, no mittens, hair flying—and were those her down bedroom slippers on her feet?—scrambling down the hill from the barn clutching something in her arms and screaming unintelligibly.

Panic galvanized me instantly. The warmth and coziness of the afternoon dissolved like the remnants of a pleasant dream, and I ran to meet her. "What? What's wrong?"

She skidded to a stop, her eyes wild. The "something" in her arms was a newborn lamb. My eyes strayed to a smear of dried blood on her cast. "There's something wrong with one of the sheep," she panted. "I was doing my homework, and I heard a lot of baaing so I ran outside to check. I don't know what's wrong. It's awful! Her insides are hanging out, and there's blood everywhere! The lamb wasn't moving, but it's alive."

I pressed the handle of my banjo case into her good hand. "Here, take this. Go inside and try to warm up that lamb. Call Dr. St. Marie. Now," I said, pushing her when she didn't move instantly. "Hurry! And if you're coming out again, for pity's sake, put some clothes on."

I dreaded what I would see in the barn. There were five expectant ewes, and one happened to be my favorite. Her name was Angel; she was quiet and regal and sweet. Of course, it would be her. And of course, it was. I knelt beside her in the fresh straw. Addy wasn't exaggerating when she said there was blood everywhere. Angel's eyes were glassed over, which I was sure wasn't a good sign. She was lying down, sides heaving, a bloody mass hanging out of her backside. I felt my eyes fill with tears.

"Oh, honey," I crooned, taking her head in my lap and stroking her face. "It's going to be okay. The doctor's coming." Hoping that the sound of my voice would be soothing, I talked to her, telling her about her baby and how much fun she'd have raising it as soon as she felt better, and how the sweet spring grass would be popping up soon, and she didn't want to miss that, did she? And hold on, please, it wouldn't be long now, until finally I heard footsteps outside and a bulky figure was silhouetted against the open barn door for a minute.

"Emerson?"

"I'm over here, Auggie." My vet, Augustus St. Marie, was an almost full-blooded Bieneki Indian, which was pretty rare. He was a giant of a man who was proud of his heritage, but humble rather than arrogant about it. His very success gave him the platform to champion the rights of his people, and I'd heard he donated a lot of his time helping with tribal affairs. His features were large, but he was undeniably a handsome man. He usually wore his long, black hair in a ponytail or braid for practical purposes, but I had seen him often enough with it flowing loosely around his shoulders to know that he was quite proud of it and rightly so.

His great size belied his gentle nature. I knew this for a fact because what kind of man's man enjoys a spot of bird-watching as a hobby? Not to say the guy could ever be taken for a sissy, because he definitely could not. Just that to look at him you'd never guess he was a gentle giant, rather that he looked like he was about to enter the ring for the heavyweight title.

"What's this then?" he asked softly as he set his vet bag down and knelt next to Angel, examining the protruding mass.

The thing I appreciated most about Auggie, apart from the fact that he was large enough to tuck these sheep under one arm while he treated them, which was a relief considering I was the original ninety-seven-pound weakling, was that he always kept a positive attitude. There was one time shortly after Danny died when I'd had a sheep torn up by coyotes, and Auggie had carried out all the disinfecting and stitching while murmuring things like, "Not bad," "Awesome," and "Good deal," under his breath as he worked. His confidence might have inspired a false sense of security, but since I tended to go to pieces during medical emergencies, I was grateful for it.

Auggie was humming a little tune under his breath as he examined Angel, and I finally screwed up my courage enough to ask, "What's wrong with her?"

He glanced over at me, surprise in his eyes at discovering me there—Auggie was also a bit of an absent-minded professor—or at my ignorance, I wasn't sure which. "Ah, sorry," he murmured. "I'm afraid it's a prolapsed uterus." It sounded ominous, but he offered the information with a tiny smile. "Don't worry. There's not much damage. I'll have her fixed up in a bit."

I blinked at him, not quite sure if I should be relieved yet. "So . . . she'll live?"

Auggie's grin split his face and his white teeth flashed against his dark face in the dim barn. "I certainly hope so!"

The tuneless whistling continued as he set about treating Angel. He gave her a shot first and then started cleaning the bloody mass hanging out her back end. He coated the whole thing with glycerol, "to lubricate the organ and reduce the swelling," he informed me absently when I asked. Shortly after he started "replacing it; you just keep petting her face, all right?" Addy ducked into the barn, her arms still full of lamb but, I was relieved to see, in full winter kit of coat, hat, gloves.

"We're over here," I called softly. Auggie was struggling with the mass, and I tried not to watch. My stomach was already feeling decidedly queasy. Addy sank cross-legged onto the straw next to me, and I could see that the lamb was feeling a lot better.

"He wants something to eat," Addy said. As if to prove her point, the little thing struggled a bit in her arms and let out a baby bleat. I was surprised to hear Angel answer it weakly with a throaty rumble.

Auggie's chuckle was nearly as rumbly. "Not yet, little guy. Hang on." He turned to Addy. "Here, give that little tyke to your mother and run out to the truck for my other bag, would you?"

Addy handed the wriggling lamb over to me and stood up, dusting off her jeans. "Where is it?"

"In the bed in the back of my truck. Big black plastic tote. Can't miss it. Thanks."

Addy sprinted for the door as if she hoped her speed would hasten healing.

Auggie turned back to Angel, and I took the opportunity to take a good look at my new lamb. Its body was a mass of tightly purled fleece which would grow into the corkscrew locks I loved to use in my spinning. A quick look determined that, yes, it was a little boy. I nuzzled his head and murmured baby talk while I studiously ignored what Auggie was doing to

Angel. I ran through a list of potential names for the lamb to distract myself further but was interrupted when Addy returned to the barn and set the big black case down with a thump.

"This it?" she asked, panting a bit from her climb back up the hill lugging it.

"That's the one," Auggie confirmed. "Thanks." He rooted around in the case until he found what he needed. "Here you go. Clip that umbilical cord and spray on some of this Terramycin."

He must have recognized the fear in my eyes because he handed the equipment over into Addy's eager hands instead.

"Seriously?" she asked, almost giddy with importance. "Uh, how?"

Auggie's face was a study in patience as he walked over to guide her through the process. I averted my eyes and started reciting names again. I was pretty successful keeping myself distracted because before I knew it they were done. Auggie with Angel and Addy with little . . . Gabriel—how perfect.

"Now let's see how his mom likes him," Auggie said, taking Gabriel from my arms and setting him down next to Angel who was standing uncertainly and looking around a bit bewilderedly. Auggie gave him a little nudge from behind and Gabriel tottered forward toward Angel's bulging udder. With a little help from Auggie, he managed to get a teat into his mouth and after a few attempts, began to nurse. Angel sniffed his backside and seemed to accept him. Auggie, Addy, and I stepped back a little and watched the pair. I don't know how the others felt, but I was overwhelmed with gratitude that both sheep were alive and well.

"I'll want to keep an eye on her," Auggie said as he began to pack up his stuff. "She'll need some follow-up care and a course of antibiotics." He handed his detritus to Addy. "Throw those in the trash, would you?"

My daughter took the rubbish as if she'd been given an important mission.

"Since you're here would you take a look at the other ewes that are expecting?" I asked, pulled away from my warm fuzzy thoughts back into more practical matters. I brought him around to the other ewes, and he checked each one thoroughly.

"Couple days yet, I expect. Won't be long now. Call me if you have any more trouble, but I'll stop by to check on your new mother tomorrow."

I walked him down to his truck and watched as he stowed away his gear. Instead of getting directly into the cab, he leaned companionably against the door and looked as though he was getting ready for a bit of a chat, something he did occasionally when he wasn't rushed and felt talkative.

"Be warming up soon," I offered obligingly.

"I sure hope so." He cast an eye on the swirling clouds overhead. The quickly sinking sun, diving into the lake somewhere behind us, turned them spectacular shades of red and orange. "The weatherman is promising mild weather tomorrow and, by all accounts, it's supposed to start looking like spring soon."

I eyed him suspiciously. "You're not in on the ice pool by any chance?"

He grinned. "Only for ten bucks. But that's not why I'm hoping it gets warm soon. I'm leading a bird-watch at Bienvenue[21] Pond in a couple weeks. Interested?"

Don't get me wrong, I like birds, loons and cardinals especially, but a bird-watch wasn't really my kind of thing. So I had to believe it was the fact that I felt overwhelmingly grateful to him for saving my favorite sheep that made me accept his invitation. "Sure, sounds like fun." It sounded like anything but fun. Still, I could always "forget" to go, couldn't I?

And I might have, too, if it wasn't for the fact that I mentioned it to Marise later that week, half kidding, and asked if she wanted to come with me. No sense suffering alone, at least that's what I was thinking, but then it struck me that it was a bit ridiculous to ask a blind person to go on a bird-watch. As much as I wanted the company, I almost wished she'd say no.

"I'd love to come," she said instead. I could tell she was pleased with the suggestion for the sole reason that it was an activity the blind didn't ordinarily participate in. It flattered her. "Should I bring binoculars? I'm not sure I have any."

I almost answered her before it struck me that she was joking. If I'd had any idea at the time how entertaining the bird-watch would turn out to be, I wouldn't have missed it for the world.

---

[21] Welcome

Chapter Eight

"No, Etienne,[22]" I admonished for the third time in the last fifteen minutes. "See? The count is one-e-and-ah. All four of those notes have to fit into one beat. They don't each have their own full beat."

It was my fifth lesson of the day, and I was starting to feel a familiar weariness come over me. I loved teaching, and I especially loved teaching my advanced students and any student who really wanted to learn how to play piano. But it was tedious teaching kids who would rather be anywhere else and who, it was obvious, hadn't touched a piano key since I'd seen them the week before.

I'd known Etienne would be one of those kinds of kids from the moment his mother had dragged him to my house for his first lesson. He just didn't care. Half the time he was looking out the window or asking me pointless questions or just breaking out with random nonsense that made me wonder what sort of television programs his folks let him watch.

But his mother was determined he was going to learn piano, and although I explained to her that kids really needed to practice between times, she seemed to think that lessons were the magic bullet, and all she had to do was make sure he had one a week and presto magico he'd be a pianist some day. I stifled a sigh and tried not to watch the clock. It tended to move slower if I watched it. Etienne stumped through some more Bach like an elephant in cement shoes, and I had to physically restrain myself from jumping up and pacing the room in frustration.

Last lesson, last lesson, last lesson, my brain chanted. After this I could take a break, walk down to Angelique's, check in on Marise, and go play with the lambs. I just had to get through this lesson first. It didn't help that the weather had done a sudden about-face and people were walking around in T-shirts even though there was still a few inches of snow on the ground. The skies were blue and a teasing breeze brought scents from warmer climes and the tantalizing promise of green things. Who could stand being inside on a day like today?

I envied Addy who had gone directly from school to shadow Auggie on his rounds. Ever since she'd helped him that day Angel was sick, she'd been talking about becoming a vet. It was as if she'd seen the veil pulled back to

---

[22] e-TEA-yen (e - as in 'e' in 'pet', yen - rhymes with pen)

reveal her calling. She had been reading medical books about animals, and she hounded Auggie every time he came back to check on the new lambs or treat Angel. She'd gotten him to agree to let her shadow him occasionally and was working on getting a job in his clinic for the summer to help her decide if being a veterinarian was really what she wanted to do.

Part of me felt relieved that she finally had some direction after an entire school career of aimlessness. No particular profession had ever sparked any interest, and I had wondered, sometimes agonized, about what would become of her after graduation. But another part wanted to rewind, wanted to erase everything and go back to before, because now she was talking about college when she graduated next year. I reminded myself that that's what kids did; they grew up and left home. People wrote whole books about the empty nest syndrome. Maybe I should buy some.

I must have sighed out loud because Etienne jumped and looked up guiltily. "Did I do it wrong?"

I didn't have the faintest idea. "Let me hear it again."

Dutifully, he plowed through the section.

"That was much better," I praised even though I wanted to wince and apologize to Bach in person. It actually was a little—almost imperceptible—bit better, and I'd discovered that praise motivated students a lot more than criticism. "Now, you promise me Etienne that you'll practice this week, all right?"

He nodded his little mop-top of blond curls so hard he almost dislodged his glasses. "I will, Mrs. Giroux."

"Okay, I'll see you next week then."

He gathered up his stuff and practically sprinted out to the car where his mother was reading a book. She honked briefly and fluttered her hand in a little wave before she backed out of the driveway.

"Come on, mutts," I practically sang as I threw the door open and stepped outside into the glorious day. I snagged a light cardigan from a hook by the door and tied it around my waist in case I got chilly. Taking great gulps of the intoxicating, warm air I let all the stress from an afternoon of back-to-back piano lessons dissolve away.

Gyp and Dash raced ahead of me but their trajectory changed just as they were passing the McCarty cottage. I felt my stomach lurch as they jumped up against the white picket fence to greet a figure who reached out to pet them. Seán. I hadn't seen him since we'd played music that day at Marise's. At first when he didn't show up, I'd felt hurt. Then miffed. Finally I'd settled on diffident. But when I saw him, none of that seemed to matter.

He looked awful. His cheeks were hollow and his face almost grey against the harsh black of the ski cap he wore. He leaned heavily against the picket fence and even petting the dogs seemed to be an effort. But when he looked up his eyes were just as clear and blue as always despite the deep lines of fatigue etched around them.

"Hey," he said softly, his voice a bit raspy as if he hadn't used it lately.

"Hey," I replied.

There was an awkward moment of silence as the dogs panted and vied with each other for attention. His hand smoothed the fur of one and then the other.

"So . . ." I ventured finally, "you've been busy I guess?"

"Yeah," he said vaguely. "Have I missed any excitement?"

I laughed. Not much around Toussaint constituted excitement. "Not unless you count the fact that Armand Brouillard[23] threatened to punch Angelique in the face if she didn't refund his money after he lost the ice pool. She had to call the sheriff to come and haul him away."

"What," he joked, "and you don't call that excitement?"

I chuckled. "Where have you been?"

Again he evaded the question. "Playing anything new lately?"

I gave up, knowing when I'd been defeated. If he didn't want to share, I wasn't going to press the issue. "Marise and I found some French-Canadian songs we really like, so we've all been practicing those."

"I'd love to get the music from you, if I could," he said wistfully. "I haven't been able to play much lately, but I hope to get the chance soon."

I shrugged. "Sure, I'll burn you a CD and make a copy of the dots[24] we found. That's what we've been practicing with."

"Are you going down to the store? Maybe I'll come with you."

"Suit yourself." I stepped aside as he swung the gate open and came around to join me. I noticed immediately that he was walking slowly, so I matched his pace, a thousand questions running through my mind. Was this dramatic change the result of the tumor's progression? It seemed awfully sudden, but then I had no experience with brain tumors. I had no idea what

---

[23] Ar-man-d Brool-yah

[24] Musician-speak for sheet music.

to expect. In the back of my mind, I guess I just thought that he'd be completely normal and then one day he wouldn't wake up.

I glanced at him sideways. It was like he'd aged since I'd seen him last—what? A week ago? Just a little more than a week, I guessed. Maybe brain tumors were quick killers. I wondered how much time he actually had and if he even knew.

When we walked in the store together, Angelique looked up from her paper and raised an eyebrow at us. I wanted to slap her but pretended to need something in the baking aisle instead and made a beeline there. Flour. I could always use flour. I hefted a bag and brought it over to the counter where Seán was already feeding the dogs their daily jerky. He had added something to our routine though. Before he gave them the jerky he made them sit. Both dogs planted their derrières on the worn linoleum as though they'd been performing that trick each and every day.

"Well, whaddya know," Angelique said, "you can teach an old dog a new trick." The look she gave me was meaningful, and her eyes were laughing. I knew exactly what she meant.

"How's Jeff?" I asked innocently.

"Jeff?" The twinkle vanished and an irritated scowl replaced it. "Blast him, that's all I can say. Blast him. Fixed my ad though. Was after him for weeks about it." With a self-satisfied air she stabbed a blunt fingertip at her ad on the back page of the paper. It appeared to be spelled perfectly. A hint of a smile played on her lips. "Got a plan though." Her chin inclined an inch or so. "Teach that dog a new trick."

Seán looked out of his depth. "Did I miss something?" he asked me on the way out.

I laughed. "Nothing important. Girl stuff."

"Where are you headed now?" he asked. He sounded lonely.

I had planned to stop by and see Marise, catch up a little before heading home, but I could hardly do that with Seán in tow. "I thought I'd go home and play with the lambs."

"Do you have a lot?"

"There are eight," I said proudly. "And they are beauties."

"I'd love to see them," Seán said hopefully.

"Well, there's nothing stopping you. Come on. Not much I like better than showing off my babies."

Our walk up the hill was excruciatingly slow. I had to bite my tongue to stop myself offering to go get my truck and drive him up. Concern for him gnawed at my gut. How badly was he doing? He seemed to be on a fast slide downhill. Was this normal for brain tumors? How much time did he have? He'd never given even a rough estimate.

"You okay?" I finally ventured, trying to keep my voice even.

"I'm fine," he assured me. "I'm moving a bit slow today, that's all."

"But overall, you're okay?" I persisted. I knew I was being what my mother would have called "nosy," but I couldn't help it. He'd dropped that tumor bomb on me and stirred up all the negative emotions about Danny's death that I'd managed to bury more or less successfully. But he had seemed fine, playing music with us, laughing, joking, living. And now he seemed inches from death.

He sighed, a deep sigh that seemed to come from his soul. "Just moving a bit slow," he repeated. "It's been a rough week."

"You haven't been around," I observed pointedly.

"No, I had to go to Montréal for a bit."

The silence hung between us like the Great Wall of China. Solid. Impenetrable. I gave up. When we reached the barn, I proudly showed him the lambs, trying not to think about the distance I felt growing between us hard on the heels of that wonderful closeness when we had played music together. Seán admired the lambs, but I could tell his heart wasn't in it. Or at least he appreciated them as much as he was able, but his whole presence was so thin, so fragile that it felt almost as though he was faded.

"I was wondering if you'd play something for me," he said as we walked away from the barn. "On the piano. I've never heard you play piano."

"Uh, sure. Do you like piano music? I don't play trad music on the piano, you know."

His chuckle was soft. "I realize that. I like classical music, too, you know."

"Okay, sure." I offered him a cup of tea, but he didn't want anything except water. He settled himself gingerly on the couch, leaned his head back, and closed his eyes.

"What would you like to hear?"

"Whatever you'd like to play," he assured me softly.

The implications were a bit subconscious but the first thing that occurred to me was the Coventry Carol which I had mastered for Christmas. It was a beautiful, haunting melody that dated to the 16th century. It had been played in Coventry as part of a mystery play called The Pageant of the Shearmen and Tailors. The haunting carol was a mother's lament for her doomed child, one of the innocents killed by King Herod who ordered all male infants under two years old in the town of Bethlehem to be slain in an attempt to kill the Christ child. Somehow a lament felt right.

As the last notes of the song drifted away I heard a loud thud on my porch. I leapt off the piano bench so fast I startled Seán who, I was dismayed to see, had tears running down his cheeks. I yanked the kitchen door open, and Mimi Bang sprawled awkwardly onto the kitchen floor. She peeked out at me through her wild red hair.

"Mary Margaret?" I croaked in bewilderment. "What are you doing on my porch?"

"Mrs. Giroux, I didn't hurt nothing. I just . . . I heard the music; I just wanted to listen." She was practically in tears.

"Mary Margaret, it's okay. You don't have to sneak around the house. Come in." I helped her to her feet, and when I turned around to introduce her to Seán, I was relieved to see he had composed himself. "Mary Margaret, this is Doctor Bachand. Seán, this is my young friend Mary Margaret Bang. Mary Margaret plays piano."

"Please, Mrs. Giroux, nobody calls me Mary Margaret unless they're mad at me. They call me Mimi."

"Okay, Mimi it is." Which was a relief because I stumbled over her Christian name every time I used it.

Mimi twisted the end of her shirt nervously in her hands. "I thought if I could listen to you, maybe I could learn something."

I laughed. "You might but wouldn't it be easier to take lessons?"

Mimi hung her head. "I can't afford to take lessons," she whispered, clearly embarrassed.

Seán and I exchanged a meaningful look over the top of her head. "Mimi, I'm sure we can arrange something. Maybe a barter?" I knew if I offered to teach her for nothing she would be offended and would never accept. But she might take me up on a barter.

"What's a barter?" she asked. I could hear hope in her voice.

"A barter is an exchange of services. You can help me with my fiber business, maybe do chores sometimes, help me prepare fiber, and I teach you to play the piano. What do you think?"

"I'd love to," Mimi breathed, clearly enraptured with the idea. "When can I start?"

I laughed. "Is tomorrow too soon?"

"No, ma'am!"

We settled on a time and then Mimi said she had to go, her face flushed, her eyes bright, a smile from ear to ear. As I watched her skip down the driveway I had a sudden flash of inspiration. "You know what? I think we may have our accordion player," I said to Seán. Behind me I heard a muffled noise, and when I turned, I was just in time to see him slump over like a sack of potatoes and slide to the floor. "Seán? Seán!"

Seán's body jerked repeatedly, and I immediately thought "seizure" as my panicked brain tried to remember anything I'd heard about dealing with a seizure. Once upon a time, when Marcel had taken a first aid class in high school, my parents had made me go along for company. I seemed to remember that they had dispelled the old "put a stick in the person's mouth so they wouldn't bite their tongue off" myth. In fact, I think they had said to simply make the person as comfortable as possible and remove anything that might hurt them. I quickly cleared away everything that was around Seán so he couldn't come in contact with it. Then I fumbled for my phone and dialed Marcel, who in addition to being a preacher and a farmer was also an EMT.

"It's Emerson," I panted into the phone after I heard Marcel's lazy hello. "Come to my house quick. I think Seán's having a seizure." Marcel tersely told me to do exactly what I'd already done and sounded so older brotherly that I wanted to reach through the phone and slap him. I had barely hung up when I heard the sirens on the outskirts of town start wailing. I felt my stomach lurch. Somehow the sirens made the whole situation that much worse.

Marcel arrived shortly after the ambulance, but by that time Seán was aware of his surroundings and mad that I had called anyone at all. "I'm a doctor, Emerson," he insisted weakly. "I can tell you right now I'll be fine."

"Well, let's see about that, shall we?" Marcel drawled, coming in the kitchen door and letting it thump behind him, which under any other circumstance would have irritated me. I turned Seán over to Marcel's capable hands and fled to the kitchen to do something useful, like make pots of coffee. That's about all I was good for in emergencies.

The ambulance crew, which included Angelique, had arrived in short order and after Seán had informed each one that he was not going to be taken to the hospital and Marcel had assured everyone that he didn't need to be, the whole affair turned into a bit of a party. I passed cups of coffee around and the crew helped themselves to muffins and cookies I put out on a platter.

"So," Angelique said, scraping a kitchen chair away from the table and settling her ample bottom carefully onto it, a mug of steaming coffee in one hand and a muffin in the other, "you two seeing each other then?"

I bristled. "No!" Which was maybe a bit vehement, but I was too shocked to say anything else.

Angelique shrugged. "Just asking." She had a smirk on her face that clearly said she didn't believe me.

"We're not," I insisted. "He's—not my type," I corrected nearly biting my tongue to keep from saying "dying." No matter, nothing I said this time could wipe the smirk from Angelique's face.

Slowly the ambulance crew filtered out of the house until I was left with Seán and Marcel who stayed to take Seán home.

"Just take me to my cottage," Seán insisted feebly.

"Can't do that," Marcel said drily. "You agreed, remember? I'll even put the red light on if you want."

"I don't want," Seán growled, clearly irritated by the attention but in no condition to resist.

I pulled Marcel aside. "Should he stay by himself? I mean, will he be safe? What if he has another seizure?"

"He's not going to stay by himself. I'm bringing him to his folks. I told him it was that or the hospital."

"Oh, that's good." I couldn't imagine Seán spending the night alone after what had just happened.

Marcel helped Seán to his feet and steadied him as they made their way out to the car. Seán avoided my eyes entirely, and I had the distinct impression he thought I was in cahoots with Marcel. Which, when you thought about it, I guess I was. I was glad he had someone to look after him. Despite what he thought, it wasn't good for him to be alone right now. When I saw his pale face staring resolutely out of the passenger side window as Marcel carefully backed the car around, my heart went out to him. I could almost see Death riding shotgun as they drove away, and it scared me. It scared me more than I could say.

When I told Marise about it the next day, she listened intently. "You think of death as the end, don't you?" she asked when I finished. "Like an enemy."

I blinked. "Of course, don't you?"

Marise smiled. "No. I think of death as more of a pause between here and heaven."

"Oh, that," I snapped, irritated that she was going to go all Christian on me like Marcel did. I mean, I was a Christian, too, for crying out loud. I had been raised as a Christian. I believed in God. I read the Bible . . . sometimes. I even played piano at church. I just didn't bring God into every area of my life like Marcel and Marise did.

They were in a different kind of league somehow. And it was never more apparent than during a crisis of some sort. It wasn't just that they kept their wits about them. It was that they seemed so anchored, so immobile, so solid. Like they were rooted in something strong beyond themselves and nothing, no matter how horrible, could move them. And whatever that something was it gave them strength beyond what ordinary people had with which to cope. They were the kind of people you turned to when you were in trouble yourself because you knew you could count on them to give you strength.

So, yes, I believed in heaven. And hell, come to that. But who cared about that really? I mean, it was out *there* somewhere. Life was here and now. Death was the end. Period. End of story. Who cared what happened after death? The thought that I might meet the people I loved who had died, Danny for instance, in heaven wasn't something that kept me going or anything. The thought was more like a bonus. If I happened to make it to heaven, and if Danny or anyone else I loved, happened to make it to heaven, then great. I'd hit the jackpot. If not, well, I preferred not to think about that.

"You're not going to tell me that there's something better waiting for him are you? That I should be happy that he won't be in any more pain or something? Because you can save your breath."

Marise smiled and patted my hand gently. "Em, I can't tell you anything of the sort. I only met the man once, and we played some music. I don't know where his soul stands. Do you?"

I glared at her. For all the good it did me.

"What I'm saying is that death, as such, doesn't frighten me. But I can tell it frightens you. So why don't you do something about it?"

"Do something? What, like discover the cure for cancer? Prevent drunk driving? Abolish murder? Outlaw old age?"

Marise sighed softly. "When you're ready, tell me, okay?"

"Tell you what?" I grumped, knowing very well what. And knowing, even as I railed against her, that I really did want to know what she knew. That I wanted to have that strength myself. That I really did want to know what. But I wasn't ready. Not yet anyway. God had never felt so far away and disinterested. How could he possibly help me?.

Chapter Nine

A week later as I walked the dogs to the store, hands shoved into my pockets because I'd forgotten my gloves and the wind was a bit sharp, I was surprised and relieved to see that the ice pool Christmas tree had finally sunken into the now ice-free lake. Now that little irritation was over. The wind kicked up small riffles on the surface, and further out I could see whitecaps. I thought absently that it would be a bad day for canoeing.

One thing I knew about Lake Champlain was that it was treacherous. It could be perfectly flat one minute and covered in foot-high waves the next. Storms kicked up in the blink of an eye. The ice could be frozen here, and not there. Never trust the lake, that's what I knew. It would always let you down.

Angelique looked even grumpier than usual when I pushed through the door and into the relative warmth of the store. She fixed me with an irritated glare that made me so uncomfortable I finally snapped, "What?"

When she didn't say anything I asked, "So I see someone finally won the ice pool. Who was it?"

"Who was it?" she snorted derisively. "You, that's who."

"Me?" I squeaked. I could feel the blood drain right out of my face, and then right back in as I got mad. "Yeah, right. I didn't put any money in the kitty. You made a mistake. I don't ever bet on the ice pool. Remember?"

"Nevertheless," Angelique said haughtily, "you won. A total of $254." She slapped it down on the counter, but I refused to touch it.

"I'm not taking that," I said stubbornly. "There's been a mistake. I didn't bet."

Angelique shrugged. "It's yours. You won. Take it."

"I didn't win," I insisted. "I didn't play."

"Look," Angelique said in exasperation, "someone put down money for you. Your name. Your bet. You won. Take the money."

"What?" My mind reeled. Who would do that? Marise knew how I felt about the ice pool. She would never, never . . . "Why would Marise do that? How could she do that?"

"Wasn't Marise," Angelique said. "Was your boyfriend."

"My . . . Seán? Seán did this?"

If I hadn't been so angry, the triumphant look on her face would have made my palms itch. I threw each of the dogs a stick of jerky—I did not make them sit first—grabbed my paper, slapped some money down on the counter, snatched the kitty, and spun on my heel. By the time I made it to Seán's door, I was practically apoplectic. I beat my fist against it until he opened the door and peered outside like he expected an armed robber. I was too mad to be grateful that he looked a lot more rested or to be curious about why he was wearing a ski cap in the house.

"What did you think you were doing?" I hollered. At his blank look I elaborated by throwing the ice pool kitty at him. The bills fluttered in the air for a moment like dying leaves and then floated gently to the ground. "I never, *never*," I eyed him icily for emphasis, "ever bet on the ice pool. Danny was killed on that lake. I refuse to bet on anything falling through the ice!" I knew I was screaming at that point, but I didn't care. "And thanks to you I won! This is blood money. I don't want anything to do with it."

I started to turn, but I tripped on one of the dogs. Seán reached out and grabbed my arm to steady me, but when I tried to shake him off, he held on. "Emerson, wait. I'm sorry, I didn't know. Look, come inside; I'll explain."

"There's nothing to explain. You put down money for me, in my name, on the ice pool, which I detest. What could there be to explain?"

Seán sighed and closed his eyes briefly as though he was summoning strength from deep inside. "Come in? Please?" He was almost pleading, and as the anger began to fade, the fight went out of me. Reluctantly I followed him inside, making the dogs wait out front.

"I'm not staying," I said when he told me to let them come in. "They can wait out there. Until you 'explain.' "

He tentatively released my arm as though he was still afraid I might flee. "I'm sorry," he said again. "I'm really sorry. I had no idea. I found out that Angelique put my bet on a time that couldn't possibly win, and she wouldn't let me bet again in my own name."

"That's crazy," I protested. "You can bet as many times as you want."

"I figured," he said ruefully. "I assumed she was just messing with me because I've been out of town for so long. But I wanted to outsmart her, so I put the bet in your name. She said you hadn't bet yet. I'm so sorry."

That sounded like Angelique. Seán bent down and started to pick up all the stray bills. "Look, I'll give the money back. And I'll buy you dinner. And I'll shovel your driveway. And I'll feed your cat. Will that make it up to you?"

"I don't have a cat." I considered for a minute and then knelt down to help him pick up the money. "You know any good charities?"

"Lots."

I handed him the stack of bills I'd collected. "Donate this and we're even."

He grabbed my arm as I started to get up. "What about dinner?"

I pulled my arm away gently and stood. "Tell you what. We're playing tonight at my house. Mimi's going to try out the accordion. You come play with us, buy the pizza; I'll probably forgive you."

Seán smiled. It was the first genuine smile I'd seen on his face for awhile, and it made me feel like smiling myself. He stood up. "It's a deal. So we're good?" The way he searched my face made me feel like it was crucial that we were.

"We're good. See you tonight?"

"Wouldn't miss it," he assured me.

"Okay then." I let myself out but he followed me to the door and watched me holler up the dogs and walk away. I fluttered a hand behind me but didn't turn around.

That evening Mimi was the first to arrive. She seemed a bit on edge, but I chalked it up to first time nerves. I asked her if she wanted anything to eat from the trays of snacks I'd put out or the boxes of pizza Seán had arranged to have delivered. All the way from Marquette. Must have cost him a small fortune I reflected, and wondered briefly how he'd managed it. No one in Marquette delivered out here. We were too 'rural.' The gesture had the unfortunate effect of giving me a pleased grin I couldn't seem to control. But it was definite proof that he was genuinely sorry. It felt nice.

All Mimi wanted to do, she said, was practice before everyone else arrived.

"I think I've got the hang of it," she told me as she got my grandfather's old accordion out of the case, "but I can't play it fast enough."

"Don't worry," I assured her. "It's a band, not a solo at Carnegie Hall. We'll keep pace. We listen for each other. They always have to slow down for me. Have you never played with other people before?"

Mimi shook her head. "No. Never. What if I can't?"

I laughed at the serious look on her face. "You can. Don't worry. You'll get the hang of it. You might even enjoy it."

Before she had time to doubt me, the door opened and Marcel came in with Marise close on his heels. They were arguing. Nothing unusual there. You'd think they'd grown up together the way they got along. Or that they were old married people. Though, come to think of it, Marcel and his wife

Agnès[25] never fought, which, I reflected, was a tribute to Agnès who, in my opinion, was a saint. Marcel was not that easy to get along with.

Agnès was a force of nature, very much her own woman. She and Marcel had things they did together: contra-dancing, auctions, road trips, and things they did apart: he volunteered and preached; she had her baking and 'Home Dem' short for Home Demonstration, a farm women's club that started in the early 1900s as a way to educate rural women on agriculture and home economics. Besides teaching women useful skills like how to use a pressure cooker, gardening, making nutritious meals, sewing clothes, and sanitation, the club meetings were a chance for rural women to socialize. Agnès's club was called "The Front Parlor Home Dem" and most of the women in it could trace their family's membership straight back to their great-grandmothers.

Nowadays it was more of a craft club. The women brought whatever craft they were working on, the host served snacks and coffee or tea, and they gabbed and gossiped all evening. Some clubs tried to make things more formal by having a speaker in or a demonstration and keeping minutes; it depended on the personality of each club. In any case Marcel and Agnès' relationship seemed to work though I had no idea how Agnès could put up with my brother.

Addy wandered in as Marise and Marcel began to tune up, the squawking of their instruments nearly deafening until Marcel told Marise to stop so he could hear enough to tune. Addy smiled at them and gave me a knowing grin. "They're still at it, huh?"

She scraped out a chair and sat down at the table nibbling on a cookie. Her back was to the door so she didn't see Seán when he came in. He stood uncertainly, looking around, until he spotted me in the corner of the kitchen. Our eyes met over the top of Addy's head. He hadn't really registered her, but she caught my gaze and turned around to see what I was looking at.

"Addy," I said before she could speak, "I don't think you've met Dr. Bachand. Seán, this is my daughter Adrienne. We call her Addy."

Seán's eyes dropped a level so he was looking at her, and a big smile began to spread over his face. "So you're Addy. It's nice to meet you." His hand went out automatically to shake hers and Addy reluctantly—I was so

---

[25] Ahn-yes if you're pronouncing it the French way, or Ag-ness if you're pronouncing it the English way.

grateful in that moment for good breeding—reached out to shake it from politeness but with no real enthusiasm. "Your mom's told me so much about you."

Addy eyed him suspiciously, and I knew she wanted to ask him why he was wearing a ski cap when it was so warm out but knew the question was rude and I'd call her on it since I was standing right there. "Yeah," she said, noncommittally, instead and then turned to me. "I think I'll take the dogs out."

"Sure." As if she needed my permission. She called for Gyp and Dash, brushed past Seán without another word, and let the door bang behind her in case I hadn't gotten the message that she was not pleased.

Seán looked a little bewildered. "She okay?" he asked.

"She's fine," I said dismissively. "She's a teenager and she does it well." That got a laugh out of him. "Can I take your coat?"

He handed over his coat, a heavy woolen affair, but made no move to take off his hat. "Are you cold? I can stoke up the woodstove."

"No, no, I'm fine." Underneath the coat he had on a thick cabled sweater. Not, I noticed, handmade.

"Like your sweater."

He glanced down at his chest as if he couldn't remember what he had on. "Uh, thanks."

"Are you guys going to join us, or are you having your own party?" Marcel's voice boomed from the other room.

"Keep your shirt on," I growled at Marcel. "We're coming."

Because Marcel was playing the pipes tonight, Seán had brought his bodhrán and some bones, an instrument I'd never seen before. So I irritated Marcel a little longer by asking for a demonstration. "We had an uncle who played the spoons," I said, watching in fascination as Seán's arms waved gracefully and percussive sound erupted from the wooden 'bones' in his hands.

"It's very similar," Seán said.

"Will you teach me sometime?"

"Sure." When he smiled, I noticed his sexy smile lines had deepened considerably.

Mimi looked like she was about ready to throw up with nerves. "So Mimi's been practicing La Bastringue. Why don't we start with that?"

The music started slowly because I'd warned the others that Mimi was nervous about playing in a group for the first time. As the tune began I could hear my Mémère LaPierre singing the lyrics, her rusty voice a perfect complement to the song.

When we began our second repeat, I started singing the lyrics:

"Mademoiselle, voulez-vous danser
La bastringue, la bastringue?
Mademoiselle, voulez-vous danser?
La bastringue va commencer."[26]

As I sang, I took the opportunity to glance around at the others. Their faces were such a contrast. Marcel had his eyes closed, he often played that way, but his face didn't register anything like rapture, rather a quiet kind of contentment. Marise looked like she was completely carried away on a magic carpet of music transported to some other wonderful, happy place. I suspected my own face usually mirrored hers because that's how playing music made me feel as well.

Seán wasn't playing with his usual abandon. I noticed that occasionally he was off-beat, and he was sweating profusely. He was probably regretting that thick sweater right about now. I worried that this little bit of social engagement was taking a lot out of him, and hoped he wasn't pushing himself because I'd made him promise to play with us. I decided to pull him aside as soon as possible and let him know he was off the hook.

Mimi, in contrast with all the others, was concentrating so hard that she wasn't even blinking. It wasn't much of a stretch to imagine her as a little kindergarten kid, tongue clamped between her teeth she was so focused. The muscles of her wrists and hands poking out of the ends of her long-sleeve black turtleneck were taut with the effort she was making to keep up. I wondered how those skinny little arms could even hold up that beast of an accordion. I'd tried to play it a few times in the past to make my grandfather happy and always found it was too heavy for me to play comfortably. But Mimi didn't seem to be straining with the weight or size of the thing, just the task of keeping up.

The strings of my banjo seemed to hum beneath my fingers as we began the third round, and I had to admit, we sounded pretty good. I knew the moment we stopped and everyone finished congratulating Mimi on her playing that Marise was going to make us get serious about a concert date. I

---

[26] Miss, won't you dance with me? The Bastringue is starting.

didn't mind concerts but I never enjoyed them as much as just simply sitting around like this playing our hearts out.

There was more pressure at a concert to not mess up and since all the music and all the lyrics were in my head and not in front of me on sheet music, it could be nerve-wracking. Here, if I made a mistake, or spaced on a lyric, it didn't matter. At a concert it felt like everyone knew. Which probably wasn't true, but that's what it felt like.

Playing for contra dances was fun, too, but I liked them in moderation. It was boring to play the same tune over and over again while everyone else had all the fun dancing. I'd seen a bumper sticker once that said, "Hug a musician; they never get to dance," and thought that about summed it up.

But dancing, in a sense, was kind of the point of this type of music. I remembered a conversation I'd had with my cousin Pascal, my uncle Eugene's son, who had taught me a little fiddling when I was in high school. He looked something like Elvis, and I'd always had a crush on him. I'd just sawed through a reel, The Gaspé Reel, and he asked me how I felt about dancing.

"I'm in favor," I'd joked.

"Dance much?"

"No, not much. Just at school. You know, school dances."

"That's not dancing," he'd scoffed. "That's full body seizures. I'm talking about contra-dancing."

"Um, no. I've never been." I'd had some vague idea at the time that contra-dances were what the old folks did after they played bingo down at the Legion.

"You should," Pascal had advised me, nodding his head sagely as though at twenty-four it contained the wisdom of the ages. "This music was written for people to dance to. There's a downbeat and an upbeat. You have to play it correctly for people to be able to dance to it. Otherwise it's not danceable." Then he'd given me this knowing look, like Yoda. "It would improve your playing."

I'd hated to admit it, but he'd been right. Later on when I played for my first contra-dance, I quickly learned how to play so that the dancers didn't end up tripping all over themselves. And it did improve my playing. Not on the fiddle though. Nothing could salvage that. But when I'd taken up the banjo, I'd seen what he meant.

Not that I'd ever advanced as far or as fast as I would have liked. I still always felt like the weak link in our little band. But even if my playing was sometimes rough, and my singing very organic, I was beginning to have a better sense of the music itself and respect for its tradition, for its longevity. People had been playing many of these tunes for hundreds of years.

While we caught our breath and Marcel and Marise argued about which set to play next, Mimi gazed around in wonder. One look at her face and I knew we had a convert; she practically shone with joy. At some point while we were playing, Addy had come back in, and she sat on the hearth by the fireplace. I knew she didn't know Mimi very well because they were in different grades and a year's difference in high school life was like a decade in an adult's, but Addy reached up to high-five the younger girl.

"That was sweet!" she said, and Mimi blushed with the praise.

We played a few more sets before stopping to take a break. Marcel made a beeline for the kitchen to grab a piece of pizza, and I set my banjo in the stand and made my way over to Seán. He looked up at me with a weary smile. "Hey," I said, perching on the arm of the chair he was sitting in. "We're good, you know." I waved my arm indicating the pizza. "I don't know what debts you called in to make this happen, but I really appreciate it. You don't have to keep playing if you don't feel up to it."

"I'm okay," he said and at my skeptical look insisted. "No, really, I'm fine. It feels good to play. Really good. You have no idea." His voice trailed away, and I had to admit he looked unbelievably tired but content.

"Okay, well, if you need to sit some out don't feel like you have to play."

"Fair enough." He chuckled softly.

Addy was watching us, and her disapproval wafted across the room. I smiled at her, but she didn't smile back. Seán watched this little interchange but to his credit didn't say anything. I was just about to ask for a short lesson on playing the bones when Marise started to get impatient.

"Okay people, what's next? Anybody got a set?"

I jumped up and went back to my banjo. "Why don't we play some more of the songs Mimi's been practicing?" I suggested and rattled off a list. Marise chose three for a set, and we started playing again. Fortunately for Marcel the uilleann pipes didn't require breath like the great pipes because his mouth was still full of pizza. I tried not to laugh as I watched him finish his slice of pizza without using his hands while he played along with us. I relaxed into the music, enjoying the moment, aware of a nagging thought that crept into my consciousness.

I don't even know who said it first, who planted it in my head. Maybe it was in those raw days after Danny's death, maybe sometime in childhood. I suspected it was a woman, maybe even my mother, because I always heard it in a female voice. "Enjoy this moment, Emerson," I could hear the woman's voice say in my head. "It's all we have. There's no guarantee that we'll have any time beyond this very moment, so live in this moment alone." Even though the thought was a bit macabre, it never ceased to ground me.

In any case, my thoughts didn't gain too much height that evening because an unsettling thing happened when we were cleaning up. Addy, who had been sweet to Mimi all evening, asked the younger girl to help her do up the dishes, and Mimi eagerly agreed. As she pulled up the sleeves of her turtleneck and stuck her hands in the soapy dishwater, I saw my daughter flinch in shock. Mimi didn't seem to notice and chattered amiably in rapid-fire excitement, sometimes even slipping into Franglais, a combination of French and English, the way my mémère and some of the older folks often did.

I kept an eye on the girls and noticed that when they finished the dishes, Mimi self-consciously pulled her sleeves back down. I wondered if she was worried about her weight, too skinny, too gangly; she was in that coltish stage young girls went though that was a mixture of grace and clumsiness. But Addy's eyes were worried, and I was glad when we finally got everyone safely out the door so I could talk to her. I didn't even have to ask.

"Mom, Mimi's cutting," were the first words out of her mouth.

"What do you mean?" I asked blankly. Was that some new teenspeak for "really cool," or "a total nerd," or was it a reference to how quickly she had picked up the accordion?

Addy rolled her eyes, exasperation oozing out of her. "Cutting, Mom, you know, self-injury? Cutting her arms?"

Maybe I was the nerd because I had no idea what my daughter was talking about. "Help me out here, Addy. What are you saying?"

Addy rubbed her forehead in frustration. "When Mimi rolled up her sleeves to help me with the dishes I could see her arms were covered with fine lines, cuts. Some of them were fresh. I don't think it's something she used to do; I think she's still doing it."

"Doing what?" I practically yelled.

"Cutting herself," Addy shot back. "She's cutting herself, cutting her arms, probably with a razor blade."

I struggled to understand. "Why? Why would she cut her own arms?"

Addy almost chuckled. "Mom, you really are hopeless. Haven't you ever heard of self-harm? Self-injury? Cutting? They tell us about it every year in health class. Kids do it to help themselves deal with emotions they can't handle. Cutting themselves, burning themselves, they get addicted to it, kind of high from the release. I'm not talking about the 'attention cutters' either," she said dismissively. "That's a different story. If she was cutting for attention she wouldn't have been covering up her scars. I think she's got a real problem."

I was reeling, partly from the thought that there was a whole dangerous world out there that had never crossed my threshold before and yet now, here it was. And partly because I'd started to really care about Mimi. She was a good kid. What was I supposed to do with this information? I was the grown-up here. I was supposed to render the wise plan of action. Addy was clearly looking to me for just such a plan. I hated to disappoint her.

"I've gotta think about this," I said finally. "I'll do some research."

"That's a good idea," Addy agreed, surprising me. "Maybe we can find some organizations or something that will help. I'll ask Mrs. Barnes in phys ed tomorrow for some advice, too. She's the one who's always harping on us about this stuff." She mimicked her teacher's high voice: "Don't do drugs, don't drink, don't smoke, don't hurt yourself on purpose."

I tried to look disapproving, but I could kind of imagine her teacher. "And what should you do instead?" I asked, egging her on.

"Exercise, eat healthy, and get plenty of sleep," Addy quipped promptly.

"Well, at least you're listening in class," I said, and then couldn't help pointing out, "just think if you'd blown off listening the day they talked about cutting. If I'd seen those cuts, I probably would have just thought Mimi had been playing with a cat."

Addy shook her head firmly. "No, you wouldn't have. You may not have made the connection but you wouldn't have thought it was a cat. They're too methodical."

"Maybe I should talk to her mother," I mused.

"I wouldn't. I'd get some information first. Her mother may not know any more than you did."

I laughed ruefully. "True enough." I reached out and gave my daughter a quick hug. "I love you," I said.

"Love you, too, Mom." She returned my squeeze and then headed down the hall to her room. "Oh yeah," she threw back over her shoulder. "That Seán guy is okay. I don't like him," she added hastily, "but he's okay."

Well, would wonders never cease. Little did I know that was only the beginning..

Chapter Ten

April was beautiful, all cloudless blues skies, the air kissed by the sun, lawns blushing green with new grass. Every soon to be living thing had begun perfuming the air with the kind of fragrance air freshener companies like to call "spring day" or "fresh grass." This was so much better. I closed my eyes, leaned on the sheep gate, and filled my lungs as full as I could. I felt giddy with clean oxygen.

The sheep were out making a determined search for the tiny green grass shoots pushing up beneath last year's dead pasture, and amazingly enough it really was growing under there. Seemed like just yesterday the whole landscape had been buried beneath piles of snow, but that was part of the miracle we liked to call Vermont. There's a Yankee saying that if you don't like the weather just wait a minute.

Little Gabriel was already a hefty woolly bundle, and he and a few of the other lambs were engaged in what I liked to call the lamb races. They would meander over to one end of the pasture, realize how far they were from their mothers, and tear back as fast as they could. On the way they'd throw in as many wild, twisting, airborne leaps as they could, trying to outdo one another. It was hysterical. Their mothers, completely unconcerned with their offspring's acrobatics, paid no attention unless they wandered too far off.

Before I had sheep I thought that peculiar bouncing run of springing off the ground all four feet at a time was purely a cartoon action. I was amazed, when I really started to watch them, to see that it wasn't. Sheep really ran that way. Not all the time. They could gallop just like a horse. But when they were feeling frisky they ran by pushing off all four feet at once and launching themselves in the air, bounding along just like in cartoons. I literally fell down onto the grass laughing the first time I saw them do it. If I remember right, it was the first real laugh I had after Danny died, and it made me feel both happy and guilty at the same time.

"What do you think you're doing?" called a breathless voice behind me.

I jumped and turned to find Marise standing in the driveway, hands on her hips, her hair piled high on her head making her look like a very charming bobblehead. Chopin stood by her side in his harness, panting in the heat. The old dog looked pretty rough. "What's wrong?"

"What's wrong? We're going to be late, that's what's wrong. You were supposed to pick me up a half hour ago."

"Pick you up? For what?" Did we have plans? Nothing came to mind.

"For the bird-watch!" I was close enough by now that I could see Marise was wearing a pair of binoculars around her neck. My heart sank. I had a million plans for today and none of them included standing around staring at birds.

"I forgot," I finally admitted, and then regarded her narrowly. "How did you know I was up there anyway?" I had a fleeting and traitorous thought that I could have escaped simply by pretending not to be there when she called me.

"I could hear you chuckling about something," she said, clearly very flustered.

I almost said, "It's just a bird-watch," but managed to bite my tongue at the last second. To me it was just a bird-watch. But I put myself in Marise's shoes for a minute—a very sensible pair of wildly colorful rubber boots I noticed—and realized that for her it was a chance to escape the little safe world of her home and do something outside that blind people didn't usually get to do. For Marise, this was an adventure. I tried to hide a smile and then realized she couldn't see it anyway. "Well, come on then. We're going to be late."

"That's what I've been trying to tell you." She frowned suspiciously. "What are you smiling about anyway?"

Which made me laugh. Honestly, was the woman really blind or was it just an act? "Nothing, come on."

Twice Auggie had given me directions to Beinvenue Pond, which in French meant "Welcome", as though by repeating himself he was insuring that I'd find it. I'd thought it was overkill at the time, but wandering around on dirt back roads, I wished I'd paid more attention. The pond was way out of the way, up by the border but not actually over it. It was on one of those kinds of roads that did cross the border here and there so you were in and out of Canada without realizing it. My grandparents had lived on a road like that, and we'd often picked blackberries in Canada a few fields over from their house.

By the time we arrived, there were a few cars parked as far into the road as they could be without actually blocking traffic. This time of year there was still so much water in the earth that if you pulled off the side you'd sink in so deep you'd have to be towed out, something I'd found out the hard way a time or two. I parked behind the last one in the line and went around to Marise's side to help her out.

"What do you want me to do with Chopin?" I asked. The big dog was curled into a tight ball at her feet where he'd been trained to ride at guide dog school.

"Can he just stay in here?" she asked. "I'm afraid he'd scare off any birds, and besides he'll get all muddy."

"How do you know it's muddy?" I suspected the real reason she didn't want the dog along was so no one would realize just looking at her that she was blind. Though I couldn't object to any of her actual reasons.

"It's always muddy this time of year," she replied loftily, swinging her legs out of the truck and testing the ground before she stood up. Chopin hefted his bulk off the floor of my old truck and climbed up onto the seat where he could sprawl out comfortably. I left the windows cracked generously so the truck wouldn't heat up, swung the rusty door shut, and took Marise's elbow to guide her along the road.

We made our way gingerly toward the group of bird-watchers, clearly old pros, in rubber boots, anoraks, and fanny packs, each sporting a walking stick, a pair of binoculars dangling around their necks. I wished someone had told me about the dress code. I could already feel water seeping in through the seams of my barn boots, which were ancient tan leather work boots. And my wool sweater, though thick and cabled, was doing nothing to cut the little breeze coming in off the pond. Marise wasn't dressed like anyone around us, either, but I thought it wise not to tell her. She so desperately wanted to blend in.

Auggie loped over like a happy Labrador, an excited grin on his face. "You came!" he exclaimed, pleased. "And you've brought a friend. Hi!"

Marise put out her hand first to avoid the awkwardness of searching for his, a little trick of hers. "I'm Marise Gaudet. Pleased to meet you." She smiled warmly and gazed up toward the sound of his voice.

Auggie reached out a massive paw, engulfed her hand, and pumped it warmly. "Welcome, welcome! A fellow bird enthusiast?" he inquired hopefully.

"Absolutely!" Marise agreed stoutly. "I love birds."

"Is this your first watch or are you a seasoned veteran?"

"This is my very first."

Auggie appeared to be mesmerized by the tendrils of hair that had escaped her upsweep. They danced prettily around her face as she bobbed her head in assent. "Wonderful," he murmured whether in agreement or admiration I couldn't tell. "Step right on over here. You're the last to arrive.

We've been listening to locate the birds with our ears first. We've identified a Winter Wren and a European Starling so far." He addressed the group. "Let's see what we can spot, shall we?"

Like a team, the experienced birders uncapped their binoculars and swung them into position. I realized I'd neglected to bring yet another piece of essential gear. Marise clamped her binoculars to her eyes and swept the woods in a pantomime of the others but since she didn't need them I asked to borrow them.

"Sure," she said sweetly. "We can share."

"I hear a Tufted Titmouse," someone exclaimed. "There!"

En masse the binoculars swung to the left trying to locate the elusive gray and white bird in the gray and brown brush. As we were all diligently searching for the Tufted Titmouse, Marise pointed overhead and proclaimed, "Canadian goose!"

Sure enough, I swung the binoculars upward and caught the distinct V-shape of a flock of geese.

"Actually, it's Canada goose." Auggie corrected gently.

"That's what I said, isn't it?"

Auggie coughed softly into his hand. "Eh, no, you said Canadian goose but the correct term is Canada goose."

"Ah," Marise said thoughtfully, but I knew her well enough to know she was being facetious. When Auggie had stepped away, I lowered my voice and asked her how she'd known the flock was there.

"Heard them honk," she murmured with a little smile, and I stifled a laugh.

I tried to enjoy myself, honestly I did, but I was cold, my feet were frozen, and all I could think about was the spinning I was supposed to be doing. It seemed like we'd been standing there forever, rooted to that one spot. Everyone's eyes were glued to some part of the brush surrounding the pond, pausing every now and then to feverishly write in a notebook.

A short wiry man with an untidy mustache sidled up to me, a clipboard out, his pen poised over it at the ready. I thought maybe he was taking a survey. "Hello," he said, his eyes a watery blue behind his old-fashioned glasses.

"Hello," I replied, smiling politely.

"How many do you have?"

"I'm sorry?"

"Birds," he elaborated. "On your life list. How many do you have?"

"What's a life list?" I asked blankly, wondering if it was anything like a bucket list.

"You haven't started a life list?" he asked, aghast. Ripping a piece of paper off his clipboard he pressed it into my hands along with a pen. "I hope this is your first outing," he said fervently, "because then you won't have lost any sightings to time."

"It is definitely my first outing," I assured him. "So . . . what's a life list?"

"A list of all the birds you spot in your life," he explained. "You'll really want to get yourself a nice journal to keep your record in, but for now just record each bird you spot on that piece of paper. You can transfer the information later. You'll want to put down the date and location as well." He glanced over to see how I was doing, and I diligently started writing down the names of the birds we'd spotted so far after writing the date and "Bienvenue Pond" in big letters at the top of the paper.

"I keep my actual records on my computer, of course," he continued, satisfied I was following directions. "I have a house list for the birds I see around my house, a trip list for birds I see when I go on trips, a state list that breaks down which birds I've seen in which states, and a wish list for all the birds I would like to see in my lifetime.

"Naturally my computer list is more like a database, a supplement to my journal, because it's impossible to enter my sketches." He laughed soundlessly at his own joke. "Would you like to see my sketches?" He didn't wait for me to reply, but whipped out a sketchbook he was holding under the clipboard and opened it at random. The pages fell open to reveal an exquisite drawing of a Horned Lark, hand-tinted, probably after the original sketch was done, but nothing could have surprised me more.

"That's truly beautiful," I breathed, unable to take my eyes off the drawing.

He blushed modestly at the praise and flipped to other drawings, each in their own way a work of art. I suddenly began to wonder if I was in the presence of someone whose name I should know, but I didn't want to display my ignorance so I hedged around for information.

"Do you sell your drawings?"

He drew back as though I'd slapped him. "Absolutely not!" he said so vehemently that he nearly spat. "Each of these birds is priceless."

I took a step backward just in case. "Right, yes, I agree. I just thought . . ." It didn't seem to matter what I thought because he snapped the sketchbook shut with vengeance and wandered off muttering under his breath.

Shaken a little, I turned back to find Marise. Auggie was pointing out a bird to her and absently handed her his binoculars. She took them and held them up to her eyes. "Can you see him?" Auggie asked.

"Not yet," Marise said sweetly. "Tell me what he looks like."

It was all I could do not to howl with laughter watching her interact with Auggie. He had no idea she was blind. I used to wonder why it was so important to her, that people not find out she was blind until they got to know her a little, but after years as a widow, I understood. It was difficult wearing a label. People automatically assumed things about you before they even knew you. But the worst was fending off their pity, spoken or unspoken. Which was probably why I was still wearing my wedding ring, I mused. It was my defense just as surely as Marise's fierce independence was her defense.

By the time Auggie decided the bird-watch was over, I had 15 birds on my new life list, and I was pretty certain they would be the only birds ever on my new life list. Birding was for the birds. I chuckled at my own little joke and helped Marise navigate back to the truck.

Chopin was happy to see us, and I opened the door so he could stretch his legs a little and go do his business. I passed him off to Marise, placing the stiff leather handle of his harness in her hand. She walked him a little way from the truck where I could hear her encourage him to get on with it. "Get busy, Chopin. Get busy."

Auggie rounded the back of the truck, his mouth opening to say something. When he caught sight of Marise and her guide dog, it clamped shut, and he stopped dead in his tracks.

"Hi Auggie," I said, amused at the look on his face.

Marise turned toward the sound of my voice, and I could see Auggie's mental struggle play out across his face as he tried to reconcile himself to the fact that she was blind when clearly he'd had no idea.

"But, but, you were bird-watching." Auggie sputtered, floundering with the concept.

"Well, technically I was bird-listening," Marise corrected him gently.

"Oh." He chewed on that for a bit. "And did you like what you heard?"

"Very much."

"I have some great tapes of bird calls. We could listen to them sometime."

"I'd like that."

She smiled and he smiled and I gaped. Somehow she'd snagged a date right under my nose—with Auggie of all people. Which one of us was blind?

"How did you do that?" I hissed to her as we loaded Chopin back into the truck.

"Do what?" She sounded innocent enough, but she looked like she'd swallowed one of the red-winged blackbirds we'd seen.

"You know perfectly well what!"

"Auggie, you mean? He's nice. I like him."

"You don't even know him!"

"He *seems* nice and he has a beautiful voice," she offered. For the first time an edge of doubt crept past her tight control. For all she knew, Auggie was a decrepit, psychotic derelict with a penchant for birds and a radio voice. "What does he look like?"

I toyed with the idea of messing with her before deciding that would be needlessly cruel. "He has long, black hair and a nice face. And he's very tall. But, he, um, looks more like someone who could lift a bus or rip off your face if you crossed him. Not that he would," I added hastily. "Auggie is the gentlest person I know."

Marise smirked. "He sounds good to me."

"But that's not the point." I remembered my argument in time to save it. "But he could have been psycho. For all you know he *is* psycho."

Marise brushed this idea aside imperiously. "I thought you said you knew him."

"I do!" I crowed triumphantly. "But *you* don't know him at all."

"Ah," she held up a rebuking finger and wagged it under my nose with a Cheshire cat grin. "But I will."

Which, I decided, I couldn't argue with.

By the time I dropped Marise and Chopin off at home and drove up into my yard, the day was pretty much shot. I climbed wearily out of the truck. My feet were numb and all I really wanted was a comforting mug of tea and a scalding shower. And from what I could see there were two things standing between me and what I wanted. One of them was Addy, and one was Mimi. They were together on the porch, and neither one looked very happy. I heaved a tired sigh, put all cozy thoughts of tea and heat behind me for the time being, and plodded heavily toward what I instinctively knew was going to be a distinctly unpleasant encounter.

Chapter Eleven

Both girls were talking before my foot even hit the porch step. I heard phrases like, "caught her stealing money," and "told you I wasn't looking for money," and "your hand was in the purse," and "needed something really bad," all jumbled up like a train wreck with a lot of eye rolling on Addy's part and hand-wringing on Mimi's.

I held up my hands like a traffic cop. "Tea. Inside. Now."

I pointed both girls to the kitchen and told them not to utter a word before I got back but to start the kettle. I changed out of my muddy jeans into a pair of worn sweats, found my coziest sweater, and slipped my feet into slippers which braced me up enough to return to the kitchen and supervise the tea making. Obediently, but with much glaring, the girls were quietly setting up mugs and getting the tea things out while the kettle whispered to itself on the stove building up to a boil.

I dripped honey into three mugs, dropped in tea bags, snatched up the kettle the moment it whistled, and poured the water while waving the glowering girls into the living room. When we were all sitting down and my hands were wrapped comfortingly around my mug, I nodded my head at Addy to begin telling her side with a warning look at Mimi to be still.

"You'll get your turn," I assured her.

To her credit Addy stuck to the facts. "Mimi stopped by to do chores, and I was in the kitchen doing homework. She came in to talk for awhile, but then I had to go get something in my room. When I came back she had her hand in your purse rummaging around."

I nodded to indicate I'd heard her and then turned to Mimi. "Now you."

The younger girl's face turned a violent shade of red, and she twisted her hands so forcefully I was a little alarmed that she might break her fingers.

I leaned forward. "Mimi, it's okay. Whatever it is, we'll figure it out. It's going to be okay."

"No!" She flung the word out at me with such force that I flinched. "No! It won't be okay! It won't ever be okay again." She jumped up and started pacing back and forth, her face shiny with sweat. "I did it; I did what she said, but I wasn't trying to steal money."

"Okay," I encouraged, "so what were you doing in my purse?"

She took a deep shuddering breath in. "I was looking for medicine." She said the last word so quietly that both Addy and I leaned forward instinctively to catch it.

"Medicine?" I asked blankly. "You mean like painkillers? Did you have a headache?"

She shook her head. "Yes, no, not those kind of painkillers. I was hoping to find something stronger."

I was starting to feel that now familiar darkness creeping toward me, drawing me into a world I'd been happy to know nothing about. "Mimi, I don't understand. Would you please sit down and start from the beginning?" Mimi stopped her frantic pacing and turned tortured eyes on me.

"I can't," she whispered, her eyes filling with tears. "I can't sit down. I need something; I need something now."

Addy's eyes narrowed, and I saw understanding begin to fill them. "Mimi, are you doing drugs?"

Mimi shook her head hard. "No! Just painkillers. Just since my dad died. He had something the doctors gave him last year when he had a back operation. They were in the medicine cabinet. I took one. After the funeral. To help me calm down. And they helped! But now they're all gone, and I don't know what to do. I need more. I was hoping you had something that would make me feel better."

"Is that why you're cutting yourself?" I asked gently.

Mimi stopped pacing so quickly she almost fell over. "How do you know about that?" she whispered.

"I saw your arms," Addy said, the accusation gone from her voice. "When we were doing the dishes. I saw the cuts."

Mimi began crying in earnest. I set my tea down on the table and rose to envelope the sobbing girl in my arms while Addy watched with sad eyes. "It's okay Mimi, really, it will be okay. We'll find some help for you."

"I miss my father!" Mimi wailed into my shoulder, her frail body shaking with each racking sob. "I want my father!"

"I know, I know," I soothed. Her grief was so fresh and so palpable that I started sobbing myself as it opened fresh wounds inside me bringing my own sadness roiling to the surface as new and familiar as if Danny had died yesterday. Addy quietly got up and left the room but not before I could see that she was crying, too.

The grief was exhausting and as it descended on me like an oppressive cloud, I had a flash of sudden clarity that astounded me, and I knew that it was time to let it go. It was time to move out from under that burden and walk on. The idea goaded me. I had no idea how to do that.

And yet here I was telling Mimi that it would be okay. Who was I to talk?

Later, after I'd driven Mimi home, had a quiet talk with her mother, and comforted my own daughter, I crept down to Marise's. She opened the door, still in high spirits from our afternoon birding but she sobered quickly when I told her what had happened.

"What is her mother going to do?"

I shrugged and held the steaming mug of tea she'd given me up to my face, feeling the warmth soak into my cheek, relishing the comfort of it. The aroma of roses enveloped me. Rose-scented Tulsi tea, holy basil, it was Marise's favorite kind of tea, and I only ever had it at her house. The sweet smell of the roses reminded me of love and Valentine's Day and Danny, and I felt my eyes welling up with tears again.

"Theresa said she knew someone who worked with troubled teens, a friend. She was going to make a call. She didn't seem surprised at all, just sad, almost like I was confirming something she already knew. Addy and I had been trying to get some resources together for her before we told her." I corrected myself. "Before *I* told her about the cutting. But as it turned out we didn't even need them. She knew more than I did."

"And Mimi?"

I shrugged again. "She was so agitated. I just hope she doesn't do something stupid."

"Stupider," Marise corrected.

"Stupider," I agreed. "But that's not why I'm here," I continued quietly.

"Oh?"

"I . . . I realized something . . . something you've been trying to tell me for a long time, I guess." I fidgeted for a minute trying to think how to adequately put into words how I felt, blinking back tears of frustration and despair. "It feels like I've been carrying this great weight around forever. I want to take a free breath. I'm tired. It's like everything I do is faded, and even when I'm happy, or I know I should be happy, I'm not. The weight is still there, overshadowing everything. Like a constant companion.

"If Danny were here," I pointed out practically, "he'd tell me to get over myself. He'd say, 'Lighten up, why doncha?' " I mimicked Danny's gravelly voice. "He'd tell me to make the best of it and put it in the past. Even Danny wouldn't want me grieving over him like this."

I sighed heavily. "The trouble is I don't know how to stop."

"But you want to?" Marise cocked her head at me as if whatever I said next had more importance than I could imagine.

I drew a shaky breath. "Yes." Then I repeated it for good measure, a little firmer. "Yes."

Whatever she heard in my voice seemed to satisfy her. "Well, you can't do it alone," she said finally.

"I know," I pointed out. "That's why I have you."

When she shook her head, her upsweep lurched violently to one side clearly having come unpinned from its moorings. Marise paid no attention. "No, I can support you, but I can't help you. Not really help you. You need God for something like this. He's the only one strong enough to carry that burden."

I felt the hair on the back of my neck prickle. Uncomfortably. Why did she always have to bring God into it? By now I was used to her response of, "I'll pray about that," whenever I asked her for advice or help. When she burst into spontaneous prayer, out loud, I didn't freak out anymore. I didn't even flinch when she quoted Bible texts sometimes to illustrate a point. But if I had wanted God's help, I would have asked him. I wouldn't need to ask her.

I'd gotten this same line of advice from Marcel a few times, too, when I asked him for help coping with Danny's death. Eventually I stopped asking. They both insisted that God was the answer to all my problems, that all I had to do was turn my life over to him, and he'd take care of everything. To be honest, there was no way I was turning my life over to God without knowing exactly what he wanted from me first. I wasn't about to get in over my head. If God was going to do me any favors and expected payment in kind, I wanted to know exactly what would be required. And until then, it was no deal.

I shook my head and then realized Marise couldn't see my response. "No, I know you think God fixes everything. But I'm not going there." I could feel myself getting irritated. "Besides, I do all the stuff I need to for God. We're good. I play piano for church, and I'm nice to people. Usually. I obey the commandments, and I even tithe. If I do all that, God ought to be helping me already."

The faintest smile twisted Marise's lips. It was an ironic smile though. There was no mirth in it. "This isn't about what you do, Em," she said quietly. "My mother used to say, 'Il ne faut pas mettre la charrue avant les bœufs.'"

"Don't put the plow before the oxen?" I translated, wondering what oxen had to do with anything.

"That's what it means, literally, yes, but the more familiar translation is 'Don't put the cart before the horse.' What you're talking about is the fruit of the Spirit, it's what shows when we have a relationship with God. The question is, is the fruit growing naturally or are you tying it on so that it looks like it's growing there? When we have a real relationship, the 'fruit' grows naturally; we do good things because they are the right things, and God gives us the impulse to do them. If we don't have a relationship we do good things for other reasons: we feel guilty, we feel pressured, we want to look good, or we want to avoid some kind of celestial punishment.

"The relationship has to come first. God works through the relationship to change us and help us. You told me what you *do* for God. Now tell me, do you *know* him?"

"Know him?" I stared at her blankly for a minute. "What do you mean know him? I know all about God. I've been a Christian all my life. Of course I know God. Otherwise why would I do the things I do?"

Marise leaned forward, an earnest expression on her face. "Em, I know all about Joshua Bell. I've listened to every song he ever recorded. I even got to go to one of his concerts, before I was blind. I was mesmerized by his performance. It was amazing. But even though I know all about him, and I've even seen him, we've never *met*. I don't really *know* him. If you asked him who I was, he wouldn't have a clue. You can know all *about* someone but still not *know them*."

I opened my mouth to say something then snapped it shut. Did I know God? I mean, sure, I knew all about him. I'd been raised a Christian. I hadn't been the most zealous attendant, but I had never completely left the church; I was there every week and had been since I was about twenty-seven when Addy was two years old, and I started bringing her for the children's programs. About that time the old pianist had retired, and no one else could play. Danny had sometimes complained about how I had to be there early every week, and he rarely went to church himself, but Addy and I were always there unless I was too sick to get out of bed.

I didn't usually make it back in during the week for prayer meeting, but I never felt like I needed to. I knew my way around the Bible. I was usually the first one to find a text when Marcel referenced one in his sermon. I was familiar with a lot of verses. I knew all the important stuff.

But Marise was right. All that didn't mean that I knew God. Just that I knew a lot *about* him. I sat back in my chair feeling a little defeated and bewildered. God was . . . invisible. It wasn't like you could sit down and have a cup of tea with him and indulge in a long get-to-know-you kind of chat. You couldn't go bowling or skiing with God to spend time together and get closer. The mechanics of getting to know someone you couldn't see and couldn't talk to were baffling.

"But it's not like God and I can start hanging out together to get to know each other," I pointed out finally.

Marise laughed. "Sure you can. Just not in the usual ways."

"What other ways are there?"

"Prayer, Bible reading, talking with other believers, going to church, helping people, meditating on Scripture," Marise recited, ticking the points off on her fingers. "Those are all ways we get to know God. If you ask him, he'll tell you all about himself. He'll show you things that you can't even imagine. Sometimes when I'm struggling with something, I'll read a Bible verse I've read a hundred times, but that day it will be just the comfort or encouragement or advice I needed. And I'll know that God is speaking to me directly."

Marise's face positively shone as she spoke, and I couldn't help feeling a pang of jealousy. I wanted that, too. I wanted that connection she had with a God who helped her when she was down or struggling. I wanted to know that I'd never be completely alone again. That God would help me through this dark time and out the other side where I was sure there would be sunshine if I could only reach it.

"Can I pray with you?" Marise asked eagerly, leaning forward and groping for my hands.

There was an awkward pause before I reluctantly met her reach, surrendering my hands, and swallowed hard. I felt as though I was on the brink of something momentous, something life-changing. I felt a bit sick to my stomach.

Did I really want my life to change? I considered the oppressive darkness that had engulfed me since Danny's death and recoiled, rejecting it completely. Yes, I decided. Yes, I desperately wanted my life to change. And for the first time, I felt ready to do whatever it took to conquer my grief and anger so I could start to live again.

"Okay," I whispered, cleared my throat, and tried again with conviction, "Okay, yes, please."

"Father, this is my friend Emerson. You know what a dark place she's been in because you've been there with her the whole time even though she couldn't feel your presence. God, help her feel your presence now. Help her to see your light. Dispel the darkness.

"She misses her husband Danny and she always will, but God, help heal that wound in her heart so that she can walk on in her life with you. Help her remember the good times she had with Danny and to cherish them in her heart. And help her to walk into the sunshine, the Sonshine of your love."

I felt my lips creep into a smile at her play on words. It was a little corny, but I liked it. I started to pull my hands away but she wasn't finished.

"God," Marise continued earnestly, "please help Emerson know you in a deeper way. She wants to know you. She wants to have a real relationship with you. Show her how to do that. I thank you in the name of your precious son, Jesus. Amen."

"Amen," I said, waiting for a thunderbolt or something. I didn't feel anything spectacular, but oddly enough, I did feel peaceful. I felt as though I'd been through a crisis but now had hope that it would all come out right in the end. It felt a bit like when you spot the first lightening of the sky after a storm. It wasn't gone yet, but you knew the worst of it was over. "Thank you," I added. Both to Marise and to God.

Marise's smile was broad. "Would you like some more tea?"

I stared regretfully at the contents in my cup, now gone stone cold. "No, thanks. I ought to get back home. I think it's going to be an early night for me."

"Thanks again for the birding trip!" Marise called as I made my way down the path to the road.

"You're welcome!" I hollered back, but my mind was too full of the spectacular sunset to really process my response. It was as if an artist had spilled all the most vibrant oranges, reds, and yellows from his paint box, mixed in a tiny bit of purple for contrast and spread it all out over the sky. It was magnificent. It took my breath away. And as it left I breathed, "Thank you," to God without feeling the slightest bit self-conscious.

I was keenly aware of the fact that when Marise had poked her head out of the door to call after me, she had been oblivious to all this incredible beauty around her. God gave each of us different gifts; Marise saw spiritual beauty, I was able to see physical beauty. For the first time I could actually see that as a gift. "Thank you," I repeated, feeling my heart fill with gratitude.

Taking deep breaths, looking out over the still lake as I walked, I became aware of music. It was Port na bPúcaí, as haunting as ever. It seemed to float up from the water, and I walked toward the sound, transfixed.

It didn't surprise me when I found myself at Seán's gate. The music came from somewhere around the back. I paused briefly before deciding to go on through and find Seán to talk for a minute before I continued on home. He never seemed to want to talk about how he was doing, and after my initial pique, I decided that maybe it was best if I didn't invest too much emotional energy into wanting to know. He was probably trying to protect me, and I had enough healing work of my own to do climbing out of the emotional cave I'd been living in. It was best this way. We could still be friends though. I marched confidently through the gate and around to the back of the house to say hello to my friend.

I found Seán sitting on his porch, or rather the McCarty's porch, a quaint, snug, secluded spot that looked out over a splendid view of the lake uncluttered from this angle with views of any of the other cottages. You could almost imagine this cottage was alone on the lake. A pair of ducks floated past below, cruising the shoreline which was newly liberated from ice.

"Hey," I said, startling him. The music stopped abruptly.

"Hey, what are you doing here?" He didn't look happy. Or rather, he looked almost dismayed to see me.

"I was walking home, and I heard the music. I just stopped in to say hi. If it's a bad time, I'll go."

Seán looked conflicted. He put the pipes down and got to his feet. "It's just that, well, I'd ask you to stay, but I'm expecting someone. We're going . . . out . . ."

When he said "out" the doorbell rang and a clear "Yoohoo!" cut through the house in a decidedly feminine voice. "Seán? Are you ready to go? I know I'm late, but the way I drive we should make good time on the thruway so . . ." The tap of high heels clicked sharply through the house, and the porch door swung open.

Seeing Trudy Livingston poke her head tentatively through the back door and walk outside to stand on the porch was like watching a traffic accident in slow motion. All kinds of emotions crossed Seán's face, not the least of which was guilt. Trudy seemed to sense something was wrong and glanced around to find me outside the screened in porch. "Oh, hello! Mrs. Giroux, isn't it? Adrienne's mother? We met at the . . ."

"I remember," I cut her off, forcing my voice to sound natural, cheerful even.

"How is Adrienne?" She was as polished as she had been that day in the hospital. Not a hair out of place, her suit looked as fresh as if it was still on the hanger, her fashionable pumps were so stylish I knew she had found them in an exclusive store in an enormous city, probably Montréal, I thought grimly. She was pretty in an "I've-never-had-anything-bad-happen-to-me-in-my-whole-life" kind of way, not classically beautiful, but she knew how to make the best of what she had. I glanced down at my worn-out sweats, mostly covered, thank goodness, by the knitted duster I'd thrown on in case it was chilly and the muck boots I'd shoved my feet into on my way out the door to hurry down to Marise's after dealing with Mimi and squirmed uncomfortably at the glaring comparison.

"Fine, healing well. I'd better be going. I'll see you, Seán." I was thankful for the darkness as I felt a hot burning flush sear my face. At least I was spared that embarrassment. And really, it wasn't like we were dating or something. We were friends, I reminded myself sternly, just friends. And the man was dying for crying out loud! So why did I feel like I'd been gut-punched? Why was I struggling so hard to muffle the sobs that were threatening to burst out of my throat?

God, please at least let me get far enough away that they don't hear me. The prayer was so natural, so real, that the irony didn't hit me at first. It took a few steps before I realized how crazy it was that my first real prayer in as long as I could remember was for the strength not to cry! I almost laughed, the kind of laughter that turns into sobbing, but I managed to keep it in.

My foot had hit my own driveway when I heard Seán's voice behind me calling my name. I pretended not to hear him and forced myself not to look back. A few more yards and I would be safe inside my own house. I could go straight to bed and put this bizarre day behind me. I could even pretend that my life was not about to go from bad to worse.

Chapter Twelve

A week later, as I struggled to orient myself, swimming up from a deep and nightmarish sleep, I reluctantly opened my eyes. The sun was shining through the window and onto my face. I lay tangled in the maple leaf quilt I had been wrapping up in at night in an ongoing attempt to soothe myself. I squinted painfully at the raw sunshine filtering in and pushed my hair back from my face. The sun was pretty far up in the sky and the house was quiet. Addy must have already left for school.

I got up, using the quilt as a bathrobe and padded to the window. Outside I could hear birds, the kind you only hear in the spring and summer, chirping loudly. That could only mean one thing in this part of the world. The weather had warmed up. I pulled the window up and poked my head out, taking a bracing breath of fresh air.

The sun felt warm on my face, and I could hear the sheep bleating peacefully from the far end of the pasture. Addy had let them out; I breathed a grateful sigh. The dogs, yawning and stretching, came to mill around my feet and whine to go out. I shuffled over to the door and opened it but ended up following them out onto the porch to experience the beauty of this day up close and personal.

Despite the lingering morass of emotions I'd been struggling with, most of them having to do with God, Mimi, Danny, and Seán—a veritable pea soup of confusion—I felt an almost giddy rush of gratitude and delight from the strong infusion of sunshine and warm air. It felt good. I decided to test Marise's idea that God was with us all the time by thanking him for what was clearly something he was directly responsible for. "Thank you, God," I said out loud. "What a beautiful day! I'm so grateful to you for blessing us with it."

I had my eyes closed so when a deep, male voice behind me said, "You're welcome," I nearly shot out of my skin. This was followed by a low chuckle and an apologetic, "Sorry; I'm kidding, of course."

I took a shaky breath. "Marcel, I'm going to kill you."

"Better not. I have a witness."

Every fiber of my being warned me not to turn around. Maybe if I just kept my eyes closed, it would all be a dream, and I could wake up and start over again. Feeling nothing short of murderous, I turned around slowly, burrowing even deeper into quilt, grateful I hadn't discarded it. They were sitting in a shadowy corner of the porch, but that still didn't explain why my worthless dogs hadn't spotted them. Two canine noses attached to two canine brains much more interested in watering the hedgerow than protecting me. I couldn't even trust my stinking dogs.

"Why are you here? So early?" I asked my brother bluntly. I ignored Seán, sitting next to him, his face a study in worry and, surprisingly, not amusement.

"Em, it's practically noon," Marcel said. "We just got here a little early. We're practicing today, remember? We thought you were down at the store. We were just waiting until you got back. We never dreamed you were inside still asleep." Marcel grinned wickedly. "If we'd known that I would have used my key and woken you up. Remember how I used to wake you up when we were kids? Remember?"

"I remember," I snapped, preferring to forget how he used to sneak into my room, usually on weekends when I got to sleep in, and dump a pitcher of ice cold water on me as I slept. Boy, did he catch it from our parents. Never stopped him though. I closed my eyes and tried to rally my still sleepy thoughts. Stupid alarm clock. Batteries must have died. It was a testament to my exhaustion that I'd slept in so late.

"Where's Marise?"

"Not here yet." Marcel shrugged. "There was a car in her driveway. Maybe she had unexpected company. By the way, you'll never guess . . ."

The phone shrilled inside the house, cutting him off. Marcel and Seán started to get up to follow me inside, but I held up a hand to stop them. "Sit. Stay."

The dogs scooted in ahead of me, and I almost tripped on the quilt trying to get to the phone. "Hello?"

Marise's voice was so choked up that at first I didn't recognize it.

"It's Chopin; he's dead."

Stunned, my brain whirled in place trying to process this news. Crisis! What could I do? In situations like these, the first thing through my mind was always: "Quick, find a grown-up." Then I would realize that *I* was the grown-up, and I'd try to pony-up to do whatever needed to be done. "I'll call Auggie," I said quickly.

"I called him already. He's here, but I want you."

"I'll be right there."

I didn't open the door to talk to Marcel and Seán, I just put my mouth up close to the screen. "That was Marise. We're going to have to cancel today. Chopin is dead."

I didn't wait for their response, but the sound of dismay in their voices followed me into the bedroom where I quickly pulled on a pair of—sadly— stale jeans from the day before with mud-encrusted cuffs from slogging around the sheep pen, and found a black, long sleeve T-shirt—appropriate color, I thought grimly.

Marcel and Seán were gone by the time I came back out, but I didn't stop to give them much thought until I hurried past the end of my driveway where I found Seán lingering. He quickly fell into step with me. "Hey," he said, studying my face as we quick-marched along.

I didn't turn to meet his eyes. "Hey."

"This is pretty bad, huh?"

"It's very bad," I agreed, not sure if we were talking about the last time I'd seen him, embarking on a date with Trudy Livingston, or Marise losing Chopin. What business did he have dating anyway? He was dying for pity's sake. And why did it bother me? It wasn't like I cared or anything.

I could tell he wanted to say more but the pace, dictated by my angry, irritated thoughts, was restricting him. He seemed to have lost a bit of weight lately, and he looked haggard. I knew he was probably struggling to keep up. Reluctantly I slowed down a little in sympathy, not enough to allow for chatting but enough so that he could comfortably keep step. When we reached Marise's door, I didn't bother to knock. I let myself in and tried to forget all about him.

He gravitated toward Auggie, who was in the process of removing Chopin's body. Marise sat on her couch, a box of tissues next to her, her eyes and nose red from weeping. When she heard the door slam she stiffened and turned toward the doorway. "Em?" she asked hopefully, her voice cracking.

I sat next to her and put my arms around her. She melted against me sobbing hard, and I rubbed her back soothingly. "I'm so sorry, honey."

I tried not to notice as Auggie and Seán between them lifted Chopin up on a sheet and began to carry him out to the truck. Tears stung my eyes as I thought about the old dog. I'd known Chopin forever it seemed. I used to drive Marise to his check-ups at the guide dog school.

When she had calmed down enough to talk, she began to spit out the story in pieces. "He was so cold. He must have . . ." A shuddering sob stopped her for a minute, "He must have died not long after we went to bed last night. He came into the room with me, and I heard him settle himself on the floor.

"Do you think he died peacefully? I couldn't tell." She grabbed my arm in agitation, and I looked over at Auggie for confirmation. He'd come back in and was standing rather uncertainly in the doorway between the kitchen and living room.

"Absolutely," he said with conviction. "His ticker just gave out. The old fellow died peacefully in his sleep."

"He never got to be a real dog!" she wailed, suddenly breaking out in fresh weeping.

"What?" Bewildered I looked at Auggie again for explanation.

"She's feeling badly that Chopin had to work all his life and never got to play like other dogs because he was tied to her. I tried to tell her that was nonsense, but she wasn't having it." He shrugged, the corners of his mouth turned down in a tiny frown as if Marise was a mystery he couldn't quite make out. And who could blame him? He'd hadn't known her very long. I'd known her for years and was still mystified sometimes, charmingly so. Marise was complicated. He'd figure that out soon enough.

I took Marise by the shoulders and shook her slightly. "Now, listen up," I said sternly. "That dog loved you! Living with you and helping you wasn't just work to him. He loved every minute of it. Do you think he'd have been any happier living with some family who ignored him half of his life? You spent every waking second with that dog."

"But he never got to run and play like other dogs," Marise sobbed.

"Marise, this is Chopin we're talking about," I reminded her. "Chopin, who loved nothing better than a long nap in a sunny spot on the carpet. Chopin, who could medal in laziness. Are you sure we're talking about the same dog?"

Marise smiled wanly. "Do you think he had a good life?" she asked me earnestly.

"Good life? You spoiled him rotten!" I put my hand on her shoulder and squeezed reassuringly. "He lived with *you*, didn't he? You loved him and gave his life purpose. He had the best life a dog could hope for."

"The best thing to do," Seán interjected in an attempt at helpfulness, "is to get a new puppy."

Marise stiffened. "Absolutely not."

Taken aback by her vehemence, Seán asked, "Why not?" before he caught the warning look from Auggie.

"First of all," Marise said stiffly, "guide dogs aren't puppies when you get them. They are over a year old and fully trained. It's not like replacing the family pet. And second of all, I don't want to go through this ever again. I'll, I'll . . . Em, what will I do? I don't want to use a cane!" She howled in anguish and began sobbing all over again.

I shot Seán a dirty look and patted her back while Auggie motioned the bewildered Seán into the kitchen where he began talking to him in hushed tones.

The screen door slammed and Marcel came in carrying a big bunch of flowers. "How is she?" he stage-whispered, joining Auggie and Seán in the kitchen. I squeezed my eyes shut. Men. Why couldn't they all go away and leave us in peace? I knew Marise had heard him, her sense of hearing was acute and knowing her she could probably smell the flowers, too, but she didn't acknowledge his presence, just continued to sob quietly into my shoulder.

I glared meaningfully at them and then dramatically stared at the door. Marcel advanced into the room anyway, pointedly ignoring me. "Marise? I'm so sorry about Chopin. He was such a good dog . . ." Before he got any further his wife Agnès barreled through the front door.

"Misère," she huffed, "it's hot out today, eh?"

Agnès had a commanding presence. You knew immediately she was not someone to be trifled with. She and Marcel had raised three boys and all of them served in various branches of the military into which they had melded almost seamlessly. A drill sergeant once told Marcel that he'd never seen green kids transition so quickly into regimented military life. Marcel told him proudly that farm life will do that to you, but really Agnès had a lot to do with making those boys so self-sufficient and disciplined.

"You, you, you," she pointed at the men and then at the door, "out. Here, give me those." She took the flowers from Marcel's hands where he stood uncertainly clutching them. Without asking where Marise kept her vases, she began rummaging and picked the right cupboard instinctively. As she busied herself filling the vase with water, the men filed meekly past her though they didn't leave altogether; I could hear them milling around outside. I gave my sister-in-law a grateful look and mouthed, "Thank you." She nodded curtly as she thumped the flowers down on the kitchen table and turned to fill the kettle with water.

"Marise, chérie,[27] have you eaten?"

---

[27] Dear

Marise lifted her head from my damp shoulder and shook it miserably. "I can't eat," she said sorrowfully.

"Mmm," Agnès murmured. She stood in the middle of the kitchen, her neat salt-and-pepper hair curling exactly as if she had just left a 1950s beauty salon, probably because she had it styled once a week at the Clip-n-Curl where Eileen Lamotte had been styling hair since the 1950s and wasn't big on change.

"Right." She pulled an old-fashioned apron off a hook on the kitchen wall, wrapped it around herself, and began to hum as she poked around in the refrigerator and cupboards pulling things out and setting them on the counter beside the stove. Occasionally she muttered something in French or hummed a snatch of song under her breath.

Auggie crept in guiltily to say goodbye. "Marise? I've had another call; I've got to run. Don't you worry about Chopin. I'll take care of everything."

"Thank you Augustus," Marise said. "I'm sorry I had to call you so soon about something so awful."

"Aw, that's what I'm here for." He leaned over and put one massive paw over her small hand, engulfing it. "I'll call you later, okay?"

Marise nodded. "I'd like that."

"Fantastic." He straightened up, a small triumphant look on his broad face.

Marise sniffed and Auggie ducked his head like a small boy trying to avoid punishment as he slunk past Agnès and out the door. Agnès brandished a spatula at him sternly before using it to expertly flip what smelled tantalizingly like French toast. My stomach growled, and I remembered that I hadn't eaten, and it was lunchtime.

Agnès seemed to have divined that I'd be hungry, too. Either that or she was counting on the fact that if she could get me to eat, Marise was sure to follow. In any case, she'd set the table for two, and when she caught my eye, I nodded. As she poured the tea and set a plate of steaming eggs down on the table beside a pile of French toast, I helped Marise to her feet before she could protest.

She shuffled to the table still sniffling. It was like the light inside her had been switched off; grief covered her like a cloak. She dropped into the chair Agnès held out, and I sank down next to her. Two steaming plates of food were unceremoniously dumped on the table in front of us, cutlery clattered down to join it. Agnès made herself a mug of chamomile tea before she pulled up a chair on the other side of Marise and slid the jug of maple syrup our way.

While I shoveled food into my mouth, Agnès made valiant attempts to shake Marise from her malaise, but she had reckoned on a far weaker opponent.

"So Marise, do you have a date set for the next concert? My husband tells me nothing."

"No. Not yet."

Agnès tried again. "How are the songs sounding?"

Marise's voice was dull. "Fine."

"Playing anything interesting?"

"Not really."

"How about the festival? How is that coming along?"

"Fine."

Agnès got up from the table and wandered over to the loom set up in the corner in a sunny spot of the living room. "Ah, you've started something new?"

Marise lifted her head almost imperceptibly, betraying her interest in this new line of questioning. "Yes."

Encouraged, Agnès bent for a closer look, her brows meeting in concentration. "But what is this, eh? I recognize this style. My mémère had one of these on her bed when I was growing up. I believe my arrière-grandmère, her mother's mother you understand, not her father's mother, made it for her. She was a weaver, too, like you," Agnès said brightly. "But this is traditional, is it not?"

Marise blew her nose on a tissue and nodded. "It's called catalogne. They date back to the 17th century, named for Sieur de Catalan. The textile started out as a carpet, but in Québec, they wove them as bed blankets. It was a way they could recycle fabrics because making them from scratch was such an involved, tedious process." She snorted a little. "Not that unraveling worn out garments and reusing them was so much easier, I guess. But if you don't have many supplies, you use what you have."

Agnès nodded and fingered the few inches of weaving where Marise had left off. "Pretty colors. The one we had in our family was quite faded. This one is so colorful."

"Yes, well, I have the luxury of using new materials dyed with modern acid dyes. Your great-grandmother had only plant dyes, which could be very vibrant in their day but weren't particularly colorfast." Marise took a shuddering breath and picked up her fork, tentatively poking it at her plate.

"Eggs are at two o'clock, French toast is at seven," I murmured helpfully. She nodded and for once didn't seem to mind the direction.

Agnès shot me a triumphant look over her head, and I tipped my head in acknowledgment. She'd done it. Like I said, the woman was a force of nature. "Maybe sometime you could show me how you do it, eh? Just a little bit. I'd like to see. Maybe I'll take up weaving myself one day." Agnès looked a bit wistful, then she laughed. "You can teach me, eh? Or am I too old and hopeless?"

"You're not hopeless," Marise retorted. "You're not even old. Besides, what fun is life if you don't keep learning new things?"

"Ah, well spoken," Agnès replied with a look that clearly said, "My work here is done." She untied the apron and hung it back up on the hook on the wall. "Marise, be sure you call me if you need anything, eh chérie? I'll stop to check on you later. I'm baking today. I'll bring you something. You need to keep your strength up."

Agnès's idea of keeping your strength up always had to do with baking, which was probably why my brother was so well padded. She quickly made converts everywhere she went because the woman could bake like nobody's business. Her éclairs alone won her prizes at the county fair every year. And her apple pie was devastating. What that woman could do with a little flour and butter.

"Do you know what I want?" Marise asked me after Agnès had let herself out.

"What, hon?"

"I want to sleep. I want to sleep and wake up and find Chopin next to the bed, like always. I want this to be a bad dream."

I reached out and patted her hand. "I know exactly what you mean. I feel like that almost every day."

"I've never lost anyone," Marise said softly. Then after a pause she added, "It feels awful."

"You must have lost pets before?" I said frowning. Surely she had lost something, someone, by now?

"No, we didn't have pets growing up, my mom was allergic to cats and dogs. All my family members who were living when I was born are still living. The only thing I ever lost was my sight."

"The acute phase will pass," I told her as a feeling of déjà vu washed over me. Hadn't we just been in the opposite situation? It was beyond ironic that I was now comforting her. "Sometimes it just takes longer than other times," I amended apologetically. I wasn't sure if I should tell her that she'd always feel a lingering sense of loss, of sorrow. That the fragrance of grief never completely dispelled. It just softened over time, like well-worn fabric.

"You know," I added hesitantly, "he really shouldn't have said it, but Seán was kind of right. I mean, not about getting a puppy, but you should think about getting another guide dog. You loved Chopin; he was your partner. There won't ever be another Chopin, but you can have another partner, one you'll love every bit as much in a different way."

As the words left my mouth, it was as if I heard someone saying them to me as well. It wasn't spoken words, more like impressions of the same thought. *You loved Danny; he was your partner. There won't ever be another Danny, but you can have another partner, one you'll love every bit as much in a different way.* I felt as though someone had taken a bead on me and got me right between the eyes. The thought was so tangible and hit home so hard I nearly gasped with the force of it.

I wanted to spit back, "No!" just as forcefully, but for the first time since Danny had died, I knew it would be a lie. I could feel it within my spirit, a subtle shift. Not just an acceptance that Danny was gone and would never return but an acceptance of the fact that just as surely my life would go on and that I was capable of loving someone else, maybe even as much as I had loved Danny. I wasn't exactly ready for that, but I knew it was the truth just as surely as I knew Marise would eventually get over Chopin's death.

In that same split second, I also realized why it bothered me so much to find Trudy Livingston tap-tapping into Seán's life. It was because a very unreasonable part of me wanted to be her; if Seán was going to date someone, why couldn't it be me? We were so compatible; I'd never met anyone other than Danny—and Marise, but she didn't count in this case— with whom I felt so comfortable and relaxed. It was like finding a matching puzzle piece; we fit together.

As clarity shot through me, it brought with it the sudden and very real sense that perhaps Seán had considered the same thing and made his choice in an attempt to protect me from even more inevitable sadness at his eventual, and presumably, very near passing. Maybe he cared about me so much he was purposely keeping me at a distance. Or maybe he didn't want to find out if he *did* care about me. If we never had the opportunity to explore a relationship, we would never be disappointed if it turned out we shared nothing more than a common taste in music and a surface attraction. In either case, we would be spared the inevitable final wrench when he passed away. No harm; no foul.

Which was ridiculous when you really thought about it, I told myself irritably. As if any of us knew when we were going to die. I could get hit by a tractor on my way down to Angelique's store tomorrow. Just because he knew his time was short, did that mean he wasn't entitled to live anymore? Of course not.

Marise sighed heavily, and I dragged my attention back to her. "You're right. I know you're right. It will just take some getting used to. I'll talk to the guide dog school today when I call to let them know about Chopin. And," she continued, coloring a little, "I suppose I'll have to apologize to Seán the next time I see him. I was a little out of my head with grief when I snapped at him."

"I'm sure he'll understand," I assured her, bringing my thoughts back with heroic effort to Marise and Chopin and away from my complicated mess of a life.

Marise did end up laying down for a nap. I tucked her in myself before heading home, closing the door softly behind me. I turned and nearly jumped out of my skin. Seán was leaning up against a tree in her yard. He pushed himself away from it with some effort and walked up to me.

"How is she?"

"She's sleeping."

"I can't believe I was so stupid telling her to get a puppy. Auggie told me about the whole guide dog process . . ."

I held up my hand to stop him. "I shouldn't tell you this, but she's going to apologize to you later. She knows what you meant. And your instincts were right. She's going to need another guide dog. She'd be miserable using a cane. Besides, she needs the company."

His shoulders came down as he visibly relaxed. "That's a relief," he admitted. "I don't seem to be able to say or do anything right lately." He raised an eyebrow at me. "Speaking of which, do you mind if I walk you home? Maybe we could talk about some things."

I could have said no. I could have pretended we had nothing to talk about. I could have pretended I didn't care one way or another. But I did care; I wanted to know if we had more in common than just music and camaraderie. And if my suspicions were right, well, if they were right, what did I want? Did I want him to tell me that he was interested in me? Found me fascinating? Irresistible? Even knowing what it would mean to enter a relationship we'd soon lose? Did I want to develop even more feelings for him only to lose him as I had Danny? Did I want to go through that pain again just when I was taking the first few steps away from it?

I looked at him, really looked at him for the first time in at least a month. He'd lost a lot of weight. There were wrinkles on his face that hadn't been there when we'd met. And he was still wearing that stupid ski hat even though it was the warmest day we'd had all Spring. But none of those things mattered when I met his eyes, his deep blue, penetrating eyes, as they searched my soul. I could see he knew that despite myself I had feelings for him, that in the face of every impossibility I wanted to explore the possible. There wasn't much sense denying it.

"Sure," I said simply. We fell into step together and for once it was an easy, comfortable silence, the kind two friends have when they don't feel like they have to fill every little gap with more words.

Turned out we would have been better off talking while we had the chance. As we rounded the corner to my driveway, I could see a car parked there that didn't have any business being there. Not for another week at least. The possibility of talking about anything significant evaporated with the first words out of my mouth.

"It's my parents."

Chapter Thirteen

Seán slowed drastically, as if his feet had suddenly become encased in concrete, but my mother had already spotted us from her vantage point on my porch. She was sitting primly on the top step, a tall glass of ice tea sweating beside her. I could see Dad, hands in his pockets, standing up by the fence watching the sheep. Maman climbed awkwardly to her feet, dusting off the seat of her linen slacks. She was incredibly tan, even tanner than usual, though she spent so much time baking in the sun now that she was retired she resembled a very brown, very wrinkled nut most months of the year.

"Emerson!" she smiled. "My baby!" Her arms reached out though she didn't take a step closer. Her fingers waggled encouragingly. "Hug, hug, hug!" she warbled.

I lengthened my strides and was encased in a bear hug that nearly smothered me. My mother didn't believe in doing things by halves. She held me out for a minute and scrutinized me, a tiny frown appearing at the corners of her mouth. "You look tired," she announced.

I tried to smile. "Un petit peu,"[28] I admitted, though at the moment I felt more than a little bit tired. I felt my stomach lurch as her eyes slid past me and landed on Seán.

"And who's this? No, wait, you must be one of Jean-Guy's kids; you favor him." Seán looked nothing like his father. She'd been talking to Marcel. I really was going to have to kill my brother; forty-eight years old, and he was still tattling on me.

Seán stepped up and held out his hand. "That's right; I'm Seán."

Mom's eyebrows shot up. "The famous Montréal doctor, eh?"

I could almost feel Seán's weariness. "One and the same," he replied graciously.

"How's my little girl?" said a voice from behind me, and I turned to see my dad, Bert, grinning at me.

"Papa!" His hug, though genuine, was as soft as being enveloped in a lace shawl. He patted my head.

"How's my little girl?" he repeated, and I knew he was thinking of Danny.

---

[28] A little bit.

"I'm well, Papa," I assured him, and for the first time since he'd started asking me that question, so innocent on the surface, so probing in its meaning, I felt as though I was answering truthfully.

"Why didn't you tell us Addy has broken her wrist?" my mother butted in. "Why I had to hear this from your brother, eh?"

"I didn't want to spoil your trip," I began to protest, but my father, always the hero, rescued me by taking my arm, and steering me up the hill toward the sheep. I glanced nervously behind me and caught Seán's eye. My mother was still talking.

"Quite a few new lambs this year, eh?" Papa remarked, his eyes glowing with interest as he watched them. My father had a farmer's heart even if his hands were no longer in the game. Although we'd had a dairy farm, Marcel's farm now, he was always full of advice for me about my sheep. The trouble was that he didn't see them as fiber animals. He saw them as livestock. "Do you think you'll try that new slaughterhouse that just opened on the islands this year?"

"No, Papa," I tried to be patient, respecting the fact that even though I'd grown up on the farm and wasn't ignorant, he knew a great deal more about animals and running a successful business than I did. "I actually have some fiber farmers lined up to buy most of the lambs for their wool."

His brow furrowed. "Didn't you tell me that this breed was dual purpose? Raised for meat and wool?"

"Yes, but I don't want to sell my sheep for meat." It was hard for him to understand my pet mentality when it came to sheep. The thought of sending my lambs to market made me want to throw up, though many successful fiber farmers did just that, and I could hardly fault them for it. There were only so many lambs you could sell, after all. But I didn't breed my sheep every year, and I was very selective about it. I usually had a waiting list for any lambs I wanted to sell. It was sheep breeding my way, but my father could never quite wrap his head around it.

"Emerson, I really think you should consider your options," my father began, but we were mercifully interrupted by my mother who was huffing up the hill while Seán dragged up slowly behind her.

"Yoohoo, Bert, there's going to be a contra-dance! You can take me dancing, eh? Like old times!" Her face was split from ear to ear by a genuine grin. How my mother loved to dance. Funny though, I didn't know of any dance coming up. "Seán says the band he plays in will be putting one on this weekend."

What? I looked at Seán whose grimace was almost comical.

"I said it was possible they could do it since we've been practicing for a concert, but not this weekend . . ." As usual my mother had put her own spin on the conversation and was seeing it the way she wanted it to happen.

"Absolutely," I said, surprising Seán and delighting my mother. "I'm sure Marise would love nothing better than organizing a contra-dance. She's been after us to set a date for a concert. But it might be a couple weeks. She just lost her guide dog today."

My mother's hand flew to her throat in horror. "Quel dommage!"[29] she gasped. "That pauvre[30] girl! How will she manage?"

My father shook his head in sympathy. "A shame, a real shame," he murmured sadly. My father, unlike Marcel, got along famously with Marise, treating her like a precious flower and not a verbal boxing partner. It irritated her at times, but she tolerated it because she was fond of my dad and knew he meant well and wasn't patronizing her, a courtesy she rarely extended to the rest of us.

"Bert," my mother said with determination edging her voice, "we must stop and see Marise on our way home. Tell her we're sorry to hear about her loss, eh?"

My father nodded even as the words flew out of my mouth, "Not today," I blurted. "We just left her and she's sleeping. Besides," I amended hastily, "she's pretty raw about it right now. Wait a couple days. She'll feel more up to visitors then. She'll want to tell stories about him, not cry on your shoulder."

"Ah," my mother said thoughtfully, "you're right. Bien,[31] tomorrow then, eh, Bert?"

Well, it was better than today. "Listen, why don't we go inside, and I can make you something. Would you like coffee or tea? I think there might be scones, or muffins, too. Addy was baking last night." I had a vague memory of being surrounded by tempting odors coming from the kitchen as I worked on a fiber project for a small exhibition on local fiber farms and ended up staying up far too late.

Marise had talked me into contributing. We were collaborating. I was making a tricky art yarn that was full of bobbles, coils, and springy bits, and she was going to weave it into something she called her "all or nothing"

---

[29] What a shame.
[30] Poor
[31] (Very) well.

weavings. She would mix and match the warp fiber—a big no-no. Either it would work and we'd love it, or it wouldn't and she'd have to cut it off the loom.

It was a bit of a gamble but that was Marise's style, and we had plenty of time to get ready. I was just tagging along for the ride. I'd seen some of the pieces she'd made this way, and they were stunning. I'd also helped her cut off a few disasters.

My mother's disgusted voice broke into my groggy recall. "Honestly, coffee? In the afternoon? I've already had my coffee." She drew herself up into that prim aggrieved pose that always set my teeth on edge.

In my fatigue and distraction, I'd forgotten. My mother had a strict rule about coffee. It was only to be taken in the mornings. Apparently this was a rule established by her mother and probably her mother's mother before her going back deep into our family roots because my flagrant violation of it always brought shocked disapproval from my mother.

My father took her arm firmly. "Come along, Pauline," he said. "We were only going to stop for a minute and that was half an hour ago. We've still got to unpack."

"But I haven't seen my Addy yet," my mother wailed, shocked out of her grievance.

"She won't be home for hours," I offered helpfully. "She's decided she wants to be a veterinarian, so she's been shadowing Auggie on his rounds after school a few nights a week."

"Auggie," my mother sniffed in disdain. "In my day we called people by their proper titles."

"Yes, Pauline," my father agreed, "in my day, too, but things change." He gave me a wink over his shoulder as he steered her in an about-face and propelled her firmly to their car, an enormous boat of a Cadillac that hulked next to my house like a beached whale.

"We expect you and Addy for lunch on Sunday," Papa said as he closed my mother's door and trotted around the car to the driver's side. Maman's mouth formed a little moue of disapproval as though she wasn't finished speaking yet, but Papa was backing the car out before she could get her window rolled down.

"In my day, they were called Doctor . . ." Her voice trailed out faintly as the car whipped backward down the driveway. My father tooted the horn, flicked his hand in a brief wave, and roared down the road toward town.

"I'll take you up on that tea if you've got something herbal." Seán's quiet voice broke the sudden stillness nearly startling me out of my skin. He had retreated to the fenceline where he was quietly watching the sheep. I'd forgotten he was there. My brain scrambled to change tack.

"It's not genetic, you know," I said by way of excuse.

He chuckled. "I understand."

I made the tea, and we carried it outside to sit on the porch and drink in the beautiful weather. In this part of the country, you didn't squander the beautiful days; there weren't enough of them to be reckless.

"So," I ventured, "maybe my mother will be the force that finally gets us all in one spot for a concert. Or maybe a dance, eh?" I could've bitten off my tongue. She'd only been here for thirty minutes, and I was already tacking "eh?" onto the end of my sentence like a French-Canadian. Some habits were hard to break. Seán didn't seem to have noticed I'd said a word.

"A relationship right now would be difficult," he observed quietly and completely out of the blue.

That was an understatement, I thought. Harrowing might be a better word choice. Risky, foolhardy, ill-advised, feckless . . .

"You understand, don't you?"

Me? I understood perfectly. Hadn't I lost a husband? How could I not understand the fragility of human life, the impermanence of relationships, the possible repercussions of tearing your heart out and wearing it on your sleeve? I knew that once we started walking down this road it would end in tears. And they would be mine. I accepted that. At least right now, at the beginning. "Of course I understand," I said finally, when it appeared he wanted to hear an answer and not just to see smoke coming out of the top of my head to indicate I was thinking.

Seán seemed relieved. His whole body posture relaxed. It was as if he'd been dreading this conversation, had seen it coming a mile away, and been dragged into it kicking and screaming. It was almost as if he expected me to make a scene, cry or something. As if he was letting me down gently and really hated to do it. This was not right somehow. I couldn't quite put my finger on it, and then it hit me as though he'd dashed a bucket of cold water in my face.

He *was* letting me down. He knew I would have accepted the risk of the relationship and the burden of grief when he inevitably died—next week, next month, by first snowfall. When he said a relationship would be difficult, he really meant impossible.

Seán had laid his head back against the rocking chair he was sitting in. His eyes were closed, and the sun bathed his face with warmth. He actually looked peaceful . . . fragile, but peaceful. I felt closer to him because he wanted to protect me than I would have if he'd been careless with my feelings. I wanted to cup his face in my hands and tell him that it was okay; it didn't matter what he said. I was going to love him, and he couldn't stop me. *I* couldn't stop me, and I'd certainly tried; what chance did he have? And what guarantee did any of us have, after all? Life was a risk and none of us were getting out alive.

If only I wasn't such a coward.

What if that wasn't his reason at all? What if he really didn't want a relationship . . . with me? Obviously he didn't mind toying with Trudy Livingston's feelings. Did she not matter? How dare he! Just because I spitefully—and childishly—wanted to hammer a nail into her forehead with one of her high heels didn't mean that he could play fast and loose with her feelings. But then maybe she didn't really care about him. Maybe she was taking advantage of him, dating him for his money, and he knew it and didn't mind. After all, they could go wining and dining at fancy restaurants, or whatever-all they did together in Montréal. Buy shoes, maybe. And when it was over and Seán was toes up in the little graveyard, probably a couple rows down from Danny, Trudy could go on her merry way and find another rich doctor to go out with when she wasn't riding herd on a school full of hormonal teenagers and resentful teachers.

Seán's eyes opened suddenly, and I was staring into their limitless blue depths feeling very venomous. "Everything all right?" he asked.

My wounded pride wanted to tell him that no, of course everything wasn't all right. I had been ready to offer him everything, ready to see if it was really possible to love again no matter how brief the time. Everyone claimed it was only I had never believed them until now, when it was too late. Instead I choked it back. He was right, after all. Developing a relationship as he was dying would not only be difficult, it could *only* end in disaster. And I would be the one to suffer the most. We were friends; why ruin that?

"Fine," I replied simply. I even managed to pull my lips into a pseudo smile. "Beautiful weather we're having."

After the first awful sting, I realized that as much as I hated to admit it, being friends without the angst of exploring anything beyond friendship was actually very freeing. It wouldn't save me a lot of grief when he passed, but he didn't need to know that.

"Gorgeous," he said, but his eyes were on my face.

Cheater, I thought. "Shut up," I said mildly, and his eyes crinkled into the smile lines I adored so much. I had the unmistakable feeling that I'd passed some kind of bizarre test.

"I love you, you know," he said quietly, leaning back and closing his eyes again.

"Love you, too," I replied in the same light voice I would have used with Marise, the kind you use with a friend. It was a safe voice; one that didn't inspire tears or recriminations.

"Why were you talking to God this morning?" he asked, eyes still closed.

I squirmed uncomfortably in my chair. My spiritual experience, what there was of it so far, was so new I wasn't sure yet how to put it into words that sounded genuine and not like some cheesy, money-grubbing televangelist. "Because I'm trying to recognize God in my life. I'm trying to have a relationship with him instead of just knowing a lot about him."

"You're a Christian then?"

It was the sort of question that used to make me defensive, like the answer should be obvious, and if it wasn't, it meant I was doing something wrong. I'd been a "Christian" all my life, but I was only just now getting to really know God. I was amazed at the difference. "I am," I admitted, and then I repeated it more firmly, "I am. And I'd like to be one in more than name only. Maybe that doesn't make sense."

"It makes sense. I've been trying to do the same thing." His eyes opened and he stared into the distance. "When you're about to meet God in person, you find you are suddenly very interested in what he might think of you." He turned to smile wryly at me. "You know, so you can figure out what pass he's going to give you: up or down."

I laughed, but there was a bitter edge to it. "I know what you mean. Danny wasn't religious at all. He never even pretended to be, like I did sometimes. When he died . . . well, it would have been comforting to know he would end up in a better place. But if what Marcel says is true, and the man may irritate me six ways from Sunday but he knows his Bible, there's only one way to get to heaven." I mimicked Marcel's voice and quoted him. "In his sermons Marcel's always saying, 'I am the way, the truth, and the life. No one comes to the Father except through Me.' Danny thought Jesus was an occasional curse word, nothing more."

"Does that bother you?" Seán avoided looking directly at me as he asked the question, and I was grateful.

I swallowed hard. "Yeah. Yeah, it does. But I've made peace with the fact that Danny made his own choices for his life. I can't tell you that living with him didn't affect my own choices, but that was my problem, not his. For a long time I loved him so much that I didn't care where I ended up after life. If Danny wasn't going to heaven, than I didn't especially want to go, either."

"What changed your mind?"

"Adrienne," I replied simply. "But not right away. I hadn't been real faithful about going to church until I had Addy. After that it seemed important somehow. It's stupid I guess. As if I thought bringing her to church would get her in the club somehow. But it did keep me from falling away entirely. And when Danny died, the people at church were really good about supporting us.

"I guess, though, that Marise is the one who finally helped me understand there was a lot more to being a Christian than I knew." I shook my head. "That woman; she's amazing, you know? She drives me crazy; I love her to death."

"She has her own way of doing things," he agreed.

"You have no idea," I muttered. "I want to be just like her when I grow up."

The sun was low in the sky and I wondered what time it was, but I wasn't ambitious enough to check. I had no appointments to worry about, and Addy wasn't going to be home until evening. It was nice to just sit and relax for a change. I leaned back in the chair and let the sun hit me full in the face. I could feel its rays soaking in behind my eyes, loosening up all the tension that had me twisted into a nervous pretzel.

"What about you?" I asked finally when I was sure Seán wasn't going to offer any information on his own.

"I want to be just like her when I grow up, too."

I laughed. "Smart aleck."

"Well, I started reading the Bible. I figured it was as good a place as any to start. I didn't have one of my own though. Your brother loaned me one. It's kind of funny, actually. It must be one he used a lot because it's all marked up. There's writing in it and a lot of the verses are highlighted. I started by reading all the highlighted ones but that was most of the book, so then I just started at the beginning."

"Really? How far have you gotten?" I was impressed. I had never read the Bible all the way through. In fact, I hardly ever read the Bible at all. Maybe I should start.

"Oh, I've been through it a couple times now. I started again yesterday."

"Through it? You mean you read the whole thing? More than once?" Now I was really impressed.

"Yeah. Why? Haven't you? I thought that's how it was done."

I shrugged. "I don't think there's any acceptable way to do it at all." I was curious though. "So did you find anything?"

Seán glanced over at me and raised his eyebrows. "Like?"

"Like, did you find any answers?"

"Answers? I don't even know the questions yet. But tell me if you think this is crazy. When I'm reading, some of the verses seem to, I don't know, speak to me. As if God's trying to communicate with me through them. Is that normal?"

I snorted. "You're asking me? I have no idea. It's cool though. I'm jealous, actually. Marise says the same thing. I've never gotten that impression myself before. But then I've hardly ever cracked open the Bible. My parents used to make us read it when I was growing up, but it just always seemed so dry."

"It's not dry," he said. "But if you don't ask for God to help you understand it, you may as well read the newspaper. Your brother told me that."

"Huh." Maybe that's what I'd been doing wrong. I'd have to try again. A sense of curiosity began to gnaw at me in the silence that followed. Finally I had to ask, "So what did God tell you?"

Seán was leaning back against the chair, his eyes closed, the last of the afternoon sun on his face. He quoted, "Heal me, O Lord, and I shall be healed; save me, and I shall be saved, for You are my praise."

I felt a cold shiver go down my spine and an acute spasm of emotion gripped me, the kind of feeling I have when I see something exquisitely beautiful or hear something that resonates with me. I felt that verse deep inside me where it rang like a bell of truth. I almost gasped. "God said that to you?"

"He said it to Jeremiah," Seán corrected. Then he smiled slowly. "And to me. I didn't really know what to think, so I asked Marcel about it. He said a lot of things I don't really understand yet, but one thing did make an impression on me. He told me that healing and salvation often went together in the Bible, that Jesus forgave people their sins, healing them spiritually, as well as healing them physically."

"So he's saying you need to repent of your sins before God will heal you?" That sounded like coercion.

Seán laughed. "We all need to repent of our sins, Emerson. As far as I can tell, that's the basis of the entire Bible, the whole relationship between God and man centers on man's sinfulness and God's forgiveness. I may not know a lot yet, but I did learn that much. When you think about it, if healing followed salvation it would seem like the natural order of things."

"I know that," I muttered, abashed. "But doesn't it seem a bit like God's holding it over your head? Get forgiveness, get healing, a two-for-one deal?"

"Salvation is sure," Seán replied, and a shadow fell on his face. "But physical healing isn't guaranteed. At least not here, not on earth. But if you think about it, in the end, everyone will be healed one day, either here or in heaven. There's that to look forward to no matter what."

His voice was so full of hope in the face of certain death that I didn't have the heart to contradict him even if I'd had a strong conviction about it, which I didn't. My thoughts were all jumbled up, and I needed time to sort them out. I made a non-committal grunt, and he didn't say anything else for awhile. I was almost dozing off when he finally spoke again.

"You know what I want?"

"World peace?"

"I want to hear you sing."

"What? A capella?"

"Yeah."

I flipped through my mental list of songs I knew that wouldn't sound half bad without accompaniment.

"Do you know Amazing Grace?" Seán asked quietly.

"Um, sure, I know that one." I fished in my memory banks. It wasn't like I sang it at concerts, but we used to sing at home sometimes or in the car when we had to drive a long ways, and Maman tested our memory for hymn singing. I took a deep breath and began to sing:

"Amazing grace, how sweet the sound
That saved a wretch like me!
I once was lost, but now am found,
Was blind, but now I see.

'Twas grace that taught my heart to fear,
And grace my fears relieved;

How precious did that grace appear,
The hour I first believed!

Through many dangers, toils, and snares,
I have already come;
'Tis grace has brought me safe thus far,
And grace will lead me home."

I snuck a look at Seán but he was gazing off toward the lake, contentment softening his face.

"The Lord has promised good to me,
His word my hope secures;
He will my shield and portion be,
As long as life endures."

I knew the next verses weren't as well-known as the others, but Maman had been a stickler and the child—usually me—who remembered the most got a prize.

"Yes, when this flesh and heart shall fail,
And mortal life shall cease,
I shall possess, within the vail,
A life of joy and peace.

This earth shall soon dissolve like snow,
The sun forbear to shine;
But God, who call'd me here below,
Will be forever mine."

The last notes drifted out, across the lawn toward the lake, carried off by the freshly scented breeze. I felt my throat squeeze tight with emotion as the words faded quietly away. And I started to get it. I was that wretch who had floundered around lost and blind. I may have left God, but he had never left me. If that wasn't precious grace, I didn't know what was.

"You see?" Seán said. "That's what I want. A life of joy and peace, if not here, then there."

I felt sad and happy at the same time, if that was possible. It was nice to know that if I made it to heaven there would at least be some people there I knew. Even while the thought was crossing my mind, I realized that wasn't the point, but still. It *was* nice. Nice knowing that when Seán died—whenever that was—there wouldn't be that uncomfortable thought of where he might eventually end up. Instead there would be a blessed assurance. Wasn't that another hymn?

"Hey," a thin voice floated over to us, and I shielded my eyes with my hand, trying to discern who was coming down my driveway. "Mrs. Giroux?"

It was Mimi. "Hello, Mimi! How are you?"

I hadn't seen her for about a week. As she drew closer she looked peaked, but she had a tentative smile on her face. "I'm fine, thank you. I'm . . . feeling better." I noticed she still had on a long sleeve shirt, despite the warmth. She saw me glance down at her arms, but she didn't say anything. "I was wondering if I could start helping you out again so I can could take some more piano lessons?"

"Sure, do you want to start tomorrow?"

She nodded, then bit her lip. "Would it be okay with you if I played with the lambs for awhile?"

I waved my hand toward the field. "Knock yourself out."

"Thanks," Mimi said simply, but her eyes spoke volumes. I knew what she meant, and I smiled reassuringly at her.

"Fair warning," I sang out after her, "my mother is home, and she wants to go to a contra-dance. I hope you're still practicing."

"Yippee!" Mimi whooped, twirling her arms like a whirligig as she galloped across the lawn to the barn. "A dance!"

Clearly she had no idea what she was in for.

Chapter Fourteen

If there is any worse way to spend a beautiful afternoon than chained to a piano listening to children attack beautiful music with a sledgehammer, I'm not sure I know what it is. Did no one practice? Ever? By supper time I had a pounding headache, and a thunderstorm was approaching on a collision course from across the lake at Mach 2. I gratefully waved off the last urchin before collapsing onto a porch rocker with relief. I was supposed to be starting supper; I had people coming over, but I was too tired to figure out what to cook.

A strong wind preceding the storm kicked up suddenly bathing my hot face with coolness and helped a little with the headache. Out in the pasture I could see Mimi scurrying around trying to finish up barn chores before the squall hit. She was almost done, but she didn't quite beat the opening deluge. As she ran pell-mell across the lawn toward the house, the heavens opened, drenching her before she gained the shelter of the porch.

She stood there dripping and gasping. The temperature drop from the storm front was so dramatic you could feel it plummet. "I almost made it," she chattered.

"Come on." I pushed myself up from the chair and propelled her before me into the house. "You'll have to borrow some clothes. I don't want you getting sick."

"I'm fine," she protested.

I tossed her a towel while I went to scrounge up something she could change into. When I came back, I found her in the living room bent over the spinning wheel. She jumped almost guiltily. "That's very pretty," she said shyly, fingering the yarn I had worked on all morning before lessons. Then she yanked her hand away as if she'd committed a crime.

I laughed. "It's okay. You can touch it. Go ahead. It's a tactile art form, Mimi," I explained patiently. "It's meant to be handled."

Her smile was slow, but she eagerly reached out again, touching the yarn as though she was afraid it might break. "How do you make it?" she asked finally.

I handed her the neat pile of clothes I'd gathered and sank onto the piano stool I used while spinning. The fact that I had a variety of piano stools around and used them for seating always made Marise laugh, but she didn't like to sit on them because they twirled.

"Get changed first and then I'll show you." She darted off to the bathroom and returned minutes later dressed in Addy's jeans and a sweatshirt which were too big and too short for her, but at least she was dry.

I unwrapped the end of the fiber from where I'd anchored it on the tensioning knob and held it in my hand, pedaling to get the wheel spinning. As the twist crept up the fiber I drafted the yarn in two sections, demonstrating coreless corespinning, a technique in which one half of the fiber is spun into a single strand of yarn and the second half is spun at a ninety degree angle to wrap the single. Every now and then I put in something fun like a beehive or cocoon as I went.

I could spin traditional yarn, but most of my work in spinning these days was to create art yarn: these were fantastical yarns, crazy yarns, Marise called them. She had taught me the basic principles of how to make them but her lack of sight limited her ability to do them well. She often got frustrated keeping the supplies in order. Once I learned, she left the crazy yarn making to me and concentrated on her weavings, an area where she felt more confident and in control.

Mimi's eyes followed my hands with intense concentration the same way they did when I taught her to play piano. Her focus was almost relentless, and it made her quick learner. For a few moments I let myself be lulled by the rhythm of the wheel and the feel of the soft, warm fiber in my hands. I needed a little fiber therapy after the day I'd had.

Reluctantly, I shifted off the stool, handing the yarn to Mimi. I could backtrack later; I wanted her to feel the fibers in her hands. She took the wool from me as though it was going to bite her and perched uncertainly on the edge of the piano stool.

"What do I do; how do I do it?" she asked.

I reached around her and placed my hands over hers. She was trembling. "Pinch the roving here, like this, so the twist can't creep up and form the yarn. That way you can draft the roving in front of where you're pinching before you let the twist go into it. See?" She pedaled and I guided her hands into the motions that created a single strand of yarn. As she gained confidence, I slowly pulled my hands back until she was spinning on her own. She was so focused on what she was doing that she didn't even notice I wasn't helping any more.

I straightened up and worked a kink out of my back, kneading the tension out with my fingers, remembering how Danny used to come up behind me and rub my shoulders. Normally a memory like that would drag a cloud of gloom with it that cast a dark pall over the rest of my day. This time it was more like the cloud drifted across the sky blocking out the sun for a moment before moving on. I felt as though I'd run my finger over an old wound and discovered the pain was gone and all that remained was a slight sensitivity. Before I could really ponder the wonder of it, the front door slammed and brought me back to the present. I had a bunch of people coming over who were expecting to eat dinner before our last practice session for the contra-dance and nothing prepared.

"Why don't I smell food?" Marise asked. "Did you make salad?"

"Not exactly."

"Did you make anything?"

I let Marise interpret my silence because I was too embarrassed to admit that I had, indeed, made nothing.

"You mean there's no food?" Her voice was filled with exasperation. "Em, I'm starved!"

"Well, come on then. You can help me." Conjuring up food at a moment's notice was not exactly my forte so much as it was Agnès', but I did have a few culinary weapons in my arsenal.

I stationed Marise by the panini grill with a loaf of bread and a block of strong cheddar cheese I'd bought from a nearby farm whose cheese won awards every year. Then I went on a foraging mission in the pantry where I pulled several jars of tomatoes I'd canned the previous fall off the shelves along with a couple cans of store bought artichokes.

Ordinarily I loved making soup, the whole process of it. I loved standing in the kitchen in my bare feet, feeling the worn tiles of the kitchen floor beneath me, rhythmically chopping vegetables. There was a soothing calm that pervaded my whole being from the heft of the sturdy vegetables in my hands to the aroma of the developing soup.

Tonight there was no time for any of that. I unceremoniously dumped the tomatoes and artichokes into my big, reliable stainless steel stock pot, added water, some vegetable bouillon, and turned the burner on high. Then I searched the refrigerator for my secret ingredient: fresh basil. Just the smell of fresh basil made my mouth water; in the fall I ate this soup every day.

By the time the others arrived, Marise had a pile of panini and the fragrant soup had permeated the entire house. Mimi had transitioned from the spinning wheel to the accordion where she sat deep in concentration practicing, not even noticing that the food was ready. "Mimi, come on, have something to eat so you don't dry up and blow away," I ordered, checking the soup one last time to see if it needed any sea salt.

"That smells incredible," Seán said, coming in the door, the last to arrive. I glanced up and the smile froze on my face. He had shaved his head. That beautiful, thick head of hair was gone, and in its place, the severe buzz cut of a newly enlisted soldier. Oddly enough the lack of hair brought his eyes into sharp focus, their blue depths never more dazzling, clearly registering my shock at his appearance. I struggled to recover my composure while he set his instruments down in the living room.

"You cut your hair," I observed lamely as he came up behind me to peer into the soup pot.

"You could say that," he agreed. A wary edge in his voice warned me not to pursue the topic, so I bit my tongue.

"Aren't you done yet?" Marcel asked, coming into the kitchen and hovering first over me at my station by the soup and then migrating to Marise who slapped his hand when he reached for a panini.

"Wash your hands," Marise commanded sternly.

"Yes, it's all ready. Grab a bowl; plates are over there; spoons are in the drawer. Don't stand on ceremony." I picked up a ladle and began filling bowls as they were proffered. My brother gave me a peck on the cheek as I filled his bowl. I turned to him, startled. Marcel's brand of affection was usually more violent and involved back-slapping or body-checking. "What was that for?"

He shrugged. "Good soup," he said. His eyes darted to Seán and then back to me, but the glance told me nothing. Did they have a secret or something? Or did he think that there was a relationship developing between us? My head was starting to hurt again.

I had just finished filling bowls when there was a tentative knock on the door. "Who could that be?" I muttered. Marcel was standing closest to the door, and he flung it open without even bothering to check and see who was standing on the doorstep. Auggie poked his head in but stayed planted on the doormat.

"Hello?"

"Auggie?"

"Come in," Marise sang happily.

"Hey Dr. St. Marie," Addy said, sitting up straighter in the chair she was lounging in while she listened to Mimi play. "I didn't know you were coming."

"Marise invited me," Auggie said. "I hope it's okay."

Marise was grinning and held out a plate of panini. "I saved you one."

"Absolutely," I said, recovering my manners. "Come on in. Here's some soup. Sit . . . anywhere."

My worn little Formica table already had six people at it, more than it could really handle, when I was ready to sit down so I decided to eat standing up at the counter. But then Seán noticed and scooted himself even closer to Marcel making just enough room for me to set my bowl down.

"Come on, you can't eat standing up. It's bad for your digestion." He dragged a piano stool over for me and patted it encouragingly. "Sit. Doctor's orders."

I sank gratefully onto the stool. While I waited for the soup to cool a little, I looked around the table feeling warm and happy just seeing everyone chatting and eating, not caring that they were crushed together, not caring that they were eating nothing more than simple soup and sandwiches, just enjoying themselves. There were times when I dreamt of having a long, scrubbed, farmhouse table where you could seat a crowd of people. And then there were times when I was more than satisfied to be crowded around my tiny ancient Formica one with all of my friends. As I felt Seán's solid bulk pressed up against one side of me, and Marcel's against the other, I decided my little table was just fine.

As my eyes roamed around the circle taking in the faces of the people dearest to me, they skidded to a stop at Auggie. The big man, who I'd always observed in his element wrangling sick animals, seemed rigid with nerves. His broad face was smiling but his tension was jarringly out of place in this grouping. Addy seemed to have reached the same conclusion I had, no doubt because she'd been spending so much time shadowing him. I felt a well of pride as she tried to put him at ease.

"Dr. St. Marie, how did that dog make out? The one that got hit by a car?"

Auggie started a little hearing his name, but seemed grateful to have something to talk about. "Oh, him? He came through great. He'll be gone by the time you come back to work."

"Speaking of dogs," Marise said, shifting in her seat and looking slightly discomfited. "I've decided to take everyone's advice. I called the guide dog school today, and they put me on the waiting list."

She smiled bashfully at the congratulatory hubbub. "They said there's been a higher than usual graduation rate lately and that it shouldn't be long before they could match me with a dog."

"I am so happy for you," Auggie said, his smile warm. He laid one enormous hand on Marise's shoulder. She beamed up at him and placed her hand on top of his.

Hrmph, I thought, my eyes narrowing as I took in the exchange. Marise had been keeping this little romance on the Q.T.; now *she* had some explaining to do. First thing tomorrow.

Since she didn't play music with us, Addy volunteered to do the dishes so we could get started. I gave her a quick hug on my way into the living room. "Thanks, Hon."

"We're here, we're here! Don't start without us!" a shrill voice yodeled from the porch just before my mother burst through the door followed by my father, looking slightly abashed, at a more sedate pace.

"Maman? Papa? I didn't know you were coming . . ." I trailed off weakly wondering who was next going to pop in unannounced.

"We almost didn't. No one didn't tell us when it was, eh," Maman said reproachfully. "I had to find out by accident from Angelique." Her eyes swept the table, and she made a *tsk-tsk* sound through her teeth. "Misère de chein,[32]" she tutted, "what a mess. You go, shoo! I'll help Addy straighten this place up. Salut, ma chère,"[33] she said, her voice warm again as she gave Addy a crushing hug and a peck on the cheek.

"Bert, park it somewhere, eh?" she ordered my father who obeyed without questioning, his only response a quizzical lifted eyebrow. Hurricane Pauline had arrived.

"Salut, Mémère," Addy replied, suppressed mirth in her eyes.

"Okay, okay, quiet down a minute," Marise was saying, her hands up traffic cop fashion, as I found a place to sit, banjo cradled on my lap. "I've got the song order. Emerson has called all these before so Em, go ahead and pretend there's an audience. We'll practice ignoring you. At the actual dance, Em will decide when the dancers have had enough," she informed everyone, "and she'll let us know when to stop. For tonight let's just play everything three times. Then we'll work on the set we'll play for intermission. Sound good? We'll start with Un-Deux-Trois Poussez."

---

[32] Literally: dog misery; figuratively an expression of exasperation or dismay.
[33] Hello, my dear.

"I love that one!" my mother exclaimed from the kitchen. "Bert, that's my favorite dance!"

"I know, Pauline," my father replied laconically.

I set the dance card, which had all the dance steps written on it, in a place where I could see it if I needed to. I knew this one well enough not to need the directions on the card, but since I played while I called, it was nice to have the card as a backup in case I blanked on a step. It had taken me a long time to do both at the same time and even longer to manage l'accord du pieds, Québécois foot percussion, while I picked. It had been quite a trick learning how to disconnect part of my brain in order to do completely different things at the same time. In effect, I had to put my feet and fingers on autopilot.

We started to play, and as I expected, it wasn't long before my mother's feet started tapping and she pulled first Addy and then my father into the dance with her. She motioned for Auggie to join them but his eyes widened in fright, and he stayed planted on the couch. No amount of coaxing moved him. But his feet tapped an accompaniment to the song betraying the music's hold on him in spite of himself.

"That's not my kind of music," he'd said dismissively when I'd first told him, a few years back, about our band.

"You prefer classical?" I'd asked.

"I *prefer* the traditional music of my own heritage," he'd said. And then he'd given me an education on Bieneki songs and pow-wows. "But," he'd admitted. "I do like classical music. It makes you think."

As I called and plucked and watched his feet jig under the coffee table, I wondered how much more thinking I could do at one time without bursting a blood vessel. We played through Galopede, The Flying Scotsman, La Bastringue, Ninepins, Balance the Star—and for Addy and my father —The Pattycake Polka, before Marise let us take a break only to put us back to work on the set we were planning to play during the intermission when the dancers took a well-deserved break.

Just before we finished up, the smell of coffee and cookies drifted around the room. I threw Addy a grateful look at her station next to the stove. Marise reluctantly conceded the end of the practice session when the smell reached her, and for once my mother made no comment on the inappropriateness of drinking coffee after breakfast. I set my banjo in its stand and leaned over to stretch my back.

Seán was slumped in his chair looking tired but content. He seemed to be feeling a little bit better these days, for which I was grateful. But it must take a toll on him having days like this which were almost hopeful only to succumb again to the slow pull of death. I swallowed hard and forced my mind away from the subject.

Seán caught me looking at him, probably thinking I was contemplating his newly shorn pate, and quipped, "Thanks for the craic."

It was one of those lulls that happen with groups of people when individual conversations hush for a moment and one person's voice carries over. In this case it was Seán's. All eyes swiveled toward us.

"Excuse me?" I managed, coloring. Was he being snotty? I hadn't made any crack about his hair.

He laughed. "The craic: the good time, the music, the fun. Don't you know what craic is?" Then he mused almost to himself, "No, I guess maybe you wouldn't. It's an Irish term, so I grew up with it. I forget you're all French."

"I'm not," Auggie said promptly. "Blue-blooded Bieneki." He held up his thumb and forefinger about an inch apart. "And maybe that much French," he conceded.

Amused Seán asked, "Don't tell me Beineki's don't have craic?"

Auggie's eyes narrowed. "The only kind of 'crack' I've ever heard of is white and snorted by stupid fools."

"That's the wrong kind. The craic I'm talking about is a term for having a good time. That's all."

"Ahh," I relaxed back into my chair and the rest of the room returned to their activities, which mostly consisted of packing up their instruments and slipping out into the night to make their way home. I relished the sound of their voices floating back through the open window. I smiled. Yes, it had been good craic.

Seán probably would have stayed, but Mimi was lingering even after Addy disappeared into her bedroom. He caught my eyes above her head and shrugged slightly before collecting his things and giving me a halfhearted wave. The screen door bumped behind him. Gyp climbed up on it to stare after Seán as if willing him to come back. I wanted to join him.

Instead, I sank onto one of the piano stools and twirled slightly from one side to the other. Mimi seemed to realize we were finally alone, and she looked up shyly. "Am I the last one?" she asked. I couldn't tell if I heard relief in her voice or surprise.

"Yes, but there's no rush. I haven't had a chance to talk with you lately. Are you excited about the contra-dance? Will your mom be able to come?"

Her eyes went dead at the mention of her mom. One bony shoulder hitched up toward her ear. "I guess."

"Don't you care?" I had no idea how Michael Bang had treated his daughter, but Theresa, her mom, had always struck me as being very capable and affectionate. When I'd spoken to her about Mimi's problems that time, she'd been concerned and determined, not indifferent. Maybe something had come up in the aftermath of that little drama.

"*She* sure doesn't," Mimi muttered under her breath.

"Excuse me?"

"My mom," Mimi said, "she doesn't care about me."

"Mimi, that's ridiculous. I know your mother. At least, I know her a little. I know she's been very concerned about you. Why would you say she doesn't care about you?"

"Because she doesn't," Mimi said stubbornly. "My father loved me, but my mother never has. She's always on my case. She made me go to counseling for the pain pills and the cutting. She took my phone away from me. I can't do anything without her hanging over my shoulder checking up on me. She watches me like a hawk. Why doesn't she trust me?"

Surely she couldn't be that dense? I offered a quick, silent prayer of thanks that Addy had never put me through such shenanigans. Other than an independent streak she'd inherited from Danny that caused us to butt heads now and then, we'd had a pretty smooth, comfortable relationship. Whenever she had problems, she confided in me. She even asked me for advice when she had an occasional boyfriend.

I knew casting Mimi's problems in her face as the cause of her mother's distrust wouldn't endear either me or Theresa to her. "Why do you think she doesn't trust you?" I countered instead.

"This is about the cutting, right? And the pain pills?" She struggled on the last words. "That's old history. I don't do that stuff anymore."

I laughed lightly. I didn't want her to think I found her situation amusing. "Mimi, it's only been about a month. Trust is earned slowly, over time. You have to rebuild it bit by bit. Tell me something, do you eat?"

She slid me a sideways glance. "Eat? Of course, I'm not anorexic, too."

"Perish the thought," I said quickly, not wanting to get sidetracked. "I only meant, you have enough food to eat?" She nodded. "And what about clothes? Do you have plenty of clothes?"

Her eyes rolled, and I could tell she was on to me. "Yes," she said, putting the patience of the saints into the one word. "Yes, I have plenty of everything. Yes, I realize it's my mother who gives them to me. Am I supposed to believe that proves she loves me?"

"Doesn't it? Who got you help to get off the pain pills and stop cutting?"

Her sigh was filled with resignation. "She did."

"And who works two jobs to provide for you now that your dad can't?"

"She does."

"And who watches over you to be sure you don't have a relapse?"

"Her."

"Mimi, what do you think love is?" She didn't answer me. I'm not sure she knew how. "That's love. When we take care of the people we love, even when we discipline them when they do something wrong in order to teach them to make better choices next time, that's love. Of course your mother loves you. She can't help it; she's your mother."

Bright lights swung through the picture window and illuminated her somber face. "That's probably her," she said, although I suspected as much, too. No doubt she'd pulled herself away from a well-deserved evening off to come pick up Mimi so she wouldn't have to walk home in the dark.

"I expect," I said, keeping my voice cheerful and light. The last thing Mimi needed was more condemnation in her life. "See you at the dance?" I asked.

"See you at the dance," she confirmed, picking up her accordion and slinging it over her shoulder.

"Mimi," I said and waited until she turned around. "It's going to be fun." She nodded and slipped out the door. It barely bumped behind her. "It's going to be fun," I repeated and hoped that I was right."

Chapter Fifteen

The morning of the contra-dance I awoke so early it wasn't even light out yet. I thought about going back to sleep, but even when I closed my eyes it felt like they were wide open. The air was a little chilly, brisk Marcel would have said, but he always seemed impervious to the weather. I pulled on a sweater Marise had knit for me years before and crept out to the kitchen to make some tea.

Lately I'd been waking up early like this, on my own. I'd taken to slipping out to the porch with my tea and Bible. I figured if Seán could read through the Bible a couple times, I could certainly make an effort to get through it once. At least, that was mainly what I'd thought when I'd started. Now I was finding something I had never expected. Instead of reading the words on the pages, it seemed like they were a conversation with God himself.

Not always, but sometimes certain verses jumped out at me, and I knew that God meant them for me. More than that, they often addressed a question I'd been wrestling with and praying about, usually something I didn't understand. I had started this journey feeling like I already had all the answers, but I was quickly realizing that I knew less than nothing about God. All I had was a handful of preconceived ideas that I'd developed in childhood. They were small consolation now as I faced the truly awesome God it turns out I didn't really know at all, and I was ready to release them and step into the exciting unknown.

The tea steamed fragrantly, its minty aroma mingling with the bouquet of all outdoors as I stepped onto the porch. The sky was beginning to lighten, and as a special gift, I heard the cry of a loon as I sank onto one of the Adirondack chairs on my porch. I chose the one with a view of the lake. It was time I started to face it again. At times I hated it so much for what it had stolen from me that I was amazed I had never moved away. But then, where would I move to? This was home. It had always been home, and I couldn't imagine myself living anywhere else in the whole world.

The loon continued to call as I opened my Bible, but my heart was so full of a sudden swelling of gratitude for life and all I held dear that I couldn't even focus on the words beneath the pool of light cast by my reading lamp. Inside slept my beautiful daughter; outside in the barn I had bundles of woolly love; Gyp and Dash had followed me onto the porch and were curled up on a braided rug at my feet, and I had friends who made my life rich with fun, laughter, and music. As the gratitude grew, I could feel it begin to displace the emptiness Danny had left behind. And that was when I made a wonderful discovery: I could feel again.

I almost set my tea and Bible down and raced to Marise's house to tell her. The blanket of dullness had been lifted! I could feel happiness and gratitude! I could thank God for these things and not feel like a liar. I leaned my head back on the chair and sang softly, just for myself and God, "Amazing grace, how sweet the sound, that saved a wretch like me . . ."

I remember crying afterward, but I don't remember falling asleep. I woke up to Addy shaking my shoulder, and when I rubbed my eyes, they felt gritty with the salt that had dried on my face. "What time is it?" I asked thickly.

"It's only seven, but I thought you wanted to get an early start today?"

"I did. I do." The whole exciting, crazy busy day crashed into my consciousness at once. "I'm playing at church this morning. But I have to do my chores first and take a shower..."

"I'll do chores for you," Addy said. "The only thing I have to do today is bake some goodies for the contra-dance, and Mémère said she'd come help me do that. Go take your shower. I've got this covered."

I squeezed Addy's arm gratefully as I passed her. "Thank you!"

She grinned. "No problem."

The morning passed in a blur. The contra-dance was mentioned at church during announcement time, and I felt a crackle of excitement pass through the congregation. Not much happened in our little town that passed for social activity, so this was a big deal. To me, and probably to a lot of other people as well, it also represented a tangible link with the past, a past many of us regretted losing, and others were slow to release. It was a chance for us to step back into our own history, a time when life was slower, kinder, and more honest in many ways than it was today. It put us in touch with our heritage, a heritage that was slipping away as our culture became more fractured with outsiders and our children started moving away in search of something different. I was caught up in the excitement myself for all of those reasons.

By the time I had the car packed later for the short trip to Toussaint Falls where we would be playing in the old grange hall, I was so keyed up my hands were shaking. "Are you sure we haven't forgotten something?" I asked Addy for the umpteenth time.

She sighed patiently. "Mom, let's go. We haven't forgotten anything. All the instruments are packed, Uncle Marcel picked up the sound system earlier and I checked to be sure he had everything, your banjo is in here . . ."

"Music!" I interrupted triumphantly. "I've forgotten my music and my calling notes."

"Right here." Addy held out the folder she'd had tucked under her arm. "Now can we go?"

"What about Mimi?" I asked. "Wasn't she riding over with us?"

"She was as nervous as a cat. I sent her ahead with Uncle Marcel to get her out of the way." She must have caught my disapproving look. "I was nice about it," she insisted. "Besides, I'm sure Aunt Agnès could use her help decorating. Make good use of that nervous energy."

"All right," I said finally, defeated. "Looks like you've thought of everything. Let's go then."

There weren't very many cars parked at the grange, but the bustle inside made up for it. Crepe paper streamers hung from the ceiling, a table in the corner was piled high with baked goods, and the Ladies Auxiliary had thoughtfully provided a cooler filled with bottled water. Contra-dancing was thirsty-making, and that cooler would be empty by night's end.

Marcel had set us up on the elevated stage at one end of the grange hall. Mimi was putting out metal folding chairs for us to sit on, and Marise was testing the microphones with Seán's help. My brother was, of course, eating something he's snitched from the refreshment table while he chatted up one of the Auxiliary ladies, probably the one who'd turned a blind eye during the snitching. I was pretty sure it was our old third grade teacher. She'd always been giving him treats at school. Some things never changed.

Addy helped me bring in my instruments, and then she went off to help her aunt who was busy making coffee and heating water for tea in enormous, ancient coffee urns that looked as though they could have been used by my venerable musical great-uncles Pacifique and Louis-Philippe back in the day. I hoped they didn't short out and start a fire.

I carried my banjo to the stage area and began to set up my stand and arrange my notes. I kept them spread out on the floor at my feet so I could glance at them from time to time if I got lost or just needed reassurance that I was where I was supposed to be in the dance. My hands were still trembling. In a way, I couldn't wait to get started so my nerves would simmer down, and I could begin to enjoy myself. I was always a mess at the beginning of a performance.

"Hey," said Seán, stepping over to set up his own instruments. He had covered his shorn head with a black silk do-rag that made him look more like a pirate than ever. "How are you holding up?"

"Nervous. You?"

He nodded but he didn't look nervous, and I suspected he was just trying to make me feel better. "Do you ever get to dance at these things?"

"Fat chance," I muttered.

"What was that?"

"Not usually," I said, louder, pushing down my disappointment. Not getting to dance was the price you paid for being a musician. Whenever I watched the dancers, I couldn't help but feel a little envious. The flushed faces, the breathless laughing: contra-dancing was a lot of fun. Not that I'd ever gotten to dance much even when I hadn't been playing the music. Danny wasn't much of a dancer. He said he had "two left feet that were all thumbs." At our wedding, when we took the floor for our first dance as man and wife, he'd clutched me around the waist and shifted his weight side to side—his version of dancing.

Contra-dancing, of course, was much different; even the children participated. It was very much a social form of exercise. Little kids, grey-haired grannies, elderly gentlemen with their canes looped over their arms, barefooted teens: the music and the dance seemed to transcend gender and race and effortlessly bridge the generation gap. There was turning and clapping and circling and walking and lots of jocularity as someone invariably went the wrong way or performed a step out of place. Mistakes were overlooked. People helped each other out. It was all part of the fun.

"Will Trudy be here?" I asked innocently.

"I don't think so. This isn't really her kind of thing. Why?"

"No reason."

I busied myself tuning my banjo before he could ask any more questions about my interest, but we were distracted by something far more shocking, so shocking it drove the thought of Trudy into the stratosphere. As I concentrated on my string, I saw Angelique sally in the door clamped on the arm of none other than Jeff Daniels, editor of our *Northern County Reporter*. It was rare to see Angelique out of her habitual overalls, but tonight she was wearing a bona fide party dress complete with lace, ruffles, and, as my father would say, "frilly gee-gaws". On her feet were a pair of sturdy 1930s oxfords with a Cuban heel, the kind that were referred to around here as grannie shoes, but paired with her dress and the way she had styled her hair tonight made me almost believe she had just stepped off the set of a World War II film. It was a shock to catch a glimpse of her younger self through the thickened, wrinkled changes age had brought.

Before I had time to marvel at this transformation, I realized what was really different. Angelique was grinning from ear to ear. It wasn't that I hadn't seen her smile before, occasionally, but as she passed the stage area on her way to the refreshment table I could see that all the dark holes in her smile were gone. She was sporting a full set of perfect, sparkly white teeth. I almost dropped my banjo. Angelique caught my eye and winked broadly before parading on.

I must have made some kind of strangled noise because Marise leaned forward. "What?" she demanded unceremoniously. "What's going on?"

"It's Angelique," I hissed under my breath. "She's here with Jeff Daniels and she's, well, she's got all her teeth."

"Her teeth?"

Right, Marise wouldn't have known Angelique was missing any teeth. "Yeah, she must have gotten dentures. Before, she only had a . . ."

"Couple of her own teeth, I know. You can tell by the way she talks."

Of course you could.

"Now that," Marise said, "is something I wish I could see. How does she look?"

"Like the cat who ate the canary," I replied dryly. "We'll never hear the end of it now. She's going to be insufferable. You know that, don't you?"

"As well she should be."

My laughter faded in my throat when I caught sight of my mother marching briskly across the dance floor with a determined look on her face. Time to stop dawdling I guessed. "Vite!" she barked in a commanding tone. "Vite![34] What's the hold up, eh?"

"We're waiting for your son." I pointed out Marcel, jaws still working, a fresh pastry in one hand, now comfortably ensconced in a metal folding chair against the wall, Auxiliary ladies vying for his attention.

My mother's trajectory altered toward this new target, and I renewed my effort to get my strings tuned before she sent Marcel scurrying for the stage. Sibling rivalry never really died, I mused with a satisfied smile.

Half the audience was lined up expectantly in front of the stage waiting for us to begin, the rest were milling around, chatting in groups. I waited until Marcel had his pipes ready, a small bag of goodies tucked beneath his chair for when he got hungry during breaks. Marise asked me where Auggie was, but glancing around the room, I didn't see him.

---

[34] Quick, hurry; colloquially "Get a move on."

"Ladies and gentlemen," I announced, "we're going to begin this evening with Un-Deux-Trois Poussez." That was always a good ice-breaker.

I heard my mother squeal as the dancers lined up. Usually there were a lot of observers for the first few rounds as shy folks worked up their courage to join, but this time almost everyone present found a partner and joined the lines. I had to split them into two groups before we could start.

As soon as I was active, placing people, explaining the steps, demonstrating, and then playing and calling, all my nervousness faded away. It was always a struggle to keep things straight, of course. It wasn't easy to play and call at the same time, and sometimes the task was beyond me and I just concentrated on calling. But it was more than that. It was the music, seeping into my soul, lifting me up, creating joy, knitting people together. Being unhappy was impossible in the midst of such infectious revelry. And even though I couldn't join the dancers, I had every bit as much fun as they did just bringing them joy.

I managed a glance at Mimi a few times throughout the evening, and she seemed to be holding up well. A couple times I saw her grinning, and once she even asked to be excused from a set so she could dance as her mother's partner. A good sign, I thought. It was rewarding to see her having such a good time. Marise kept asking me if Auggie had showed up, but I still hadn't seen him. "Probably had an emergency," I told her, to which she nodded.

I felt a well of cultural love and pride as I looked out over the whirling crowd predominantly full of quintessential French-Canadians, their faces all stamped in roughly the same mold, instantly recognizable if you knew what made them unique. Here were the few still grasping their roots with both hands, determined not to lose the good of the past in the headlong rush into the future. They were the people who would rather trek down to the Legion to play bingo than sit mindlessly in front of the latest television show. The ones who decorated their kids' bikes for the town parade. The families who still gathered for Sunday dinner even when it wasn't a holiday. I loved them for all of it and more. I loved being one of them.

When the last note of the last set faded into the night and the dancers came to a slow stop, I heard Angelique call out, "Let's give our musicians a hand, folks!" I looked out over the sea of smiling, flushed faces and was grateful for being part of their joy. Smiling foolishly at the others, I reached out and grabbed Marise's hand, giving it a squeeze. She grinned and squeezed back.

The Auxiliary ladies were already starting to clear up the mess, and the dancers began to talk amongst themselves, retrieving their coats and purses. Marcel and Marise started to put away their instruments. Seán turned to Mimi before she could follow suit and asked her if she knew Olivebridge Waltz. Mimi shook her head.

"Pity," he murmured. "Well, can you play something slow and pretty for us?"

"Sure."

I had just set my banjo back on its stand when he reached out and took hold of my hand. "Can I have this dance?" he asked.

"What dance?"

"This one," he repeated. Giving Mimi a firm nod he pulled me to my feet and lead me down the little flight of steps to the dance floor. Instead of setting his hands awkwardly around my waist, he placed his left on my waist and took my right hand in his in a comfortable, experienced way, and I remembered Marcel had said the Bachands were a musical family. Before I could panic and explain that my dancing skills were likely to be inferior to his own, Mimi breathed life into her accordion and the theme from Titanic floated out into the hall. As the tune registered, Seán and I stared at each other not knowing whether to laugh or cry.

The next thing I knew we were dancing, and I forgot all about being self-conscious or not knowing what I was doing or the implications of the song or of anything at all except that small space of existence in Seán's arms. The music floated around us, haunting and beautiful. Seán's embrace was strong and his steps sure. I relaxed and let him and the music carry me to a beautiful place that existed only right now. When I looked up, I found Seán staring at me, absorbed in watching the expression on my face. Nothing and no one existed for the two of us in that moment except each other. I smiled at him, wishing the music would never end, that we could dance like this forever.

A few of the lingering couples decided to take advantage of the encore and joined us while others looked on enjoying the music but not feeling the need to participate. I tried fiercely to imprint the memory in my brain as it came to me that in Seán's condition, this might be the only time we ever had a chance to dance like this. The thought brought me to earth so suddenly that I stumbled. Seán caught me effortlessly, and I forced my feet to keep moving, not wanting to miss one second of the beautiful experience.

When the music inevitably ended, we drew reluctantly to a stop. "Thank you," I told Seán, my voice choking with emotion. All my life I had imagined dancing to be exactly like that. I felt as though I'd been granted a wish. "That was incredible."

I expected him to laugh off my sincerity but he didn't. Instead he took my face in both hands and lightly kissed me. "Thank *you*," he returned, reminding me of that first night we'd played music together. Around us folks who had danced with us started a smattering of applause for Mimi and we joined in.

As I fanned myself with my hand and Seán went to collect our instruments, I savored the wonderful feeling of happiness that washed over me, crowding out the bittersweet. This had to be what Seán referred to as craic; I liked it.

My mother sidled over to my side. "I didn't know you and the famous doctor were such good friends," she remarked, a glint in her eye. "Maureen says he doesn't have much time left but maybe enough time to get married, eh? Then you'd be set."

I was so stunned I froze, my heart pounding, blood whooshing in my ears at a furious pace. My father, standing nearby, overheard her. His whole face went tight, and his lips formed a thin line. Maman jumped when his hand snaked out and smacked her on the fanny. She flushed guiltily. "Pauline," he barked crisply. "Now."

Maman pecked me quickly on each cheek and meekly followed my father outside while I stood rooted to the spot, face flaming, the entire evening lying shattered like broken glass around my feet. I became acutely aware of the fact that Seán might have overheard her crass remark as well. Holding my breath and using only my eyes, I scanned the room to locate him. He was chatting with Angelique and seemed oblivious; certainly he was too far away to have heard. Slowly my heart rate returned to normal, and I unclenched my hands, little half moon indentations carved into my palms from the pressure of my squeeze. I counted slowly to ten, trying to put the exchange out of my mind.

"Ready to go?" Seán called, striding toward me, a relaxed smile on his face. It struck me all of a sudden that he looked better—healthier—than he had in a long time.

"Yes!" My quick reply was a little too bright and eager, but it was better than just slinking off like a whipped dog, which is what I really wanted to do. "I just need to find Marise and Addy."

"Present and accounted for," Marise said, coming up behind me on my daughter's arm. For the first time I realized how vulnerable and alone she looked without Chopin.

"Did I miss it? Is it over?" Auggie burst through the door and surveyed the room with increasing dismay before his eyes fell on our little group, pinpointing Marise in particular. "I'm so sorry. Car hit a cat. It was pretty bad."

Smoothly, Marise released Addy's arm and slipped her small hand into the crook of Auggie's elbow. She smiled up at him. "But you saved it?"

The anxiety on the big man's face cleared like storm clouds banished by the sun. "I did, yeah, I did."

"All's well that ends well," Marise quipped.

"You aren't angry, then?"

"Of course not! You were saving a life. What could be more important than that?"

Auggie's smile was broad. "That's a relief."

"I'll tell you what," Marise continued. "Let's celebrate."

"Because of the cat?" Auggie was clearly puzzled, but I had an idea that I knew where this was going.

"Because of the cat," Marise agreed, "and because we're finished the contra-dance so we don't have to practice so hard now—for awhile," she amended. "And . . ." she paused dramatically, "because I heard from the guide dog school in Montréal. They've got a dog for me, so I'll be going away for a few months."

This obviously wasn't news to Auggie, but it was news to the rest of us. I could tell from the shock on our faces. Diverted by the congratulations, I wasn't able to prevent the disaster, but I saw it coming. Marise held up her hand for silence and said, "Let's have a little dinner party at my house. I've been wanting to cook some traditional French-Canadian favorites my way."

"You cook?" Auggie asked, surprise fighting with admiration in his voice.

"Of course," Marise smiled sweetly.

His face lit up. "That's fantastic!"

I groaned inwardly. He had no idea. When she said "my way" she meant vegetarian, and there wasn't much about traditional French-Canadian food that was vegetarian. It made for some . . . interesting . . . dishes. I'd sampled them before.

"I'll need some time to get a menu together and get prepared. A couple weeks from now?" she suggested. "Let's do it the weekend before I go away. A real send off." She beamed and looked so satisfied and pleased with herself that I didn't have the heart to make excuses.

"Sounds great!" I enthused.

Addy and I made our way home, the country roads quiet. We rolled down the windows and took great lungfuls of air. Seán, who was in the car behind us, tooted when he pulled off into the McCarty's driveway. I tapped my horn in response. Minutes later I turned onto my own driveway and drew the car to a stop. Addy and I filled our arms with my instrument and equipment, lugging them into the house.

"Good night, Mom," Addy said, giving me a quick hug and peck on the cheek. "You guys did good. It was a great dance."

"Thanks, chérie," I returned the hug, giving my daughter a tired smile.

"Are you going to bed?"

"No, you go on. I'm going to stay up for a bit."

Physically, I was exhausted, but my mind was racing. Swirls of color continued to dance in my mind, whirling in time to a reel. I wandered into the living room and put my banjo in the corner. My trusty vintage record player was in the same corner, and I put an old La Bottine Souriante record on the turntable. As the needle caught in the grooves, thin, scratchy French-Canadian music and French voices filled the space. I dragged my spinning wheel into the middle of the floor and maneuvered a piano stool into place. A basket nearby held wool roving. It was last year's shearing back from the mill. Burying my face in the softness, I inhaled. It was a little sheepy smelling and very comforting.

I pulled a hank of the roving from the bag, drafted it into strips the width of my thumb, and attached one to the leader on my bobbin. Treadling quickly, I let the twist creep up the length, pinching and drafting as I worked it into the roving, creating yarn. Every so often I picked up a clump of bright, colorful recycled sari silk and let it twist into the yarn. The fibers tangled together making a plump cocoon of color like dancers spinning around the floor.

I worked quickly and rhythmically. When the record reached an end and the needle hit empty space it turned itself off, but I barely noticed because it continued in my head, music from the record, music from the dance tonight, music from practice sessions; they all formed one long continuous reel made up in my head as bits and pieces from multitudes of songs all blended together. I kept time with my foot, depressing the treadle to the beat of the tune. As the yarn formed on the bobbin, the energy of the evening passed from my brain through my fingers, sore from the metal banjo strings, into the fiber until finally the bobbin was full and my mind was empty. I blinked a few times almost feeling as though I was coming out of a trance. I was both incredibly tired and incredibly happy.

Turning out the light I walked down the hallway to my own room, the dogs rousing themselves from their comfortable spots on the sofa to pad softly after me. It was two in the morning. I wouldn't get much sleep, but I was willing to bet it would be sweet. I didn't know it as my head sank gratefully onto my pillow, but I was about to lose that bet.

Chapter Sixteen

It was the incessant ringing that woke me up. I was the kind of tired that makes your limbs feel as though they are made of cement and glues your eyes shut. I could hear myself groaning as though I was coming out of anesthesia as I struggled to move my body, to force it upright. Prying my eyes open I glanced at the display on the alarm clock. It read 3 o'clock. Slowly it registered in my brain that the ringing was coming from the phone in the kitchen.

As both thoughts collided, I felt as though someone had dumped a bucket of ice water on me. The phone did not ring at this time of the morning to herald good news. Ever.

Seán was dead.

Flailing for the light switch, I hurtled across the room tripping on one of the dogs who was curled up on the floor in front of my bedroom door. As I rounded the corner I saw Addy emerging sleepily from her room. "What is it?" she asked.

"I don't know yet." I was afraid the ringing would stop before I reached the phone, but it didn't. It continued to shrill, demanding to be answered as I stood over it, my hand frozen, my mouth dry, my heart racing. I didn't want to know.

It had been like this with Danny. In my mind, he'd been alive all evening, having a great time with his friends. He'd been alive to me even after he'd gone into the water, under the ice, because I hadn't known yet. In that protected time between death and knowledge of death, he had still been alive. Even after they told me, hope flickered faintly until the police found his body a week later, his boot wedged into a crevice of his sled, trapping him beneath the water. But for me the moment of his death had been when I'd found out, not when his heart had stopped.

Seán was alive to me at this moment and would be until I picked up that phone and someone informed me that he was dead. My fingers were frozen over the phone, hesitating. And while I struggled to find enough courage to lift the receiver, Addy's hand snaked beneath mine and snatched it.

"No," I moaned, my throat already closing in a spasm of grief.

"Hello?" I could hear words, indistinctly, on the other end of the line. The tone deep, a man's voice: it sounded like my father. "We'll meet you there," Addy said before she hung up. She turned to me, her expression grim.

"It's Grand-mémère. She's had a stroke. They've brought her to the hospital. I told Pépère we'd meet them there."

"Mémère?" I echoed dully.

Addy put her arms around me, and I could feel her sympathy. "You thought it was Seán, didn't you?"

I hugged her back fiercely. "I did, but this is no better."

"She's alive," Addy replied simply. "That's better. Come on, let's go."

I pulled myself together enough to drive, but it was a grim trip. Addy huddled against the corner of the car sniffling. Driving in the darkness of the early morning hours felt surreal and unnatural. We didn't pass a single other car before reaching the hospital. I trailed behind Addy into the building, letting her lead the way since she remembered it better from her recent visit.

We found the room easily enough. My parents, Marcel, and Agnès were gathered around a bed where a frail shape lay draped with white blankets. Mémère looked peaceful, but different. The left side of her face dragged downward, the muscles slack, as though an artist had started to erase it and then changed his mind.

The unnatural lighting washed us all out, as though we'd had all our blood drained on the way to her bedside. Marcel was holding one of Mémère's hands, his head bowed, his lips moving in silent prayer. Agnès stood next to him, her hand on his shoulder, her head also bowed. My mother busied herself tidying up the bedside table; my father, grim-faced, paced at the foot of the bed. He looked up as Addy and I entered the room. I felt my throat constrict when I saw the pain in his eyes, and I threw my arms around his neck.

"How is she?" I murmured. My father gave me a brief, business-like hug before releasing me.

"She's stable, they said. The one that was in here before, she said it could have been much worse. My mother is fortunate." He seemed to struggle with the veracity of his own statement. "That's what they said," he repeated as if trying to convince himself. "She's fortunate."

"She *is* fortunate," Agnès agreed. "The night nurse found her when she was doing her rounds. Mémère woke up and said something to her and then," she tipped her head toward the bed, "this."

"When will she wake up?" I asked. My eyes tracked Addy as she put her arm around my mother. They stood together by the bedside. Mom reached out and took Marcel's hand and bowed her own head, joining him in prayer. Addy did the same.

"They aren't sure."

"What can we do?" I felt that same crushing feeling of helplessness I always felt when confronted with serious illness or death. Unreasonably, I wanted Seán to be there. I wanted his reassuring presence. I wanted his support. But just wanting those things from him made me feel small and weak and selfish. Seán had enough to deal with; he didn't need to be put through the additional grief of our situation. Anyway, this wasn't his problem, and I wasn't his responsibility.

Where then, I wondered, could I find the strength I so desperately needed? It was then I looked up, and my daughter caught my eye. She smiled through her tears and held her hand out to me. I walked over and took it, bowing my head and joining in prayer with her, my mom, Marcel, Agnès, and my father. Together we faced tragedy. We faced the possibility of loss. We faced off with the unknown by fortifying ourselves with the only strength that was ever available to anyone in that kind of circumstance: God.

We prayed for his mercy. We prayed for more time with someone we all loved. We prayed for the doctors to have the wisdom needed to treat her in the very best way possible. We prayed for a quick recovery and no lasting effects from the stroke. We entreated God to give us the strength we needed to accept any outcome while leaving it squarely in his hands. We thanked him for the time we'd had with Mémère and in turn we talked about our best memories of her, our favorite times together, the funny, and often crazy, things she'd said or done.

Marcel read the twenty-first Psalm, and we all joined him and then the two of us, together for the first time in many years, sang Amazing Grace. I had forgotten what a rich, deep baritone my brother had. His voice was as smooth as dark chocolate. To my surprise Addy joined us. She rarely sang, and I was never sure if she simply didn't enjoy it the way I did, or if she didn't like the quality of her voice. She had inherited my deep contralto and had always been slightly sensitive about it. I knew what it was like to be put in with the altos and sometimes even the tenors in chorus while all the other girls hung out in the soprano and alto section. The music teacher had always called me a "gravel Girty" and told me I needed to reach up high so I wouldn't be singing in the basement. But while alto was usually attainable, the quality of my voice suffered when I struggled to reach high notes.

When we finished praying and singing, the room was starting to lighten, the sky outside a chilly summer gray. Even in summer it wasn't unusual for the temperature to plummet at night. The others headed off to locate the cafeteria to see if they had started serving breakfast yet, but I stayed behind. Pulling a chair up close to the bed, I took my grandmother's papery thin hand in my own and laid my head down on my arms to pray some more, but I was so drained from the concert and lack of sleep that I could feel exhaustion overtake me even while I fought oblivion.

The next thing I knew the morning was far spent. Hot sun glancing through the hospital window struck my face and woke me. I glanced around, disoriented, trying to get my bearings. My family was gone, except for Marcel who was dozing in a chair in the corner of the room. I was no longer sitting beside the bed where I must have passed out shortly after I sat down. Instead, I was in another of the plastic hospital chairs along the opposite wall of the room. As I became fully awake I realized I was covered with a thin, white hospital blanket and cradled on the broad chest of the person in the chair next to mine. A strong arm was wrapped protectively around my shoulders. My father? I craned my neck, pushing myself up slightly to see who was holding me. My slight shift resulted in an answering movement, and I knew I'd woken him.

I looked up directly into Seán's blue eyes.

I was so startled that even though my first reaction was the kind of embarrassment you feel when you realize you've fallen asleep on the shoulder of the person sitting next to you on the bus, I ignored the impulse to hastily push away and mumble an apology. Instead, I smiled and burrowed deeper into his arms. He responded by holding me tighter, almost as though he were clutching me to keep me from drifting out to sea.

I'm not really sure how long we stayed like that because I dozed off again. The next time I woke up, Marcel was gone. I wanted to pretend that I was still asleep and go on being held but I must have stirred. "Why didn't you call me?" Seán asked quietly.

"How did you find out?" It was easier to parry with a different question than try to explain how I hadn't wanted to drag him to the edge of the grave when he was close enough himself to spit inside.

"I've been prayer walking with Marcel in the morning," he replied, as if I'd know what that was. "We'd planned to go later this morning because we figured we'd both be tired from the dance last night, but he never showed. When I called him, he explained what had happened. I came as soon as I heard."

"How long have you been here?"

"Since ten o'clock maybe."

I pushed back from his chest so fast the blanket slid off and fell to the floor. "What time is it now?"

"Maybe one o'clock. Why?"

"My animals, my lessons . . ."

"Addy took care of all that. She left with Agnès earlier to do your chores. I stopped and let your dogs out on my way over here."

"You? But how . . ."

He chuckled. "You don't hide your spare key very well. In the flowerpot on the front porch? Really? You should at least make it a challenge."

I colored. "What about my lessons?"

"Addy said she'd call the parents, explain. I'm sure they will all understand."

"Did anyone tell Marise?"

"I left a note taped to her door," Seán replied.

I should have caught the teasing tone. "A note? But she's . . ." When I realized he was kidding, I swatted him. "Does she know?"

"She knows. She said she would be praying for her. We should probably stop there on the way home."

"We?" I hated to ask, hated to discuss something that had the fragile, temporary feel of a cobweb. I wanted to leave it unspoken, assumed, that the illusion I felt at that moment was reality. Was there a "we"? Could there even be a "we"? I didn't want to think about that. Instead, I had to be practical. "What about my car?"

"Addy took Agnès home in it so they could leave Marcel's, and he wouldn't be stranded here. He's gone down to get something to eat, but he'll be back soon. He's planning to stick around until she wakes up, but he had a few quick errands to run. I think the others said they were going to come back this evening to check on her. There's really not much more anyone can do right now."

I glanced toward my grandmother's still form on the bed. She didn't appear to have moved, but her face seemed to have better color this morning than it had the night before and the drag marks pulling her mouth and cheek slack seemed less fierce. "She hasn't woken up then?"

"Not yet." Seán reached out and smoothed the hair back from my forehead tenderly. "But the last time a nurse came through she said her vital signs were improved from when they'd brought her in."

"Really?" I felt a surge of hope. I turned back to Seán, and for a moment I thought he was going to lean over and kiss me. His eyes were soft, and his hand cupped the back of my head, tilting me toward him. I savored the delicious thrill that flooded me. I wanted that moment to last forever, and I didn't want it to last another second. But in the next instant, Marcel sauntered back into the room, steaming mug in one hand, Bible in the other.

"Morning," he said indolently, apparently oblivious to the moment he'd just rudely interrupted. He noisily pulled a plastic chair over to the bedside and spread his Bible out on his lap.

Seán smiled ruefully, released me, and looked over at my brother. "Hey, I'm going to bring Emerson home. Are you good to stay here for a while? Do you need anything?"

Marcel waved the Bible with a flourish. "Nah, I've got everything I need right here. If anything happens, I'll call you," he told me. Then in a pleasant, conversational tone, he began reading to Mémère from the Bible. "In the beginning . . ."

Seán grinned. "Wonder how far he'll get before she wakes up?"

Feeling almost normal for the first time since I'd gotten the phone call that morning, I joked back, "Only until he skips something. Mémère was always a stickler for the whole story. I used to read to her while she was quilting, and she always knew if I skipped over something. Even if it was just a boring part, she'd make me go back and read it over."

I kissed my grandmother on the cheek, praying again that she would wake up soon, gave my brother a rare hug even though I would have preferred slapping him, and followed Seán out to where he'd left his vehicle. As I climbed into the big, green Explorer, I remembered the first time I'd seen it parked at the gas pump at Angelique's. It felt like a lifetime ago. The "tall, handsome, stranger" Marise had prayed for that day so long ago had become a precious friend I couldn't imagine my life without.

To distract me from where those thoughts inevitably led, I said, "Tell me about prayer walking. Is that some new scheme of Marcel's? He sure likes to be different."

I was joking, but Seán answered me with all seriousness, full of enthusiasm. "It was new to me, too. We happened to run into each other one morning on Craig's Hill when we were walking, so we joined up. Your brother explained to me that he was walking the whole town, and as he walked, he prayed for every person who lived on that road, even if he didn't know them. He said he figured God knew them even if he didn't, and God would know what their needs were."

I'd never heard of such a thing, and I struggled to take it in. "He's walking the whole town?"

"Not all at once," Seán assured me. "We only walk about five miles every day. But he does have a map and highlights all the places he's already been so eventually, yes, he'll have walked through the whole town and prayed for every person in it."

That explained why Marcel was looking fitter these days. "He never said."

Seán glanced at me then quickly returned his eyes to the road. "You can come with us if you like. I know Marcel would love that."

"You think?" I smiled to reassure him that I was teasing. Although Marcel and I got along like oil and water most of the time, we had the sort of deep loyalty to one another that all brothers and sisters had . . . whether they admitted it or not. "I'd like that."

I hadn't noticed, but Seán was taking us home the back way, along an older route that ran parallel to the highway. I became aware of my surroundings as he slowed and pulled in to the parking area in front of a small diner called Mac's Grill that had existed for as long as I could remember.

"Hungry?" Seán asked.

"Starving," I admitted.

The waitress looked like she was still in high school and the short-order cook, who I could see through the waist-level swinging doors, didn't look any older. She was a plain girl with eyes the color of beach glass, and she stood poised over the grill like a sprinter at the starting blocks. I scratched my nose to hide a smile. Seán found us a booth with a window that overlooked the lake and after slowly setting down her paperback, the waitress sauntered over and slapped a couple of menus down on the table.

"The spaghetti is out-of-this-world good here," the waitress informed us and then lowered her voice and leaned over the table. "But don't order anything with steak in it." She jerked a thumb over her shoulder to indicate the cook. "The meat's questionable, but the boss is making her cook it anyway. Guy just left here and puked all over the parking lot." She shook her head. "Wouldn't listen to me."

She snapped her gum and smiled brightly. "You ready to order?"

Seán and I exchanged looks. Without looking at the menu he said, "We'll have two spaghettis. Thanks."

"Right. Coming up." She scrawled the order on her pad, picked up the menus, and returned to her book. As soon as the slip of paper was clipped to her station the cook sprang into action. I had no doubt we'd have food in front of us in record time.

Seán chuckled. "Maybe we should have gone somewhere else. I remember this place from when I was a kid. It was always a real treat when Dad brought us here for dinner. Made us all feel so grown up." He scrutinized the dining area. "The old place is looking run down. I don't think a trip down nostalgia lane is worth a case of food poisoning." He considered me with a worried expression. "Do you want to leave? I can cancel the order."

"What? Are you kidding? This is the most adventurous thing I've done all week. Besides, I think you'd break her heart." I tipped my head toward the back room where the young cook was slaving away. "I think she's trying to set a land speed record to get that food out here. I'm sure it'll be fine. There's no steak in spaghetti."

"So it looks like there's going to be a wedding this fall," Seán remarked, mercifully changing the subject, though the sudden shift left me disoriented.

My stomach lurched. "What? Who?" If Marise had shared news with him that she hadn't even shared with me, we were going to have words.

"Angelique and Jeff Daniels, of course," he said, looking surprised that it wasn't obvious. "Mrs. McCarty says they told her last night they were engaged. Finally. Apparently it's the longest running intermittent courtship in recorded history."

I laughed. "That old dog. Good for her. She finally got her man."

The cook slapped her spatula victoriously onto a bell on the counter like a runner breaking through the tape at the finish line, and the waitress put down her book with obvious reluctance and unhurriedly fetched our order. Seán's face brightened at the sight of the two steaming plates of food. When the waitress set a basket of garlic bread on the table, he smiled broadly. "I'd forgotten about that. You guys have the best garlic bread I've ever had."

The waitress snapped her gum. "Leftover rolls." At our blank expressions, she elaborated. "The owner makes us save all the leftover rolls from the bread baskets, and he cuts them up to make the garlic bread. Enjoy your lunch."

Seán leaned over the table and dropped his voice so low I had to lean toward him to hear. "I'm so sorry." He mouthed, more than spoke the words. "Is that even legal?"

I laughed. "Just bless the food, and then we won't have to worry about it."

Shyly, Seán reached across the table and took my hands in his. He bowed his head a little self-consciously, and I tried not to notice the waitress watching us with interest. I'd never prayed in public before, and I felt awkward, but I followed Seán's lead, closed my eyes to block everything else out, and gripped his hands.

"Lord," he whispered fervently, "I ask You to please bless this food, and I thank you for Emerson's company. Thank You for giving us this time together. We ask You to be with her grandmother in the hospital. Help her to heal quickly. In Jesus' name. Amen."

"Amen," I repeated.

We ate in silence for a while, and I took the opportunity to study Seán surreptitiously. The scruff on his cheeks almost hid a lingering gauntness that accented his high cheekbones, but I suddenly realized that over the months since he'd come to live at the lake he had undergone a slow transformation. It was almost as if he was getting . . . well.

Seán caught me looking at him. "What? Do I have food on my face?"

"No," I said, waving my fork dismissively. "Not at all. By the way, how have you been feeling? You never mention it." *Even though I've tried to ask you before*, I thought.

His face grew guarded. "Not bad," he said. "I have good days and bad days."

"Yeah, but not a lot of bad days lately?" I hedged.

"No, thank God, not a lot of bad ones lately," he agreed.

I got bolder. "What do the doctors say?"

He grinned, but his eyes were sad. "You mean, how much longer have I got? The jury is still out."

It was the most he'd ever talked to me about his brain tumor since the night he'd told me he was dying, but I could tell he wanted to change the subject, so we started talking about the night before, and then he told me stories about playing music with his family when he was growing up. Eventually the waitress wandered over and collected our empty plates. "Do you want dessert?" she asked dubiously.

"No," Seán said firmly. "Thanks anyway."

She shrugged. "I'll meet you at the till, and you can pay there."

I followed Seán and stood silently as he settled the check. "I used to come here as a kid," he told the waitress conversationally. "Hasn't changed much."

"Yeah?" She eyed him. "I didn't know it had been here that long."

I felt Seán jerk as he passed me and realized he was stifling laughter. He made it out the door before I could.

"Please tell the cook for us that the food was great," I said.

The waitress nodded. "I hope it worked," she called after us.

I turned back. "Hope what worked?"

"The prayer. I hope you don't get sick. Have a nice day!" She waved cheerfully, and I let the door close behind me, setting off the bells announcing we were leaving. Catching up to Seán, I told him what she'd said, and we both laughed until we were leaning against the SUV trying to catch our breath.

"I am so sorry, Em," Seán gasped when we could finally speak again. "We should have gone somewhere else."

"No," I protested. "This was great. The spaghetti *was* out-of-this-world good."

"If you get sick, I'll never forgive myself," he replied. In an instant, the moment grew serious and before I even knew what was happening, he pulled me close, tipped my chin up with one hand, and gently placed his lips on mine. I returned his kiss, leaning against him for support, not wanting the moment to end, but he broke away, holding me away from him, looking stunned. "Emerson, I . . . I . . ." There was anguish on his face. "I shouldn't have done that. Please forgive me."

"Seán, there's nothing to forgive." I attempted to step back into his arms, but the moment was gone, shattered, and he opened the door for me so I got into the Explorer instead, wondering if it was something I had done. Or—I shuddered to think—had things gotten serious with Trudy, and he regretted our intimacy for that reason?

Seán started the engine, but he let it idle for a moment.

"That was inexcusable." He turned to look at me, his blue eyes troubled. "Will you forgive me?"

"Of course," I said lightly, but I sensed he needed serious reassurance. "Of course," I repeated more firmly. "Seán, don't worry. I know where things stand. I won't get the wrong idea."

He held my gaze for a few moments. "I love you, you know."

I smiled but refused to let my words betray any emotion I felt when I replied. I kept my tone light and noncommittal. "I love you, too." I broke eye contact and glanced out the side window. "And if I get food poisoning, you're going to come over and hold my hair back for me while I vomit into the toilet."

He chuckled and seemed to accept that his actions hadn't caused any permanent damage between us.

"You got it." He put the vehicle in gear and backed out of the parking lot. I watched the scenery go by, listening to him talk about inane topics to distract me, but inside I marshaled every ounce of strength I had to keep my broken heart from shattering into a thousand tiny pieces.

I managed to do it until I watched him back out of my driveway, waved, and made it into the soothing quiet of my own bedroom. Then I buried my face into one of my Mémère's quilts and wished with all my heart that I could let go enough to cry.

Chapter Seventeen

I saw Seán a few days later at the store. Truthfully, I sometimes suspected he timed his trips to Angelique's in order to run into me. I was able to smile cheerfully, and as far as I could tell, our relationship had fallen seamlessly back into its previous track, the hiccup we'd experienced forgotten.

"How is your grandmother?" Seán asked, flipping the dogs some jerky despite my warning glare; one treat every morning was more than enough.

"She's stable. I'm headed down there this afternoon. I thought I'd bring her a bouquet of gladiolas from my garden."

"Flowers! That's a great idea." He looked thoughtful but didn't elaborate.

That could have been because it was difficult to get a word in edgewise with Angelique gushing about her upcoming nuptials and flashing her ring around. Her hands danced so much while she was talking that if she'd been conducting the Flight of the Bumblebee, the orchestra would have been playing double-time. The ring's sparkle distracted me from gawking at her mouth, resplendent with that perfect set of shiny, white teeth. Their dazzle competed with her ring for attention. The new teeth made her look like a different person; I wondered why she hadn't gotten the dentures years earlier.

"Have you picked a date yet?" I asked quickly when she paused finally for breath.

"Christmas Eve," she replied. "Can you picture it? Poinsettias, garland, fake snow, tinsel?" She sighed dreamily.

I tried to hide a smile. Apparently it never changed, the excitement of beginning a new life with someone you loved; no matter how old you were, true love didn't fade. I was so happy for Angelique that I couldn't even work up any irritation at the insufferable way she droned on and on about her wedding plans. I glanced over at Seán to see if he was getting antsy and found he was regarding Angelique with a mixture of amusement and envy: a strange combination.

"Jeff wanted to get married by a justice of the peace without no ceremony or nothing," Angelique was saying. "He don't want no fuss." She snorted. "Tant pis.[35] I waited a long time," she gave us an arch look and repeated, with emphasis, "a *long* time, to get married, and I want all the

---

[35] Too bad, tough.

trimmings. Now it's Jeff's turn to wait." She laughed, making no sound, her shoulders shaking with mirth.

"I don't blame you," I agreed stoutly. "You stick to your guns."

Still sporting a Cheshire grin she waved us off, at last, and Seán walked out with me. We meandered slowly back up the road in a companionable silence, the dogs running circles around us, herding us home.

"I have to give a piano lesson in a half hour, but there's time for tea if you want to come up to the house," I said, keeping my voice light and friendly.

"I wish I could," Seán replied ruefully, "but I have an appointment this morning. Can I take a rain check?"

"Of course. Always. You know that. Did you want to go to the hospital with me later on?"

"I really wish I could," he repeated, looking anguished.

I could feel his eyes on me, but I studied the horizon and shrugged. "Another time." I turned in his direction without meeting his eyes. "You know where I live," I joked.

"Emerson . . ." He stopped in front of his house and stood uneasily, digging his hands into his pockets. He seemed to be having an internal struggle with himself. I waited, curious, but finally he sighed and said only, "Have a great day."

"Sure. You too." I turned and headed up the road with the dogs. When I glanced back, he had gone inside, but I saw Trudy pulling into his driveway. She gave me a little smile and a wave which I returned before I quickened my steps to get out of sight. *Appointment, right*, I mused darkly, *date, more like*.

Before I could speculate on what exciting plans they had for the day, I spied Mimi's lurking form silhouetted on the porch. This was not the cheerful Mimi I had seen two days before playing music and having fun. This was a stormy Mimi, dressed completely in black, her face a thundercloud. One of the long sleeves of her T-shirt had crept up revealing the tail end of a thin, fresh cut. She saw my eyes go to it and quickly tugged the errant sleeve down to her bony wrist.

I said nothing and sank down in the chair next to her. We sat in silence for a few minutes, the time pressing on me. I knew that a car would pull up shortly, disgorging a homeschooler who was my idea of a prodigy—a student who actually practiced—and our time would be cut short.

"Don't," she pleaded, red-rimmed eyes lifting to meet mine, "don't yell at me."

"I'm not going to yell at you," I said, keeping my voice soft. "Why would I yell at you? You aren't about to step off a cliff."

My attempt at levity wasn't lost on her, and she almost smiled. "Everyone yells at me," she said softly.

"Everyone, huh?"

She sniffed. "My mom, she hates me!"

I struggled to be patient. "Mimi . . ."

"Don't say she doesn't hate me!" she cut me off hotly. "You don't know. You aren't there. She expects me to do everything: clean, make dinner, haul groceries home on my bike! It's like I'm her little slave, not her daughter."

And what, I wanted to ask, *is she doing in the meantime*? But I didn't need to ask; I knew. Theresa was working. I also knew it would make no difference to mention this to Mimi. She was a kid; she had no idea of the responsibilities adults faced. In her eyes, she was being asked to do an unreasonable amount of work at home, work her mother should have been doing, the same mother who was yelling at her for not doing it, presumably.

I closed my eyes for a moment. *Lord*, I prayed silently, *tell me what to say to Mimi. She's hurting and I feel helpless. I can't bring her father back. I can't take the weight of responsibility from her mother. I can't fix their relationship. I can't give her the true comfort she needs, or the tools to handle her situation, only You can do that. Please use me to reach her. Thank You.*

When I opened my eyes Mimi was staring at me, her dark eyes accusing. "What are you doing?"

I swallowed hard. Caught. Might as well fess up. "Praying."

"Why?"

I took a deep, steadying breath. "Because, Mimi, there's nothing I can do for you, humanly speaking. I can't change any of the circumstances in your life. All I can offer you is friendship and advice and donuts." She almost smiled again. "You need supernatural help."

"What, like God?" Her eyes narrowed to slits, and there was the slightest hint of scoffing in her tone.

"Not 'like God', no. Exactly God. Only God. Totally God."

She deflated a little, her shoulders slumping. "I go to church," she protested. "I pray. Sometimes."

"That's great," I said. "That's a step in the right direction. But that's not what I'm talking about. God is more than someone you meet at church, or throw a prayer at now and then. He's someone who wants to help you in everything, every little thing. He wants a relationship with you." I wished mightily that Marise or Seán or Marcel could trade places with me. Having a relationship with God was something I was only just beginning to understand myself. Better to admit that up front and not get caught out later on. "Look, I know this can be hard to understand. I don't even really understand it myself yet. All I can do is tell you what God's done for me."

Mimi looked skeptical, but she didn't stop me, so I plunged on. "Do you know about what happened to my husband? Danny?" A brief nod. "It was years ago now, but at the time I felt like my life was over, ruined. I didn't see how I could live without him. A heavy, dark cloud has followed me ever since then. I haven't been able to shake it."

"But your brother is the preacher," Mimi protested, interrupting me.

I shook my head. "That doesn't matter. That's what I'm trying to tell you. It's not my relationship with my brother, or anyone else that matters. Because their relationship with God isn't my relationship with God. What matters is my relationship with God, and I didn't have one. I play the piano at church every week, but that doesn't mean I listen to the sermon or that I even care about it. Marcel is the preacher, and he has his own relationship with God, but it's not mine. You can't experience God's power through someone else's relationship; you have to have one of your own."

"So God made you all better and now you have a new boyfriend, is that it?"

I jerked back as though she'd slapped me. "What? What are you talking about?"

Mimi rolled her eyes. "You know . . . you and Seán? I know he likes you. I thought you liked him, too."

My heart pounded wildly in my chest, but I didn't let any indication of it cross my face. "Mimi, Seán and I are friends, that's all. Seán has . . . He's . . . not available." Mimi exuded a sympathy for me that nearly made me break down and cry. "Look, that's not the point. Whether or not I ever have a new boyfriend or get remarried, that's not important. What is important is that I started talking to God and listening to him. That dark cloud that's been around me for so long, it's lifting. I'm starting to be able to enjoy life again. I'm learning to trust him to take care of me and to help me handle the things that he allows in my life: like Danny's death." *And Seán's*, I thought to myself.

"I don't get it," Mimi said bluntly, shaking her head with irritation. "God's not here. You can't even see him. How can he possibly help you handle stuff?"

"By changing you on the inside, by changing your perspective," I said simply, feeling as though I had just discovered something important as the words passed my lips. It was true, I realized. That's how God was making things different for me; he was slowly changing me on the inside. My outward circumstances hadn't changed at all—Danny was still gone—but inside I didn't feel as crushed by his death. Because of God's help, I felt able to cope with it, to rise above it even. "Marise says that the Bible is God's living Word, and that means he can use it to change us. He might change our circumstances, but he always changes our hearts. That's what she says, and I have to admit, that's what he's done for me."

"Do you think he'd do that for me? Help me with, you know . . ." She tugged at her sleeve.

"Yes, I do. Would you like me to pray with you?"

Mimi looked both embarrassed and frightened, something I could relate to when it came to praying with other people, but in her eyes I could also see desperation and longing. "Do we have to?"

I laughed to break the tension. "No, but I'd like to. Would you?"

"I guess." She was skeptical, but she bowed her head anyway, so I followed suit.

"Dear Lord, I bring you my young friend, Mary Margaret . . ."

"Mimi," she hissed without looking up. "He should call me Mimi."

I dug my fingernails into my palm to keep from laughing. "My young friend, Mimi," I amended obediently. "Help her to feel your love and strength, Lord. Show her how very much you love her. Be present in her life and give her the strength she needs to deal with her difficult circumstances. Send your Holy Spirit to guide her and instruct her. Teach her how to have a relationship with you. Thank you, Lord, for forgiving us and for saving us. Amen."

Mimi looked up. "Now what?"

"Now you read your Bible and pray and ask God to keep talking to you."

"I don't have a Bible."

"I think we can fix that." Before I could get up to see if I could locate an extra, a car pulled into my driveway. A young boy hopped out of the vehicle clutching a folder that flapped wildly as he pelted up to the porch.

"I'm sorry I'm late, Mrs. Giroux," he gasped, "my little brother's diaper had a blow-out, and Mom had to change him before we could leave."

"That's all right, Marc," I said. Standing to follow him into the house I turned to Mimi. "We can talk more later, and I'll find you a Bible." Suddenly, a thought occurred to me. "Why aren't you in school, anyway?"

She waved a hand in dismissal. "Teacher convention. I've got the day off."

"In that case, why don't you take Gyp and Dash and move the sheep into the pasture by the road? After that you can muck the barn. And after that, we'll have a lesson."

"OK." She stood uncertainly on the porch for a moment. "I don't feel any different yet," she said, looking slightly worried.

I smiled and patted her on the arm. "It's not about feelings, Mimi. And it's not magic. Don't worry. God is there, and he will help you."

I had two more lessons after Marc left, and it was lunchtime before I made it out to the barn to check on Mimi's progress. The only spare Bible I'd been able to locate was a green pocket-sized version I'd been given as a college student by someone from the Gideon's. "It's just the New Testament and Psalms, I think," I told her, "but it's a start. I'll get you a better one as soon as I can."

She took the little Bible from me and slipped it into her pocket. "Thanks," she said, leaning on the pitchfork. Tipping it, she indicated one of the sheep out in the pasture. "He's my favorite."

"Little Gabriel?" He wasn't so little any more, but it was hard to stop calling him that. Most of the other lambs were spoken for, some had already gone to their new homes, but I hadn't been able to part with Gabe, even though I didn't really need to add to my flock.

At the moment he was lying back to back with his mother Angel. They looked like mirror images of each other, calmly chewing their cuds surrounded by rich, green grass. If contentment could be painted, they would make worthy subjects. Maybe it was the exercise, or just being in a pastoral setting around the animals, but Mimi's eyes seemed calmer as she watched them. She seemed less hectic, less troubled. *The peace of God passes all understanding*, I mused to myself.

"Are you ready for your lesson?" I asked.

"Almost," she said. "As soon as I dump this wheelbarrow, I'll be finished."

"I'll go make us some lunch then," I told her. "Come down when you're finished, and we'll eat first. I don't know about you, but I'm starved."

My garden was minuscule by local standards and lingering frosts had killed a lot of my early plantings. Poking around, I managed to find a couple of early tomatoes and a puny basil plant in the cold frame. Paired with a baby mozzarella I'd picked up at the co-op and a loaf of bread from the local bakery, we had the makings of a meal fit for a king.

"What do you call this?" Mimi asked later, staring down at the plate where her lunch steamed, blissfully scenting the crisp air.

"That, my dear, is a panini," I informed her. "It's like a grilled cheese for grown-ups. Try it. You'll love it."

She pushed aside the dill pickle wedge and apple slices I'd marshaled around the sandwich and picked up one half of it. Tasting it delicately, she chewed as though she wasn't yet committed and would spit it out if necessary. Fortunately, it wasn't necessary. Her eyes widened in surprise, and she didn't even wait until she'd swallowed before blurting out, "This is good!"

"I'm glad you like it."

"No, I mean, it's really good. Like, it's crazy good. You could start a restaurant or something."

"Thanks, Mimi, but I don't really think . . ."

"I'll do it, then," she said. "I'll learn how to cook like this, and I'll start my own restaurant. I'll call it Mimi's, and I'll serve crazy good stuff like this."

I laughed. "A star is born."

"You don't think I could do it?" she asked, looking hurt, mistaking my remark for doubt.

"I absolutely think you could do it," I corrected her emphatically. "You can do anything you put your mind to. I've known that about you since we first met. Anyone who can teach herself to play piano by listening to the radio can do anything she decides she wants to."

A flush crept up Mimi's cheeks. "You really think that about me?"

"No, I know that about you. Let me ask you something, Mimi. How many other girls your age have taught themselves something so complicated?"

She gave my question a little thought. "No one I know, I guess."

"And how many are working like slaves so they can learn even more about something they love?"

"No one I know," she repeated, her voice stronger, more confident, a slow smile spreading across her face.

"Exactly. You can do anything you want to do. If you love to cook, then you'll be a terrific cook. You have the two things you need to succeed: determination and perseverance." I leaned toward her and lowered my voice.

"And when you have your own five-star restaurant do me a favor: don't make the cook sell spoiled steak."

While we ate I told her the story about my lunch with Seán at Mac's. It turned out she knew both the short-order cook and the waitress from school though they had graduated the year before. The cook had been in her band class. "She played the French horn," Mimi said, "badly."

After lunch, Mimi helped me clear the table and wash up our few dishes. We left them in the drainer to dry and settled ourselves at the piano. Mimi struggled because she could play better than she could read music at the moment. She could sit down at the piano and replicate (after a fashion) something she'd heard on Vermont Public Radio after listening to it a few times, and she was frustrated at being stuck in a "kiddie" piano lesson book. It was like being able to speak fluently but not being able to read; Mimi was still at picture book level.

I never timed Mimi's lessons. We just worked until we reached her frustration point. Some days that came earlier than others. Today she managed to maintain her focus longer than usual and when someone called, "Knock, knock," and pushed open the kitchen door, I had to straighten out a kink I'd gotten in my back from leaning forward before I could turn to see who it was: only Marcel. Mimi had done well, fortunately, and she had a look of satisfaction on her face. I left her studiously going over a tricky section that used both hands while I went to see what Marcel wanted.

Not standing on ceremony, he'd wandered into the kitchen and was picking at the grapes I'd left out on the counter. "Help yourself," I said, but my sarcastic tone was lost on him.

"Thanks."

Suddenly, I worried that he'd come to bring me bad news. "Mémère's not worse, is she?"

"Worse? No, she's a lot better. She's talking."

"Talking?" How was that possible? The woman had suffered a stroke. Last I heard she hadn't even been conscious.

Marcel shrugged. "According to the doctors, it's a miracle." He grinned. "And they said they don't use that word lightly. One of them threatened to call me a liar if I repeated it."

I felt as though a great weight had lifted. Until that moment, I hadn't realized how much concern for my grandmother had been weighing on me. "Is she still at the hospital?"

"At the moment," he said. "But they want her out pronto. They said she's been trying to make a match between a doctor and a nurse. Seems they've been sweet on each other for a while, but neither one had the courage to make a move."

"And she found that out in a matter of hours?" I asked incredulously. The woman was unbelievable.

"No, apparently she heard a lot of what was going on while she was "unconscious". She overheard the nurse confide in a co-worker about her feelings for the doctor and cry on her shoulder about how she'd never find out if he was interested in her or not because he was like an absent-minded professor, focused completely on his work and not interested in mortal trivialities like love."

I doubted the nurse had described her love interest in exactly those words and suspected they had come directly from the mouth of my grandmother who dearly loved to sensationalize such things. It proved, more than consciousness did, that she was back among the living. I couldn't help grinning.

"It's like a soap opera!"

Marcel shook his head. "Wait, it gets better. So as I heard it, the doctor was examining her when her eyes flew open, and she grabbed his arm with her good hand. She said, 'I have a message for you, me. Dere's somebody in dis place what calls herself Claire dat loves you, only you is too blind to see dat, what's right in front of your nose, you. Stop dat and tell dat girl you love her.'" He mimicked our grandmother's voice so perfectly I laughed out loud.

Marcel held up a restraining hand. "Oh, that's not all," he said. "Then she told him that he was getting too old to put off something as important as getting married and that if he knew what was good for him he'd go find 'dat girl' right now and get things settled once and for all."

"She didn't!" I gasped, laughing almost too hard to speak.

"The doctor—it was Doctor Gadbois, do you remember him?—well, he was pretty shaken up. According to the nurses, he staggered down the hall to the nurses' station looking like he'd seen a ghost. The poor man was so rattled that he didn't even realize Claire was one of the nurses in the group when he told them what happened. She turned beet red and fainted dead away. They had to revive her with smelling salts. Meanwhile, one of the others had the presence of mind to go check on Mémère and found out that, sure enough, she was awake and coherent, if a little obnoxious.

"She kept demanding that they do something about 'dose two'. And that was when they called us. Well, they called Maman and Papa who called me; they asked me to let you know. The folks have already headed up to the hospital—the hospital staff insisted—to see about arrangements for moving her back to the nursing home tout de suite.[36] I'm going right now. I'm sure they'll need some help. Do you want to come with me?"

"Are you kidding? I wouldn't miss this for the world." I checked my watch. I didn't have any other lessons scheduled until after supper. Addy would be home soon, unless Auggie had an emergency to deal with, and could do evening chores if I wasn't back in time. I wrote a quick note to let her know what was going on and taped it to the door. "Mimi? We're going to run up to the hospital to see our grandmother. Do you want to stay here and practice, or are you headed home?" I hated to kick her out, but she scooted off the piano bench willingly enough.

"I need to get home anyway," she said. "It's my turn to cook dinner. Thanks for the lesson. I'll keep practicing."

I looked pointedly at her wrist. "Will you be okay, do you think?"

She caught my meaning and colored. In reply, she fished the little Bible from her pocket and waved it at me. "I think I'll do some reading when I get home."

"Good deal," I said, giving her a thumbs-up.

"What was that all about?" Marcel asked me, sotto voce, as he followed me out the door.

"I'll explain on the way," I replied. A flash of color caught my eye just before I got into the truck. The gladiolas!

"Just a minute, I want to pick some glads for Mémère." Marcel waited with no hint of impatience, one his best qualities if you asked me. I gathered the spikey, showy blooms into a thick bouquet and cradled them in my arms like a baby.

Marcel's pickup truck was only slightly more reputable than my own, and I climbed in gingerly. I had to shift a pile of parts belonging to some contraption off the seat and shove empty soda cans and fast food wrappers to one side on the floor just to have a place to put my feet. "Why don't you clean this mess?" I complained.

"Shut up," Marcel said blandly.

I knew I could rant at him for hours, and he wouldn't take offense.

---

[36] Immediately

Sometimes it was annoying. I glanced out the window as we passed Seán's house. His SUV was parked in the drive, but the windows of the house were dark. Still out with Trudy. I wondered where they had gone and what they were doing. And then, I tried not to.

Chapter Eighteen

"But you have to help me," Marise insisted stubbornly. I was surprised she didn't emphasize the demand by stamping her foot and setting her ponytail bouncing. For someone who normally wouldn't allow me to dry the dishes she was now just as adamant in the opposite direction.

"Sweetie, you know I'd be happy to help, but I don't know how to make traditional Québécois dishes vegetarian." Most people I knew would have considered that a form of sacrilege. Case in point, over family dinner at our parents' house on Sunday when Marcel had blabbed what Marise was planning, Maman had informed us bluntly that if you took the meat out of Québécois food you might as well eat dirt.

As I'd helped her clean up the kitchen later, I'd heard her muttering to herself about the impossibility of making tourtière—meat pie—without meat. "What would you call it then?" she'd demanded, "air pie? Empty pie? Just pastry?" I'd laughed at the time, but I really didn't know. What did you use to fill a meatless meat pie?

"You don't need to know how to cook them yourself," Marise wheedled. "I have recipes. I just need help making them. It's a lot of work, you know."

I knew, all right. I'd been roped into helping the last time she'd hosted a dinner party; it was Mexican food that time and much easier than this fiasco was promising to be. At least then I'd known that at the end of the day the food was going to be edible. I had no such assurance this time. In my heart of hearts, I'd been hoping that she'd reconsider, change the menu, or decide that it was all too much work, but she was just as keen on the idea now as she had been when she'd extended the initial invitation.

I wasn't sure how to tell her that a party featuring the sort of food she was planning to make was going to be a disaster. Even if I'd been able to speak with the tongues of angels she'd never have listened. Marise was the most determined person I knew.

I relented. "How early do you want me here?"

"You'll help?" she squealed in delight.

"Of course, I'll help," I said, trying to force my voice to sound bright. "But you'll have to tell me exactly what to do."

"Naturally," Marise said sweetly, beaming in triumph. "Oh, Em, this is going to be the best dinner party ever!"

I doubted that very much. I doubted it even more when she sat me down at the table and dictated the menu to me:

Tourtière (of course)
Fricot a la belette
Poutine
Tarte ou sirop d'érable (maple syrup pie)
 and Pet de soeur (with the leftover pastry scraps)

I tapped my notebook thoughtfully with the end of my pencil. Fricot I knew; it was French-Canadian ragout: meatballs in a roux of browned flour gravy. The distinguishing flavor was cloves. In my family, it was served over boiled potatoes. But I wasn't sure how the "weasel" part of the recipe title fit in. "What, exactly, is fricot a la belette?"

Marise laughed. "Since you're going to help me make it, I suppose I'll have to tell you, but I swear you to secrecy."

"On Marcel's grave," I replied mildly.

"There really is a Fricot a la belette," she began.

"Naturally."

She shot me a dirty look before continuing. "In lean times, when there was no meat to put in the fricot, the inference was that the cook was sly as a weasel for leaving out the meat."

"And in your already meatless version?"

"Fake meat."

"Ah." Of course. Naturally. Fake meat.

"It's meant to be a joke," she explained rather unnecessarily. I didn't tell her that serving vegetarian versions of meat-filled dishes was already a joke.

"This menu is kind of heavy," I pointed out. "There aren't any vegetables. Did you want to have a salad, maybe?"

"Salad?" Marise shook her head. "No, I don't think so. I want it to have only completely authentic, traditional French-Canadian dishes."

They were going to have to bring the Jaws of Life to get us out of her house after this meal. I wanted to tell her to put the ambulance on stand-by, but I didn't think she appreciate it. Instead, I said, "What authentic, traditional meat did you have in mind for the tourtière?"

Marise ignored my sarcasm and sat down at the table next to me. She honestly looked so happy that I decided I'd better stop ribbing her, or I might kill the fun. "The tourtière is kind of amazing, actually," she said. "It's filled with different types of meat substitutes. It's really quite good."

"I believe you," I said firmly. "What time should I be here to help you start cooking?"

"Early."

"You got it."

It wasn't quite the crack of dawn when I found myself shuffling down the road to Marise's, but it was close enough. Addy was already gone. She'd left me a note explaining she'd run into town to help Auggie with an emergency and would catch up with me at Marise's. I worried about her. She'd been walking around lately with dark circles under her eyes from staying up late to study so she could shadow Auggie as much as possible.

"I'm definitely going to be a vet," she'd confided not long ago, her eyes shining. "I need to get used to long hours."

The day was just starting to heat up. The dogs circled me like little furry satellites, and I was glad I'd brought them along, though I didn't really know why. Their presence felt comforting somehow. Especially when we walked past Seán's house which was dark, his SUV in the drive; he was home. Alone, I thought smugly, even though I could have kicked myself for even caring. He'd made it pretty clear that he wasn't interested in anything but friendship with me. Why couldn't I let it go?

I shook myself sternly. I had to get a grip on this. In just a couple hours, he'd be sitting at Marise's table. It was bound to be awkward. I wondered if Trudy had mentioned (maliciously? innocently?) that she'd seen me. Did he know that I knew they'd gone out after he'd blown me off that day? And what on earth had they been doing together? Who went out on a date that lasted all day?

Maybe they had been hiking the Long Trail together, I thought morosely. But try as I might, I couldn't picture Trudy hiking those challenging trails in sensible foot gear, and I'd never seen her wear anything except high heels. Besides, something that strenuous seemed a little ambitious for a guy who was dying of brain cancer. And it wasn't like Trudy was a doctor and could intervene if he had another seizure or got into medical trouble somehow. Though I had to admit, he'd been looking almost healthy lately, not at all like someone dying of cancer.

I shoved my thoughts firmly to the back of my brain and steeled myself not to think about it. Dinner was going to be challenging enough without that. I'd just be my usual cheerful, if maybe a bit distant, self and let him squirm.

"That'll teach him," I muttered to myself as I pushed Marise's door open.

"What did you say?" asked Marise, seated at her kitchen table, her braille Bible open in front of her, a steaming mug of chai in her hand. Immediately I felt a flood of guilt for my selfish, petty thoughts.

"Nothing important," I said. "Can I join you?"

Praying with Marise shifted everything back into perspective. I was almost happy. This was partly due to the revelation while we were praying that if I couldn't wish Seán well in his relationship with Trudy then I didn't really love him as much as I thought I did. If I truly loved him—and by now I was willing to admit, even if it was hopeless, that I did—I would want him to be happy, regardless of whether or not that happiness included me. In fact, I felt so magnanimous at this thought that I selflessly suggested to Marise that we should have invited Trudy, too, for Seán.

"Why?" she asked, turning her head sharply in my direction. "What has Trudy got to do with Seán? What's going on?"

I squirmed uncomfortably, sorry now that I'd brought it up. "Nothing, I don't know, I've just seen then around together . . . a lot."

"And you think he's in a relationship with Trudy?" Her face mirrored the astonishment in her voice. "But he's dying. Why would he start a relationship? And if he's going to be in a relationship, it should be with you!"

I sighed unhappily. "I think they've been going out for a while. I didn't realize it was quite so serious, but it must be. He . . . well, he kissed me a couple weeks ago and then apologized. They seem to be together all the time lately. Not long after the . . . well, they were gone all day long."

Marise harrumphed and knit her lips together in a tight line. I knew she was struggling not to say something unkind. Reaching over, I patted her arm. "It's okay. I want him to be happy." I really thought I meant it, too.

A couple hours later, I was checking on the tourtière when my cell phone rang. It was on the table and since my hands were deep in the hot oven, I asked Marise to answer it.

"No, she's doing something in the oven," Marise was saying as I struggled to lift the heavy pie out so I could test it and see if it was done. Her voice sounded strained, like she wasn't happy with whoever was on the other end. Marcel, I decided. "What's going on?"

Marise continued to make noises to indicate that she was listening as I manfully hoisted the pie back into the oven. I nearly dropped it when I heard her say, "Well, if you make it back in time why don't you come over anyway. And bring Trudy with you. She's invited, of course."

It felt as though I had to wait an age listening to her clipped monosyllabic answers before she finally said goodbye. "Who was that?" I demanded the second she ended the call.

"Seán." Her voice was dark. "He's not coming. Seems he's in Montréal and can't make it back in time. He wanted to know how I knew Trudy was with him."

"And you said?"

"I said nothing, but he didn't sound pleased at all. Does he think he's keeping her a secret?"

I was stunned. Seán wasn't coming. Any pleasure I had in the coming dinner party left me with a *whoosh*. I felt deflated and so sad I could have cried. It was one thing to suspect something, or even believe it but have no confirmation to back it up. It was quite another to have sudden, irrefutable proof. Seán wasn't at home getting ready to come to Marise's dinner party as I'd thought when I walked past his house a few hours ago. He was in Montréal with Trudy and had probably been there overnight since it was unlikely they'd headed up there before daybreak. I wanted to throw a dishtowel over my head, drop into a chair, and sob my eyes out.

Fortunately, Marcel prevented me. He burst through the door at that precise moment with more excitement than I had seen since he got his first tractor. "You are not going to be believe this," he said. "Come see."

I had to queue up behind Marise and the dogs to get out the door although, technically, I was the only one who was going to be able to "see" what he wanted to show us.

"What is it?" Marise demanded before I even got around the side of the truck so I could tell her.

I peered into the interior of the truck bed at the blanket wrapped lump hog-tied there and knew immediately. "It's a piano." Bewildered, I turned to Marcel's beaming face and tried to make sense of what I was seeing. "What? You've decided to take up piano?"

He rolled his eyes, exasperated. "Tête dure,"[37] he muttered. "No, my hard-headed sister. It's for Mimi." He enunciated each word to highlight my stupidity. Thumping the side of the piano he said proudly, "One of my

---

[37] Hard head

parishioners was going to haul it off to the dump, so I asked if I could have it."

"Does it play?" I asked dubiously. Who knew what sort of junk Marcel would be willing to haul home.

"Of course it plays. It's a nice piano," he retorted in defense. "Now, I need to use my truck to haul some hay, so can I leave it here?"

"How?" Marise asked. "We can't help you lift it out of there."

"Good point," Marcel mused, thoughtfully sizing us up.

"Don't even think about it, Tête Dure," I said sarcastically.

"Well, never mind, then. I'll just have to figure something out." He opened the driver's side door, then turned to us with a warning look. "Not a word to Mimi," he cautioned. "I want it to be a surprise."

"Absolument,"[38] Marise and I chorused together with mock solemnity.

By the time we'd returned inside and rescued the dishes we'd abandoned in our excitement, I had, if not forgotten, at least come to grips with my despair over Seán. "Thank You, Lord," I murmured, my words swallowed up in steam as I bent over a double boiler with the maple syrup and other ingredients I was boiling for the maple syrup pie.

"This smell reminds me of sugaring," I said aside to Marise who was setting the table. "Too bad we missed sugaring this year. We should go to Marcel's next spring when they're sugaring and make some sugar on snow. I haven't done that since I was a kid." About the only maple treat we had during sugaring was my mother's traditional crapeau. Just thinking about it made my mouth water. Though why maple sugar dumplings were called "toads" in French was beyond me. Marcel always suggested it was because they looked like little toads swimming in syrup. Which they kind of did.

"We should," Marise agreed. "Maybe Auggie could come, too," she added hastily and with a blush that shot up to the roots of her hair.

I grinned. "Yes, that's exactly what I had in mind," I said with all innocence. "For Auggie's benefit, we should definitely do it."

"Stop smirking," Marise snapped, but she couldn't help smiling.

"Knock, knock," Mimi poked her head in the door. "Am I the first one here?" she asked, astonished. "That's kind of unbelievable." She sauntered in and slid into a chair at the table, unconsciously straightening some of Marise's crooked place settings as she inhaled deeply. "What smells so yummy?"

---

[38] Absolutely

"Maple syrup. How did it go today?" I had asked her to fill in for me down at the church since I was helping Marise with the cooking and couldn't be in two places at once. It was her first time as an official pianist.

"It was fine. My mom practically blew up she was so proud. I haven't seen her smile that big in a long time."

I didn't say anything, but I was glad to hear it.

"Reverend LaPierre was acting all weird though," she observed. "I'm not sure he liked it. I didn't make any mistakes, honest. Even though they added a song we hadn't gone over. It was pretty easy, and I might have played it kind of slow, but I played all the right notes. I'm sure of it. I thought it sounded really good, actually." There was a certain note of satisfaction in her voice that filled me with pride.

"I'm sure it was fine," I assured her, glancing at Marise who was struggling to keep a straight face. I wondered if pinching her arm would be helpful or if she'd only yelp and make Mimi even more suspicious.

Instead, I jerked my chin at Mimi, indicating she should finish straightening the place settings without letting Marise know she was doing it while I made sure that all the dishes we were serving would be finished at the right time.

Marcel and Agnès arrived before Auggie and Addy only because they'd had a slight emergency to attend to before they could come.

"Porcupine quills," Addy explained, breathless and flushed with excitement. "It was awful, poor thing."

I looked at my daughter in admiration. It seemed she had really found her calling. I wasn't sure how much longer she could keep up such a punishing schedule, but she seemed to be thriving.

When everyone was finally seated, we started with the poutine, which was pretty standard because it was already mostly vegetarian. Marise had me make a brown mushroom gravy rather than a meat-based sauce brune like my mother would have made, but it was a pretty good substitute if I did say so myself. Agnès's eyebrows rose slightly at the first bite, but she cocked her head as if to say "not bad" and kept eating. Marcel, who would eat anything, didn't even seem to notice the change. Addy ate the way only teenagers could, and Auggie tucked in like it was his last meal. Only Mimi seemed curiously reticent to try the food, and I wondered why. As I surveyed the table I felt a pang of regret that Seán was missing our dubious feast. He was a part of our group and without him the table felt empty. To me, at least.

The rest of the meal plowed on, more or less a success, which made me grateful for Marise's sake. She presided like a queen at the head of the table and insisted on jumping up to serve courses and refill the water pitcher, though she barely picked at her own food. Her excitement was contagious though and despite Seán's absence and the scandalous food, I discovered that I was enjoying myself.

The pièce de résistance was the maple syrup pie, but no sooner had Marise distributed slices, *à la mode* with vanilla ice cream, then she was circling the table with the plateful of pastries we'd made with the leftover pie dough.

"Pet de soeur?" Marise asked sweetly, wafting the platter in front of Auggie.

The big man choked on a mouthful of pie. "What did you call me?" he asked, his eyes wide with shock. "I only took a couple semesters of French in high school, but even I know that's not polite."

Marise reddened, perhaps realizing that offering the man of your dreams a nun's fart wasn't in the best of taste. As with many French names and expressions, it was easy to forget what they really meant when they'd been part of your lexicon forever. Some things you just took for granted, like the strange, inexplicable names your forbears had given to things, until you found yourself suddenly having to explain them.

"That's what they're called," Marise said bravely. "Silly, isn't it? But I don't know any other name. Do you?" She appealed to the entire table, but our blank expressions said it all.

"Maybe we could come up with another name for them ourselves," suggested Mimi helpfully. "Like cinnamon snails. They kind of look like little snails. And they have cinnamon in them."

"Very clever," Agnès said heartily. "I like it!"

"Cinnamon snail, then?" Marise asked, rephrasing with an audible sigh of relief.

Auggie's face split into a wide grin. "Sure, if you insist."

"You aren't eating much," Addy observed, glancing over at Mimi's plate.

Mimi blushed crimson and my warning glare at Addy went unnoticed. "It's just, well, I'm vegan now, and this is all kind of . . . kind of . . ." She floundered, apparently searching for an accurate description that wouldn't be taken as an insult. "It's kind of heavy. But really good," she added hastily. It was okay. Marise and Auggie had their heads together at the other end of the table and were oblivious to what she was saying.

"I've been studying nutrition a lot lately." Her eyes slid to mine. "After we were talking that day about opening a restaurant," she explained, "I went in to see my guidance counselor. I think that's what I want to do, so next year I'll be taking some business courses. When I told my therapist, she started talking to me about nutrition. It's so important, ya know?"

She leaned across the table to Addy and said earnestly, "Do you have any idea what they put in most food these days? It's awful! All the chemicals and pesticides. I watched this movie . . ." She seemed to become aware suddenly of where she was and broke off abruptly. "Well, anyway, I've been eating a lot cleaner."

"What does your mother think about that?" I asked.

The girl grinned. "She wasn't too crazy about it at first, but I got some vegan cookbooks from the library and started cooking from them. She likes most of it."

Without being obvious about it, I studied Mimi. She looked more self-assured and confident. Not exactly outgoing, but then, becoming healthier wasn't going to change your whole personality. She seemed as if she had found the right track after suddenly being knocked off course as she had been by her father's death. I was glad. I only wished I had been able to help her find it.

"I have an announcement," Marcel said loudly, bringing all conversation to a screeching halt like a traffic accident. "Well, more of an unveiling." He scraped his chair back and stood with a groan. "I don't think you'll have to make me any supper, Agnès," he said in a loud whisper.

"No," she agreed bluntly. "You packed enough food away to last you for a week at least, eh?"

Everyone laughed and stood to follow Marcel, but only Marise and I knew what he was up to.

"Come on, girls," I urged, when Addy and Mimi lingered, engrossed in their conversation. Addy gave me a look that clearly asked, "Do I have to?" But they rose to their feet and followed everyone out the door.

Seán was hustling up the driveway as we clustered around the tailgate of Marcel's truck. My brother hauled himself onto the bed with difficulty and started unwrapping the bulky object covered with blankets. As Marcel fumbled with the straps and knots, Seán sidled up to my side, and I forced myself to turn to him with a smile.

"Hey, you'll be glad you made it back for this. Keep an eye on her face," I nodded toward Mimi who was guilelessly watching Marcel.

"Ta-da!" Marcel announced with a flourish, yanking the blankets back dramatically and nearly toppling over when one got stuck under a rope and made him lose his balance. Everyone whooped and cheered, even Mimi, though it was obvious that she was clueless. Slowly she became aware that all eyes had turned to her, to see her reaction, and the blood drained from her face.

"What?" she asked.

"It's for you," Marcel said gently. "Do you like it?"

To our collective horror, she burst into tears. After that, pandemonium broke loose. Agnès hustled over to comfort Mimi, Marcel stood uncertainly in the truck wringing his hands, Marise attempted to explain to Mimi where the piano had come from, and everyone else tried to calm her down all at once. The net effect was that nearly everyone was talking and no one was listening.

Agnès held up her hand for silence, and, miraculously, all conversation staggered to a halt. "Now then," she said briskly. "What's all this fuss about? Look, cherie, do you have room in your house, do you think, for that monster? Because I'm certainly not taking it home. It would be a shame if it had to go to the dump, eh?"

At the word "dump", Mimi's head snapped up. "What? No! I'll take it! I want it!"

Auggie lifted her up into the truck bed so she could see it better, but before she examined it, Mimi threw her arms around Marcel's neck. "Thank you," she said fervently, "from the bottom of my heart."

Marcel patted her back awkwardly and went pink. "No problem," he said eloquently. "I'm glad you like it."

"That piano couldn't have found a better home," Seán observed with a grin as Mimi's fingers danced over the keys, and she gave us an impromptu concert for a few minutes.

"I think that's an understatement," I agreed. I glanced up at him. "I'm sorry you missed dinner, but there's plenty leftover. If you want to eat, that is," I amended. "I know vegetarian French-Canadian food is a bit of a farce, even if Marise won't admit it."

He laughed, but there was an edge to it, and I could feel his eyes on me when I wasn't looking, as if he was trying to determine how mad I was that he had missed the party or that he had been with Trudy. I wasn't sure which. I did wonder what made Montréal so special that they kept going up there. Was it the anonymity? Did they not want to be seen together around here where they were known for some reason? Where, come to think of it, they were never together. They were really too old to care what other people said about their relationship. It didn't make sense.

"I'm starved," he admitted. "I haven't eaten all day. The trip to Montréal was . . . spur of the moment."

"Ah," I said noncommittally. It was hard to act as though I didn't care when I was dying to know why anyone would rush up to Montréal on the "spur of the moment." But it was none of my business what they did. "I'll make you a plate," I said.

To my dismay, he followed me into the kitchen.

"Emerson," he said, and I was surprised to find that he sounded angry. So angry that my hand, holding a ladle full of gravy, halted on its way to the fries I had carelessly piled onto a plate for him and hovered there wobbling. "Emerson, you realize if things were different . . ." He didn't go on, and I wasn't sure if I did realize, but it seemed less complicated to nod as if I did.

He tried again. "If there was any way . . ." But he never finished that sentence either and left it hanging like I was.

"Look, Seán," I said finally. "It is what it is." I wished I had any idea what exactly "it" was.

He closed his eyes and a range of emotions flashed across his face. He looked like a man trying to talk himself down from a ledge. When his eyes snapped open suddenly, his gaze drilled me with an intensity that took my breath away. "Emerson, do you trust me?"

"I . . . do," I said, with less conviction than I felt.

"I see," he said sadly.

I wanted to say I was sorry, that I really did trust him, but it felt as though Trudy was standing there in the room with us, smiling at me smugly and shaking her finger. "Keep away," smug Trudy said. "He's mine." And I knew that no matter what words came out of my mouth, I didn't really trust him. Not the way he seemed to be asking me to trust him.

What kind of hold did she have over him anyway? Why couldn't he leave her if that was what he wanted to do? Or was that really what he wanted? Was he trying to tell me something else entirely?

I turned back to the stove feeling overwhelmed with confusion, but he put his hand on my arm to stop me from continuing to fill his plate. "Don't. Thanks, but I'm not hungry anymore."

I froze there, the place he'd touched on my arm tingling as though it had been seared by electricity. Tears stung my eyes as I heard the screen door slap shut behind him. Music from the piano was still tinkling outside along with the sound of people talking and laughing. I set the plate down before I dropped it and sagged against the counter. I wasn't sure how much more of this I could take.

Chapter Nineteen

Something between Seán and I had changed. It was particularly evident at Marise's final concert for the Champlain Summer Music Festival, which took place the evening before she was leaving for Montréal to stay at the guide dog school and build a relationship with her new guide dog. She would be gone a couple of months, and I already missed her. The snap in the air dictated warmer clothes, and I had to rummage around in my wardrobe for something appropriate. Half the time it was blazing hot this time of year. In Vermont, the time between seasons could be challenging to dress for. If you weren't too hot, you were too cold.

I found a wool dress Marise had helped me make back when I was learning to knit. It was constructed from a bunch of knitted squares of all sizes and different gauges put together like a patchwork quilt. This would have been a real faux pas normally because constructionally, knitting required a delicate balance between tension and gauge to create the desired structure. But in Marise's world it was considered creative, and I had to agree.

The dress was one of my favorites. I'd used varying shades of gray and blue. It reminded me of the moods of the ocean, which reminded me of a trip I'd taken to the seaside once with Danny. It had been our honeymoon, in fact, spent beachcombing along the shores of Maine. Sometimes this reminder made me nostalgic. But as I hunted for some tights and boots to wear with it, I realized that tonight I only felt happy and a little sad.

His voice stopped me when I stepped onto my porch, and I froze as though I'd been shot.

"Nice night."

I turned to face Seán, who was sitting in the corner. He looked the same; he looked great actually. But there was something in his voice, a distance that had never been there before. I was probably the only one who would have noticed it, and it made my heart drop.

He was dressed up. Not in a suit, but in dressier clothes than I had ever seen him wear. He cleaned up well, as they said. His hair had grown out into a crew cut over the last couple of weeks, and he'd even shaved. And he smelled positively delicious.

"Well isn't this a nice . . . surprise," I stumbled at the last word, hunting for something appropriate. It was really more of a shock.

He stood up slowly. "I thought I'd walk down with you. If you don't mind."

"Mind? Of course not! I'd love it." My words were a lot more honest than my thoughts. It was true that I'd love to walk down to the concert with him, would like nothing better, but it felt as though the air between us was a few degrees colder than the air around us, and I almost shrank away from him.

I struggled to breach this sudden wall I felt; what I really wanted to do was beat it down with my fists if necessary. Despite everything that had happened between us, despite the fact that it felt as though Trudy was practically a physical presence whenever we were together, we had always shared a comfortable closeness. Tonight it was gone, and I wanted it back more than anything.

As we walked slowly down the road to the Champlain Inn where the concert was being held, we chatted. We even laughed a little, but instead of melting the coldness, it only served as a reminder of how much I had come to love this man who now felt like a stranger. By the time we reached the Inn, I was practically in tears and had to excuse myself to go to the ladies room and get a grip.

When I came back, Trudy had joined Seán, and I dithered on the edges of the crowd not knowing what to do. It wasn't like we were on a date. For all I knew, he'd walked down with me but intended to attend the concert with Trudy. After all, he hadn't formally asked me to attend with him. He'd just shown up at my door like any neighbor and friend might so we could walk down together.

As I stood there, uncertain what to do, I noticed something peculiar. Trudy was chatting with Seán as animatedly as she usually did when I saw them together, but he seemed as standoffish with her as he had with me. He was making conversation with her, but the whole time his eyes were darting around the room, looking for something. Or someone. Me? Trudy didn't seem to notice or care.

Before I could puzzle out exactly what this meant or decide what to do, Marise appeared at my elbow, having been guided by, as far as I could tell, no one at all. She seized my arm and nudged me in the direction of the stage at the front of the outdoor pavilion.

I protested feebly. "I came with Seán."

Marise took almost no notice. "Did you? Where is he?" she asked, not waiting for an answer.

I hesitated and then gamely said, "Talking with Trudy."

"Well then," Marise said, as though that explained everything. "I've had them set aside a seat right at the front just for you."

Someone had been hard at work decorating. Potted trees, ornamental arches, and the entire raised platform that served as the stage were wreathed in twinkling lights. It looked positively magical. The very first few rows were cordoned off, clearly marked "Reserved." A smattering of people were already occupying some of the seats, perusing their programs.

I gave Marise an encouraging hug before she left me, but I could tell she didn't really need it. She never suffered from stage fright like I did. Instead, it was as though she glowed, and it seemed as if a field of electrical energy crackled around her. She was positively radiant.

"The seat next to you is for Auggie," Marise explained. "In case he shows up." She frowned a little. "He probably won't," she added. "He called not long ago and said he'd been called out to help a horse that was having a baby. But he said if he finished in time, he'd come, and I promised to save him a seat."

She threaded her way, tapping along with her cane, the sea of bodies before her parting like the Red Sea. I took my seat and followed the example of those around me by studying my program to see what we were going to be hearing, remembering how Marise had complained about the complexity of the pieces at the beginning of the season. I was unfamiliar with most of them, but then, I wasn't overly familiar with classical music.

"There you are," a voice beside me said. "I wondered where you'd disappeared to." Seán dropped into the seat Marise was saving for Auggie and gave me a mild look as I tried not to show my dismay (and my sudden elation that he'd come looking for me.) "Is this seat taken?"

"Marise is saving it for Auggie," I apologized, fully expecting him to vacate it and find another.

"That's too bad," he murmured, making no move whatsoever to leave.

"He's out on a call," I explained nervously, trying to make him understand that he couldn't sit there in a polite way. The musicians finished tuning up and the house lights—some spotlights set up on poles around the perimeter of the tent and stage—blinked, indicating that the concert was about to start.

Seán leaned toward me, and I felt a sudden rush of emotion at his closeness. "Shh," he whispered. "They're about to begin."

Helplessly, I watched him coolly settle back as the concert began with, according to the program, "Psalm 51: Tilge, Höchster, meine Sünden" an adaptation by Bach of Pergolesi's Stabat Mater in which Marise was playing not her violin, but a viola as in this piece it was being given a "gloriously active part that enriched the texture of the whole ensemble." I agonized whether or not I should insist that Seán move, torn between loyalty to Auggie and my desire to share the concert with Seán, until the two visiting soloists, an alto and a soprano, opened their mouths and began to sing.

Suddenly, it didn't seem to matter whether Auggie had no seat if he arrived. It wasn't my problem anyway, was it? Relieved to have reached this conclusion, I sat back and let myself relax as the beautiful words of Psalm 51 (albeit in unfamiliar German) wafted over me like a benediction. I followed the English translation in the program, and halfway through I realized that Seán was leaning toward me, following along with me in my program, his own unopened in his hand. I was so transported and uplifted by the music and the beautiful words of the Psalm, and so filled with gratitude to God for forgiving me and loving me, that I felt a rush of love and joy that I couldn't hide when I looked up and found Seán staring at me intently.

Our eyes held and in his I saw such stark love that it took my breath away. Just as suddenly, a shadow blotted it out and instead of love, his eyes were filled with agony. I swallowed hard and turned away, fastening my gaze intently on the program, and keeping it there studiously. Not for the first time did I wonder why he always seemed conflicted toward me. Had I been a stronger person, I would have asked him outright. Instead, I kept miserably silent as always.

By the time the program reached Bach's Concerto for Two Violins, Strings and Continuo in D minor I was so uncomfortable sitting next to Seán that all I really wanted to do was bolt out of my seat the moment the house lights came up. Instead, I forced myself to remain, to make polite chat, to congratulate Marise when she finally pulled herself free from her other admirers and made her way over to us.

Having her there broke the ice a little. She was in such good spirits after her stunning performance that she didn't seem to mind that Auggie had never arrived, or that Seán had managed to sit next to me after all, though I did notice she placed herself rather protectively between the two of us.

I had to say goodbye to Marise that night since Auggie had insisted on driving her to the school early the next morning. I would only get called upon if he had an emergency, and something told me there wasn't an emergency dire enough to prevent Auggie from going with Marise. I almost wished there would be. I didn't want her to leave. I especially didn't want her to abandon me to the almost sole companionship of Seán who was about as approachable as an iceberg now.

"You'll write?" I asked pathetically.

"Of course I'll write," she assured me. "I'll tell you all about my dog. And I'll be home before you know it. Make sure you keep everyone in shape. Have a couple practices while I'm away." She hugged me hard, and then she was gone, weaving her way back through the crowds, tapping her white stick imperiously when people didn't move out of the way quickly enough.

No doubt, Seán blamed my quietness as we walked home on being sad about Marise leaving and that certainly was a large part, but the fact that the Great Wall of China might as well have been between us for all we connected was smothering me. I sensed that the distance distressed Seán as much as it did me. But while I had no idea how to repair our formerly close relationship, I had the distinct impression that Seán not only knew how to restore it, but that he was keeping a tight grip on himself to prevent that from happening. I wildly speculated that maybe he'd made Trudy some rash promise to marry her before he died. Any feelings he had for me would be a moot point, in that case. And he wouldn't live long enough to regret his choice, either.

That last thought brought me to my knees every time it crossed my mind over the next few weeks. I had the constant sense of waiting for the other shoe to drop. Seán seemed to have good days and bad days and whole weeks in between when he seemed to get no better and no worse. As far as I knew, he hadn't had any more seizures, but then, who was likely to inform me if he had? He certainly wouldn't.

As fall dragged on, life settled into a weird, quiet slog of lessons and chores and spinning. Addy spent even more time than ever with Auggie, and Auggie worked even longer and harder than usual with Marise gone. I felt a stab of loneliness every morning when the dogs and I walked past her quiet, dark house, and then I felt another stab as I walked past Seán's, though for an entirely different reason. At least Marise would be coming back someday. I wasn't sure the same could be said for Seán. Each new day saw us drifting even farther apart.

Even my daily visits to Angelique's store changed. In order to avoid the awkwardness of running into Seán every morning, I began to vary my trips, sometimes going early, sometimes later after I'd given a few lessons. I felt like a fugitive sneaking down the road, scuttling past his cottage, trying to peer over out of the corner of my eye to see if he was outside.

Seán seemed to cotton onto what I was doing and after managing to avoid him for a couple weeks, he suddenly developed a second sense about when I was going to be there. I strongly suspected that he was watching out his front window, because he had an uncanny habit of leaving his house at precisely the same moment the dogs and I happened to be going by. He'd saunter out casually, as though he had been planning to walk down to the store all along and wasn't it a happy coincidence that I just happened to be going by.

At church he began to sit in the front pew, on my side of the church. When I wasn't playing, I had no choice but to sit next to him. He never said a word, but he looked plenty pleased with himself.

To tell the truth, I found it all frustrating in the extreme. He made constant excuses to see me and positioned himself in my life with the cunning of a chess player, yet though we were polite to each other, the distance between us was so great that we might as well have been strangers.

I had hoped Marise would be home by Thanksgiving, but she wrote to me shortly before the holiday explaining that she had decided to extend her trip somewhat because a couple of the graduates she'd befriended lived in Seattle, and she was going to return with them for some "sightseeing". She was beyond excited about "seeing" the Pacific Ocean for the first time and planned to explore the fiber arts community while she was there, hoping to return full of new ideas and new projects.

She didn't expect to make it back home until the week before Christmas, so I tried to be happy about that. We could still do our yearly nursing home crawl in which we took the band to play carols at the area nursing homes. I wasn't sure how I'd face my mémère if we'd had to cancel that. She was so proud of knowing "the band", and because of this lofty position became somewhat of a temporary celebrity beginning the day after Thanksgiving— old folks took the holiday celebrations to the nth degree.

I received a few letters from Marise while she was away. Getting mail at any time was so rare it was a treat, but Marise's letters were written entirely by hand—her own—and just looking at the loopy, meandering script on the wad of pages she managed to cram into a single envelope filled my heart with love. I missed her so much.

Her dog, she wrote, was called Mozart, and she was already in love with him. Her letters were full of praise about his intelligence and his sweet disposition. The only thing that was missing was a picture. Even though I asked for one, she never sent it.

Thanksgiving—the meal at least—turned into a quiet affair at Marcel's house. Agnès carried it off single-handedly with aplomb, and I was thrilled that two of my three nephews were able to make it home. I hadn't seen them in months and the contrast between their military bearing and my brother's slouchy, laid back demeanor was so marked that I poked him in the ribs a couple times in a vain attempt to smarten him up. He brushed me off with his usual lack of respect and paid no attention to me whatsoever.

Irritation with my brother was not the reason I decided to walk home after dinner, but it probably contributed to what happened after that. Stuffed with all of Agnès' good food, I needed exercise. The dogs were only too happy to oblige, and Marcel just lived a few miles from my place. Addy promised to drive the truck home for me when she was finished visiting with her cousins. They had all become embroiled in a cutthroat game of pool. It reminded me of when they were children. They were arguing good-naturedly over the rules they'd invented as I slipped out the door.

The air had a bite to it, promising there would be snow soon. I stuffed my hands in my pockets to protect them from the cold. Walking home might have been a bad idea. I wasn't exactly dressed for the weather. Cold stung my legs straight through my tights, and I walked faster to try and warm up. Gyp and Dash thought this was a game, and they raced around me barking.

By the time I reached my own road, I was angry with myself for not turning back in the first place, and when Seán trotted out of Angelique's store and hustled to catch up with me, I turned on him, letting loose all the pent up emotions I'd kept trapped inside for months.

"What are you doing?" I screamed.

He skidded to a stop and held up his hands in surrender. "Going home?" he offered hesitantly. "Unless you'd rather I didn't."

I know it was meant to be a joke, but I was beyond joking. I was cold and miserable and fed up with his confusing treatment.

"Why do you always follow me around? And show up wherever I am? Why do you want to be around me so much when all you do is treat me like a . . . like a . . . horrid old aunt with . . . with . . . bad breath." I finished lamely, not quite knowing how else to put it.

Seán laughed, which made me scowl at him deeper. He patted the air in front of him with a placating gesture. "Okay, okay, let's be calm . . ."

"I can't be calm!" I wailed, struggling not to start crying right there in front of him. The only way to prevent it, I knew, was to get angry. So I got good and angry. "You're always around, but you're never *here*," I said savagely. "You might as well be a million miles away. I can see you and I can hear you, but there's nothing . . . there's no connection between us anymore. Why don't you just . . . just . . ." Just what? I wanted to say, "Just go get lost," but the words lodged in my throat and wouldn't come out.

"Emerson," Seán said, suddenly serious. He leaned forward and grabbed my upper arms, pinning in me in place. "You have to trust me, and you don't. Can I ask you to trust me? Just for a little while longer?"

"What? No! Why should I trust you?"

"Because I need you to," he said so softly that I had to lean forward to hear him. The wind caught his words and blew them away. But I was certain he'd said them.

I was confused. Why would he need me to trust him? Again, as always, I had the feeling that there was something going on, something big and important that he just wasn't telling me.

"Emerson, please, will you trust me?"

"Something's going on," I said stubbornly. "Something you're not telling me. What is it?"

His eyes shifted away from mine and again, it was as though a curtain dropped over his face. If he hadn't still had me firmly by the arms, I would have reached out and shaken him. "I can't tell you."

"But you expect me to trust you?" I asked, my voice dripping with bitterness. "Fat chance."

His grip slackened and he stepped away from me. Suddenly, I regretted my impulsive words, my anger, my stubbornness. He had already turned away when I reached out to grab hold of his arm. "Seán wait, I didn't mean . . . that is, I'll . . ."

Whatever I was going to say hung there between us as Marise's voice hollered, "I'm home!" Auggie's truck drove slowly past us. He was beaming inside behind the steering wheel and Marise had her arm stuck out the passenger side window waving wildly.

"She's early!" I exclaimed, feeling a surge of relief and excitement at the sight of Marise, but one look at Seán's woebegone face pushed my happiness at Marise's return aside. His shoulders slumped dejectedly as he turned to follow Auggie's truck to where it had pulled to a stop in Marise's driveway.

I swallowed hard. Should I say something? Should I try to make it right? He wanted me to trust him, but how could I do that when he refused to tell me what was going on?

"Seán, I'm sorry," I said, taking extra large strides to catch up with him. "Can we maybe talk sometime? I want to trust you, I really do."

Seán stopped and turned toward me. He studied my face for a moment and then he smiled. But it was not a smile of relief and joy. It was the sad smile of someone who knows there is no real solution to their problem, only temporary, insufficient patches.

"Sure," he said, nodding even as I knew it would never happen. "I'd like that."

"Come meet Mozart!" Marise was yelling from her driveway where she stood beside a big black and tan dog as Auggie wrestled her luggage out of the back of his truck.

"Come on," Seán said, striding up the hill. "Let's go meet Mozart."

"I'm so glad you're home," I hollered to Marise as I hustled to keep up with Seán.

He joined Auggie to help with the suitcases while I gave Marise a backbreaking hug. Mozart regarded me mildly, neither excited nor guarded. But there was something in his eyes that seemed to size me up. I looked at the large dog, noting the intelligent but soft brown eyes, the erect ears alert for any danger, the way he was tuned into Marise like she was the only radio station worth listening to.

"He's not a Labrador!" I exclaimed, unable to resist stating the obvious.

"He's not?" she wailed in mock horror, a huge grin on her face. "Is he a dog at least?"

I laughed. "Why didn't you tell me they gave you a German Shepherd?"

Marise reached down and stroked the dog's head while he stared at her in adoration. She shrugged. "Because I wanted to see the look on your face when you met him. He's incredibly handsome, isn't he?"

"Hey," Auggie protested. "Have I got competition now?"

"Jealous are you?" she teased.

Auggie eyed the dog and looked genuinely worried. "Maybe."

"Why are you home so early?" I asked.

Marise shrugged. "Seattle was nice, but I cut my trip short. I got a sudden rush of Christmas spirit and wanted to be home. We have a ton of work to do, you know."

I groaned. Home less than ten minutes and she was already warming up her whipping arm. "Can't we at least take some time to appreciate the holiday season before we have to fill it up?"

"Nope," Marise said. "I want us to sound our best for the nursing home crawl. You know how those people depend on us for good Christmas music. Unless," she said innocently, turning her head in my direction, "you've been practicing?"

"Not exactly," I mumbled.

Her triumphant smile was delightfully wicked. "In that case . . ."

I sighed with resignation, but I couldn't help the tickle of excitement in my chest. Marise could be such a pain in the neck. It was great to have her home.

Chapter Twenty

Marise hadn't even unpacked before she began demanding that we get everyone together to rehearse Christmas songs for the nursing home caroling. I had tried to corral everyone a few times while she was away for the very same purpose but hadn't had any luck. They all had an excuse for every date I picked. To say I was miffed when Marise managed to pull it off less than twenty-four hours after returning home would be putting it too mildly.

But I had to admit a grudging admiration for her. When Marise said jump, most people jumped and asked, "How high?" on the way up. She had that effect on people.

We met at my house. I made my mother's ragout, the traditional way for the meat eaters and a batch of vegetarian ones for Marise and Mimi. Having helped Marise with her dinner party, I had an idea for the "meat" balls that I wanted to try. I was surprised to find that I rather preferred them, but nothing would have induced me to admit that to Marise.

Everyone blustered in at nearly the same time, and I was kept busy taking coats and sweeping up the snow they tracked in so it wouldn't melt into puddles. Seán came in with all the others, laughing with Marcel about something, his arms full carrying his instrument.

He gave me a genuine, albeit slightly wistful smile, but he didn't get a chance to say anything before Marise demanded that we get a move on.

"We've got a lot of practicing to do," she said in the tones of a drill sergeant. "Don't think I don't know how lazy you've all been while I was gone. Eat up so we can get started."

"I wasn't lazy," Mimi piped up, then immediately turned scarlet. "I mean, I didn't practice traditional Christmas songs, but at school our band has been practicing Christmas pieces."

"Very well," Marise conceded. "Everyone but Mimi was lazy. We've still got a lot of work to do."

We were all so comfortable with each other by now that we crammed in around my table not caring that we were practically sitting in each other's laps. Everyone chattered at once, talking to those sitting next to them and those across the table with equal enthusiasm, and my heart squeezed with happiness as I took it all in.

"Thank You, Lord, for this family of friends," I whispered.

Seán seemed to sense my thoughts. He looked over at me, and I wondered if he'd heard me. For an instant, as our eyes met, I could see him as clearly as I had before the wall had grown up between us. His heart, too, seemed to be brimming. His brilliant blue eyes swam with unshed tears, and he blinked them away.

Thank You for sparing him, Lord. Thank You for giving him another Christmas with the people who love him. Trudy's smiling face popped into my head, but I pushed the image away resolutely. She could have him for the rest of the holiday, but tonight he was here, and that was good enough for me.

We managed to cram three practice sessions in before the date we picked to go around to the nursing homes, a week before Christmas. I left Addy home making a "surprise" for us to return to when we were finished and drove Marise and Mozart into St. Croix in my truck.

"You've been quiet since I got back," she observed mildly over the furious blowing of the fan as it tried to heat the frigid interior of my old truck. "What is it you're not telling me?"

"What do you mean?" My voice sounded innocent enough, even to my ears, but I knew I couldn't fool Marise.

She sighed patiently. "Em, what's going on with Seán?"

"I don't know," I said quietly. "He . . . he asked me to trust him."

Marise's brow furrowed. "Trust him? Why? In what?"

"I don't know," I replied. "He wouldn't say. And that's the whole problem. Something is going on, something he's not telling me, but he expects me to trust him."

"I see." Marise was quiet for a few minutes. "Do you love him?"

My grip on the wheel tightened at the question. Of course, I loved him. Wasn't that the whole problem? "Yes, absolutely."

"Then trust him," she said simply.

I didn't dare take my eyes off the road to stare at her, so I stared at the road instead. Trust him. Easy for her to say. She didn't know what he was hiding. *I* didn't know what he was hiding. Why should I trust him?

"Trust him because you love him," Marise continued, whether reading my thoughts or finishing hers I couldn't tell. "Anyway, what other choice do you have?"

"Exactly," I muttered. "What other choice do I have."

We were silent for the rest of the trip. I pulled into the snowy parking lot at Mémère's nursing home, at which we played first, naturally. Marise insisted on carrying her fiddle in one hand as Mozart guided her with the other, ignoring all my harping that she'd slip on the ice and break her neck. She seemed to believe Mozart could protect her from anything, bad weather and all.

I'd gotten to know the dog a little since she'd come home, and he was like a very serious, humorless old man. It was as if nothing existed in the world for him except Marise. He didn't even play with Gyp and Dash the way Chopin had. In fact, he seemed to regard them as foolish creatures he was forced to tolerate for Marise's sake.

There were about five residents shepherded by a few nurses all lined up waiting for us when we trudged in from the snow-drifted parking lot with our instruments. Mémère, of course, was the unofficial leader (by virtue of bossing the others around, I guessed.) She was puffed up with self-importance for being related to musicians in "the band."

"Bonjour, Mémère," I said, greeting her with the customary kiss on each cheek. "Comment ça va?"[39]

"Très bien,[40] Emerson," she said, her voice high with excitement, her cheeks flushed. I worried that all that excitement might affect her blood pressure.

"Mémère, maybe you should let me get you a wheelchair," I suggested.

"Bah," she spat mildly. "I'm fit as a fiddle, me." Her eyes narrowed at me. "Not *your* fiddle," she elaborated unnecessarily. "I still remember the way you play fiddle, me." She shuddered and brought her arms up to mime someone playing the fiddle who, it appeared, was also scratching multiple bug bites at the same time. I tried not to be irritated.

"Quel dommage,"[41] she said, shaking her head sadly. "Your pépère now, he could play, him. And your cousin Pascal." She gave me a frank, sorrowful look, as if I had been born with a tragic malady and couldn't help it. "I don't understand, me, why you should like that plunky thing." She made a dismissive gesture toward the banjo case in my hand.

Marcel had watched this exchange with a wry smirk. He didn't have to worry about her censure in his choice of instrument. Mémère had always loved the pipes. She claimed that as a young girl she had been quite good at the sword dance, an energetic, graceful dance in and around the four quarters of two crossed swords laid out on the ground in the shape of an "X". One of

---

[39] Hello Mémère, how are you?

[40] Very well.

[41] What a shame.

our uncles, a Scot, had apparently taught her and played the pipes while she danced. There was some speculation, mostly by my mother, that this was wishful thinking at best and a pure fabrication at worst. In any event, the uncle was long dead and there were no pictures, so no proof.

"Marcel, cheri,"[42] Mémère said, latching onto his free arm. "You may escort me, you." She led the procession of band members and nursing home groupies with so much obvious pleasure that I found it difficult to be offended by her opinion of my fiddle playing—I wasn't *that* bad—or her prejudice against banjos.

I hefted my poor maligned instrument and fell into step behind Marise who was chatting with great animation to Mimi as Mozart led her confidently down the hall. Seán walked next to me but made no comment though he'd heard every word my mémère had said. He seemed deep in thought.

As we played our collection of Christmas carols, many of the residents sang along in their quavery voices. (None of them so loud as my mémère.) I couldn't help but feel a rush of gratitude to Marise for insisting that we do this each year. It was a lot of work in a season that was too busy already, but for me it embodied the spirit of the season more than almost anything else.

You would have thought we'd be all played out after we finished trudging around to two nursing homes and a rambling old house that had been turned into a private care facility, but no. Spirits high and music flowing through our veins, we returned to my house where Addy was waiting with hot, mulled cider and freshly made cider donuts to eat and talk and sing and play even more music.

This, I mused to myself, *is what Christmas should always be like.* Somewhere between the commercialism and the social pressures, we always seemed to miss the true point of the holiday. For the second time in as many weeks, I looked around at the smiling faces of my friends and family and wanted to preserve the moment in some way. Who knew what might change by this same time next year.

It felt as though a dark cloud passed over my mind at the thought. But I reminded myself that eternal life was the original Christmas gift. When Jesus was born as a baby all those years ago, He was God's gift to the world for all time. I didn't know about anyone else, but an end to death and sin and sorrow was the best possible gift I could imagine in this world that was so often characterized by pain and loss.

---

[42] Dear

Our collective adrenaline started to peter out around eleven, and one by one, instruments were packed up and people said their good-byes and slipped out into the cold night air letting wintery gusts burst into the kitchen. I threw another log on the fire Marcel had made in my tiny fireplace.

Seán was the last to leave. Addy had already gone to bed for the night, so it was just the two of us. He stood doddering around the kitchen door looking nervous while I started to tidy up the kitchen, unaware that anything important was about to take place.

"Emerson, there's something I'd like you to have." Seán stooped to pick up a bundle of blankets he had placed in the corner when he'd arrived. He handed the bunched up wad to me gingerly. "Careful," he cautioned. "The wrapping is crap," he apologized, "but since I'm a guy, I'm hoping you can overlook it."

I took the awkward bundle, which wasn't heavy, only unwieldy. "Seán, I couldn't . . ."

"Just open it first," he said gruffly, doing a mighty poor job of hiding his anticipation of my reaction when I found out what was inside the blankets.

Carefully I peeled them back to reveal an A.C. Fairbanks Whyte Laydie No. 7 Banjo circa 1903 and gasped. This was the instrument of my dreams. "Seán! I can't accept this! It's too much. It's . . . it's priceless!"

He snorted. "Not hardly. As a matter of fact, that one didn't cost me a dime. It belonged to my aunt, and she doesn't play anymore because her fingers are crippled by arthritis. She was happy for me to take it off her hands. She didn't want money for it; she wanted it to belong to someone who would love it."

I turned the instrument over and over, admiring the extraordinary pearl inlays, the colorful wooden marquetry on the bottom rim of the pot, the carved heel. "I don't know what to say," I breathed. "It's exquisite. Thank you so much."

"That works for me," Seán said. His voice was perfectly normal, but his eyes were shining.

I leaned toward him, brushing my lips against his rough cheek. "Merry Christmas, Seán. Here hold this. I have something for you, too." I smiled shyly at him and ran to get a squishy bundle from under the tree. "It's not much," I warned, "but I made it myself from start to finish."

Seán grinned and plucked gingerly at the wrapping paper before abandoning etiquette and tearing it off. When he saw the mittens inside, he smiled like a schoolboy.

"You made me mittens?" He turned them over and over in his hands. "I haven't had a pair of homemade mittens since my grandmother passed away. Man, we used to be able to make the best snowballs with these." He slipped them onto his hands and clapped them together. "I love them! Thank you!"

I beamed. My worries about his reaction to a gift from me, and the nightmare of logistics in how exactly to give it to him, fled in an instant. I was overcome with a feeling of holiday bonhomie. That was the only explanation I could give for what happened next.

"Everybody I love has something I knitted. I figured it was time you did, too," I blurted out and immediately regretted my hasty, unplanned words. I reached my hand out blindly as if I thought I might be able to snatch them back. My fingertips landed on Seán's arm and the muscles beneath the soft flannel of his shirt felt tense. The look on his face was a mixture of elation and despair.

"Seán, I am so sorry. I didn't mean . . ."

He ripped one mitten off and pressed a finger to my lips so fast the shock alone stopped me.

"Emerson, don't say it. Don't say anything."

I stood there staring at him, my eyes wide. He closed his and took a few deep, centering breaths before opening them again. And just like that, it was gone. The wall of distance that had been between us since Marise's dinner party had melted.

"Seán . . ." I began, but he put pressure on my lips.

"Goodnight, Emerson. Merry Christmas." Leaning forward, he replaced his finger with his lips, giving me a kiss so light it was like a whisper. And then he was gone.

A cold breeze from the closing door behind him snapped me out of the trance I seemed to be in. Should I go after him? Forget it and pretend it had never happened? Or should I let things settle and then approach him, try to explain? Clutching the banjo, I wandered into the living room in a sort of daze.

It might have been an accident, saying I loved him, but it also happened to be the truth. I should have told him months before, I knew. I sighed. Better late than never, I supposed.

How I wished I could understand the contradiction I'd seen written so plainly on his face. He'd had the desperate look of a man who'd been given the keys to the kingdom and then watched them sail over the edge of an abyss.

"Stop," I told myself sternly. Clearly, yes, there was something between us, something Seán at least recognized even if he wasn't interested in acting on it. And then I reminded myself—again—that he was *dying*. The thought never seemed to be far from his mind, though I seemed to be unable to retain it. Why was I always forgetting that simple fact?

Because, I realized suddenly, I didn't want to believe it. I didn't want to believe that God had helped me get over Danny's death *finally* only to lead me to the only other person on the planet with whom I was interested in spending the rest of my life. How could God be so cruel? He was snatching Seán away in his prime, depriving his dying patients of his skill and me of the only man I could imagine ever loving.

Miserably, I tuned up the banjo and plucked out a tune. I was almost through it when I realized I was playing O Come, O Come Emmanuel. The words were going through my head, but I'd been oblivious.

O come, O come, Emmanuel,
And ransom captive Israel,
That mourns in lonely exile here
Until the Son of God appear.

I felt a sudden stab of conviction. Why was I always blaming God for Satan's works? I wondered. God was not the source of sin in the world, Satan was. God gave; Satan stole. God loved; Satan hated. God redeemed; Satan destroyed. Why was it so hard for me to remember that? How quickly I could forget that God was on my side, and Satan wasn't.

"I'm sorry, Lord," I murmured. My fingers had continued to pluck out the melody for O Come, O Come Emmanuel, and tentatively, I began to sing along with it. My voice in the quiet room was soft at first, but as I began to feel the words resonate deep in my heart, my voice became stronger and louder.

"Mom?" Addy's sleepy voice interrupted me just as I was beginning the last verse, and I jumped guiltily. "Why are you still up? Why are you still *singing*?" Her half opened eyes caught sight of the Whyte Laydie on my lap and flew open with surprise.

"Wow, nice! Where'd you get that?"

"Uh . . . Seán gave it to me," I said, seeing no other alternative. "For Christmas," I added defensively.

Addy chuckled softly. "Someone's in love," she crooned, making the word "love" sound like "luuuuuv."

"I'm not . . ." I started to protest hotly and with a total lack of sincerity, not to mention veracity, but she cut me off.

"Spare me, Mom. I meant Seán, but if the shoe fits . . ." With that parting shot, she shuffled back down the hallway to her room, leaving me cradling the banjo guiltily and blushing.

I saw Seán at Angelique's wedding, of course. We didn't have a chance to talk much because Angelique and Jeff had asked "the band" to play the music at their reception. (I also had the honor of playing piano for their ceremony, which was, in sharp contrast to their reception, simple and short.)

Judging from the number of people present at the reception, I figured Angelique had invited everyone in the entire village, which wasn't surprising when you considered that between them, she and Jeff were probably related to most everyone somehow. The dance floor was so packed I had to get really creative calling sets so people wouldn't crash into each other. No one seemed to mind.

It was the most carefree, joyful celebration I'd ever attended and probably had something to do with the attitudes of the bride and groom who appeared to be trying to out-smile each other. I'd never seen two people so exuberantly in love. It was infectious.

I looked over at Seán and wondered what it would feel like to be that free to love him. I was immediately embarrassed by the thought. How selfish of me to consider my own happiness at the expense of Trudy's, I chided myself, and turned resolutely back to calling the dance I was in the middle of with so much energy that when it was over, people collapsed into chairs panting and whisked bottled water from the coolers where they were crammed in cheek by jowl on beds of ice.

While they were catching their breath, I studied the surroundings to distract myself. Angelique and company had turned the humble hall into the manifestation of her winter wedding dreams. It was really quite lovely with tiny twinkling lights strung everywhere entwined with mercury glass stars and swags of small snowflakes festooning the walls and dripping from the ceiling and wrapped around pretty much everything that wasn't moving.

"I don't know what's gotten into you," Marise hissed suddenly in my ear, "but play a waltz, would you?" She picked up the handle of Mozart's harness and said one word: "Auggie."

I couldn't help but grin as the big dog obediently led her directly to Auggie who was sitting at a small table near the stage where we were playing.

"Let's play a slow one for Marise and Auggie," I suggested. "How about Tabhair Dom Do Lamh?"

"Give me your hand?" Seán asked innocently, translating the title of the song, but there was a wicked glint in his eye.

"It's a wedding waltz," I answered weakly, suddenly flustered and wondering if I'd gotten my tunes mixed up. "Isn't it?"

Marise put Mozart into a down-stay and took the floor with Auggie before the music even started. The bride, not to be outdone at her own wedding, quickly hustled the groom onto the dance floor before he could tuck into his second slice of wedding cake. Slowly others followed suit and since I didn't have to call steps, I put the Whyte Laydie through her paces, enjoying her singular sound.

Closing my eyes, I concentrated on hearing Seán's pipes in the cacophony of sound and weaving counterpoint harmony around his melody line. My fingers danced on the fretboard, first hiding on the melody, then playing peek-a-boo with it, now dancing with it. As the song drew to a close and I opened my eyes, I was surprised to see Seán grinning at me. Before I could think better of it, I grinned back at him.

During the intermission, he brought me back a bottle of water when he fetched one for himself. "Great reception, huh?" he asked, looking around and twisting the top off his bottle.

"It's great," I agreed. The bottle he'd given me was slippery, and I had trouble twisting the top off. It stuck stubbornly.

"Here, let me," Seán said. He took the bottle from my hands. While he was opening it, he remarked casually. "A little too many people though . . . for my taste."

"Oh?" I looked around in surprise. It *was* awfully crowded. "I suppose so."

"Now if it was me? I'd skip all the pomp and circumstance." He handed the bottle back to me, minus the cap, and continued with a faraway look on his face. "I'd sneak off to a justice of the peace for the legal part and then whisk my bride off to a secret location, just the two of us."

I gulped. "Really?" I wistfully imagined that tantalizing scenario before it suddenly occurred to me that maybe he'd done just that. Maybe he and Trudy had gotten hitched already and . . . "A place like Montréal?" I asked, hoping to catch him out.

"What?" He frowned, looking disgusted. "No, nothing like Montréal. Too crowded. No, I'm thinking of a secluded place, somewhere we could be together with no distractions. Some quiet spot where we could get to know each other and focus only on each other. Not have to answer to anyone and not have to live up to anyone's expectations. That's what a honeymoon should be like, shouldn't it? Not running off to some honeymoon spot filled with other people and jumping through the required sightseeing hoops."

I swallowed hard. "Sounds perfect to me," I breathed.

No way, I decided. If he and Trudy had gotten married, she'd be here tonight. I glanced at his hand surreptitiously. He'd be wearing a ring; he wasn't.

"If it was me," he repeated, staring at me significantly, "that's what I'd want. What about you? What would you want?"

I cleared my throat and took a big swig of water. If it was me? I'd marry him in a second and wild horses couldn't keep me from joining him in a secluded place where we could "focus only on each other." I couldn't tell him that, obviously. "I agree," I finally managed to say. "This is nice, but I'm a more reserved person than Angelique." He laughed, but I wasn't finished. "A little cabin in the woods somewhere, maybe, sounds like the perfect place to join two hearts."

He didn't respond, but as we finished our water and watched everyone talking and laughing, I couldn't help but feel that this conversation wasn't over. And I wondered why, exactly, he'd brought it up.

Chapter Twenty-One

Angelique and Jeff's wedding, the big event of the winter, had so warmed the hearts of the entire community that the Christmas spirit seemed to linger far into the blustery spring. I saw Jeff occasionally after the wedding now that he lived just down the road. Outwardly, he looked like the epitome of a hen-pecked husband as he trotted outside in the rain to collect the newspaper or dutifully held doors open for Angelique. But in his eyes smoldered the smug, self-satisfied look of a man who had gotten exactly what he'd wanted.

Winter flew by, mostly because I didn't want it to. In just a few short months, Addy would graduate. Lately, when she wasn't studying or shadowing Auggie, she'd been busy with her friends, many of whom would be scattering to the four winds after graduation, off to college or new lives, spreading their wings. My stomach clenched every time I thought of it even though Addy had been accepted at the University of Vermont and wouldn't need to leave home in order to go to college.

Still, despite the fact that she was staying home, I felt an almost constant sense of foreboding. Change was in the air, and I didn't like it. I got into the habit of listening to CDs of the Bible while I sat in the living room spinning yarn. The steady rhythm of treadling calmed me as the narrator's soothing voice reminded me that no matter what changes came in life, God was in control. In the great battle between good and evil, Jesus had already won. It was simply a matter of time before we could trade this dark old world for heaven and a New Earth. It was hard to worry much once that message sank into my soul.

Seán, I noticed, looked better than ever. He seemed to be regaining a lot of the strength he had lost. I wondered if it was all the walking he'd been doing with Marcel. All winter they had continued to hike around the village praying for people as they went. When they'd covered the whole village, they set off to walk the more outlying areas. I don't know how far they'd walked, but even Marcel looked fitter than he had in years.

Seán's hair had long since grown back out to the tousled mess of loose curls I loved. Every now and then he mentioned getting a haircut but didn't seem inclined to follow through—for which I was secretly grateful. It was hard to recognize the beautiful, tortured stranger who had blown into town more than a year ago in the vibrant, carefree man he had become. I wondered if it was the lack of stress and responsibility that had caused the change or his newfound relationship with God.

It was such a remarkable transformation that even Marise noticed.

"Seán's looking good lately, isn't he?" she innocently remarked one day when I was helping her warp her loom to make a blanket with some wool I'd just spun.

"How do you know that?"

"I can hear it in his voice," she said, for once not leaving me to wonder how she could discern such a thing. "He sounds happy and . . ." She thought for a minute. "More relaxed." When she continued, her voice was nonchalant, but there was something about her face, a funny look she got when she was hiding something, that told me it was possible she knew more than she was letting on. "He stopped by the other day."

"Did he?" I was so startled, I dropped the reed slaying hook and had to fish it out from under the loom. Marise and Seán hadn't been on particularly good terms since her dinner party, but apparently they'd made an uneasy truce if he felt comfortable enough to drop in. "Any particular reason?"

She laughed. "There was, but I'm not free to share it. He wanted help with something. You'll know soon enough."

I glowered at her despite the fact that it was lost on her. I hoped she could feel the beams of my displeasure radiating in her direction. "You're really not going to tell me?"

"I'm really not."

"Some friend you are," I muttered, busy pondering what Seán could possibly want Marise's help for . . . Marise's help and not mine.

"Ha," she said smugly. "You just wait and see what kind of friend I am."

Curiosity about this revelation would probably have given me enough food for thought to keep me busy speculating for weeks if I hadn't had Addy's graduation looming in front of me like a skyscraper about to topple over and crush the life out of me.

"There *has* to be a party," my mother insisted. "It's her big day." We were out in her back yard, and she was hunched over a flowerbed, weeding.

"Sure," I agreed, "but I thought we'd have something small at the house."

"Oh no, no, no, no." My mother had that mulish look she wore when she got the bit between her teeth. "We'll have it here. I insist," she added before I could protest. "Bert and I will pay for everything." She patted my arm, a scheming gleam in her eye. "Don't you worry about a thing, eh?"

"I can't let you do that," I sputtered. In my mind's eye, I could envision exactly the type of gaudy, hideous, over-the-top kind of party she had in mind. It was precisely the sort I'd had to suffer through: relatives galore (most of whom Addy wouldn't know), decorations out of the 70s (not, mind you, "of that style" but actual decorations she'd saved from *my* graduation party that had been saved from someone *else's* graduation party even earlier than me), and mismatched music from several generations (in an attempt to please everyone.)

"Why not?" my mother demanded stridently, as if I'd offended her. "Why I can't give my granddaughter a party, eh?" I knew she was getting angry because her English was deteriorating.

I held up my hands in surrender. "Okay, okay, fine. If it'll make you happy."

Her ruffled feathers smoothed down immediately. "Well, then," she said. Her gears were spinning already. I could tell.

"Just let me know if you need any help," I offered, knowing full well she wouldn't.

"Oh, it's nothing." She brushed me off. "Now, let me see . . . where did I put those decorations we had, remember? When your cousin Pascal had that . . ."

She was off, her short legs carrying her rapidly back to the house. "Bert! Bert! Viens vite!"[43]

I sighed. Already I dreaded telling Addy, but she must have had more of my mother in her than I imagined. She was tickled pink when I told her over supper.

"Wow," she breathed giddily. "Just think of all the money and presents I'll get if Mémère invites as many people as you say."

"Adrienne! That's not the object . . ." She cut me off.

"Mom! Of course it is! Why would anyone have a celebration otherwise?"

She had so much confidence in her opinion that I actually began to doubt myself. But since my own opinion hardly mattered anyway, I bit my tongue.

The day of Addy's graduation I was a bundle of nerves. Marise showed up an hour before we were supposed to leave to go to the high school. Addy had already left to join her class and prepare for the ceremony, completely oblivious to the fact that I was struggling to come to grips with the realization

---

[43] Come quick!

that my baby was growing up. Today, as she walked across that stage, she'd be walking out of my life. At least, that's what it felt like.

I wanted to throw up.

But even more than that, I wanted Danny to be there, beside me, watching our baby grow up but knowing that as she made ever greater orbits around and away from us, we would remain, constant, at the center of her world. Instead, there was only me. I was sick with self-pity, but Marise was having none of that. It was like she could feel the negatively charged air the minute she walked in the door.

"We are going to pray," she said firmly.

"Pray?" It hadn't actually occurred to me to pray about the way I was feeling. "Right now? I'm not even dressed for the graduation yet."

"Which is more important: looking good or feeling good?" she asked practically.

I knew resistance was futile, but I felt a certain sense of relief as we made our way into the living room, the dogs scurrying around with pleasure at seeing Marise, but puzzled by Mozart's disinterest in them. Marise knelt down beside the sofa and Mozart dropped to his belly beside her. I joined her hesitantly, still shy about praying with other people. Fortunately, Marise started.

It always amazed me to listen to her pray. Although I felt as though my relationship with God had grown, I wasn't as comfortable with it as Marise was in her relationship with him. I could easily imagine her climbing up onto his lap the way a small child would with a beloved parent, to be cuddled and consoled as she poured out all her troubles. I longed for a relationship like that.

As she prayed, I felt a wave of peace wash over me. The tension and worry bound up tightly inside me slowly eased away. I realized then, for the first time I think, how much I had relied on Addy after Danny died. I had resisted her independence for the same reason I resisted her next step into adulthood: I was afraid to be alone.

I felt as though I'd been dashed in the face with cold water. All this time, all the mental anguish I'd suffered. At the root of it all was this unreasonable fear of being alone. I looked across at Marise, not only alone but blind, yet totally reliant on God for everything. Her complete faith in him to provide for her, to be her everything, humbled me so much that I was barely able to squeak out an, "Amen," when she finished praying.

"Lord," I gulped, glad Marise couldn't see the flush of shame that burned my face, "help me to lean on you completely. Be my everything. Fill me up with yourself so that I won't be empty anymore."

I felt a strong sense of comfort wash over me. It was as though, after all this time, my soul had been stripped down. But as it stood naked and trembling, God covered it with a thick, warm, comforting blanket and placed a protective arm around it, around me. And I knew, in that moment, that I had finally and completely stepped free from the fear that had held me prisoner for so long.

Yes, Danny had gone. Yes, Addy would leave soon, too. But no matter who came and went in my life, God would always be there. His presence would be an irrefutable fact in my life forever, from this moment on. I would never be alone again.

"I'm not alone," I whispered to Marise as we stood up, and I brushed tears of joy from my eyes. "I'm not alone."

"No," she smiled softly, and I could tell she knew exactly what I meant. " 'Be strong and courageous' " she quoted. " 'Do not be afraid; do not be discouraged, for the Lord your God will be with you wherever you go.' "

It was as if I could hear God's voice speak to me through Marise's lips. The message was exactly what I needed to hear. It was confirmation of what I felt. If God was going to walk with me, then I would hold my head up. I would not cower and worry about a tomorrow that hadn't even arrived yet. I would take this one next step with God by my side. And then I'd take the next and the next. As long as I did that, I could be confident that life would never overcome me again. And neither could death.

After all, what was death really but a pause between places? A comma in a sentence? It was as narrow as the threshold of a door. Someday we would live forever without the interruption of death. And when it came time for me to step through that portal whether it was tomorrow, in a week, or years from now, God would be with me even then.

I threw my arms around Marise, and she jumped a little in surprise but patted me soothingly on the shoulder. "You're going to be okay," she said confidently.

I was crying so hard with relief and joy and the sheer taste of *freedom* from the tyranny of fear I had lived under for so long that I could barely control my voice. "I'm going to be okay," I sobbed. "I'm going to be okay."

"You're also going to be late," Marise pointed out practically.

The thought of being late to Addy's graduation shocked me so badly that I gulped back my sobs in a hiccup of laughter. "I can't be late!"

"Then you'd better hurry."

If I hadn't chosen my outfit the night before and laid it out in readiness, I have no idea what ghastly thing I might have put on, such was my mental state as I shoved arms and legs into clothing, twisted my hair into a messy-on-purpose knot high on my head, and put makeup on so fast I was fortunate not to leave skid marks. I ushered Marise out to my truck so quickly she squeaked in protest and even Mozart gave me a disgruntled look. After skillful driving that was much too fast, according to Marise, along with some creative parking, we managed to find seats in the crowded gymnasium before the ceremony started only because my parents and Marcel had saved some for us.

I was so lighthearted that it felt as though I didn't have enough weight to remain in my chair. I wouldn't have been surprised to find that I was floating several inches above it. Marcel kept shooting me puzzled looks, which was perfectly understandable considering that he'd dropped by last night suspecting how I might feel having gone through graduation no less than three times himself. Needless to say, he'd found me in pretty low spirits.

I smiled sweetly at him and pointed upward. When he shot a worried glance at the ceiling, I almost laughed out loud. I might have, too, if the band hadn't chosen the exact moment to strike up "Pomp And Circumstance" cuing the graduates to begin filing in, flowing down the aisles, the boys on one side in blue cap and gown, the girls down the other in white.

I spotted Seán halfway through the ceremony. He was sitting in the middle of a crowded section and gazing thoughtfully at the proceedings, but I could tell his mind was miles away. He seemed tense and on edge, as if he expected bad news at any moment. I was pretty sure it had nothing to do with the occasion or the graduates themselves. I didn't think he was there for Addy; he must have had a niece or nephew graduating.

Trudy was flitting around in her official capacity as principal, but he barely seemed to register her presence. She looked like an exotic, glossy black bird in her cap and gown as she swanned back and forth across the stage tripping lightly along on the highest heels I'd ever seen. They were so high, in fact, that they made her taller than Seán. I noticed this—not uncharitably but with a small sense of satisfaction that I couldn't control—after the ceremony when they were talking together. She'd drawn him aside slightly and was gesturing and chatting animatedly while he listened. Eventually, he seemed to brighten up a little and began to smile. What happened after that I didn't see, because I turned myself firmly away.

We didn't stick around very long after the graduation because my mother was anxious to get her party started. After Marcel had bought their farm, my parents had moved into a small beach cottage right on the lake in Marquette, the next town over from Toussaint. As I had suspected, my mother was in her element, buzzing around like a queen bee from one knot of guests to the next, the decorations every bit as hideous as I had feared, both house and lawn every bit as jam-packed with people as I had expected. I hung off to one side, uncomfortable with the noise and press of people in the small house. It looked to me as though my mother had invited every living relative we had.

When I heard fiddle music from the front lawn, I went out to investigate. Sitting on a metal folding chair, battered fiddle tucked against his chest, cigarette hanging from his lips, was my cousin Pascal. His eyes were closed as he played, so I leaned up against the house and listened until he stopped for a minute.

Before I had the chance to push away from the house and make my way over to him, the crowd parted in the opposite direction, and Marise tapped-tapped her way straight—more or less—at him. I had convinced her to leave Mozart at home and use her cane because I knew how crowded it would be at my parents'. She hadn't been happy about it, but I could see it hadn't slowed her down any, either.

As they became aware she was blind, my relatives made way for her, parting like the Red Sea all the way up to Pascal's chair. She planted herself squarely in front of him. "That was pretty good," she said, "but this," her hand snaked out and whipped the cigarette right out of his mouth, dropped it onto the lawn, and crushed it vehemently beneath her heel, "this will kill you. How can anybody in this day and age not know that?" she demanded.

Pascal's mouth was hanging open as he stared at her. "Are we related?" he asked skeptically. He seemed to take in the white cane at about the same time he realized she was blind, and he touched his lips gingerly, probably wondering how her aim was so accurate and grateful she hadn't missed.

"What difference would that make?" she asked. "Where's she been hiding you anyway?"

"She who?" Pascal asked, bewildered.

"Me," I laughed, fighting my way through the knots of people talking and laughing. "Pascal, meet my friend Marise." I touched her arm, but I doubted she needed that reassurance to know where I was. "This is my cousin Pascal.

He lives in St. Croix." I gave my cousin a quick hug. "I only get to see him at family stuff. How have you been?" I asked him.

"Been good," he said vaguely, but I could tell his mind wasn't on me or what I was saying. He was enraptured by Marise.

"Pascal tried to teach me how to play the fiddle when I was in high school," I explained to her.

"Ah," she said. "I bet that was a dismal job."

"Hey," I protested.

Pascal threw back his head and laughed. "She had no rhythm at the time," he agreed.

"At least you tried," Marise said sympathetically. "If it's any consolation, she picks mine up every now and then, and she's not terrible. But she's much better on the banjo."

"You play?" he asked Marise. He turned to me, his eyes twinkling. "I like her. She's got spunk."

He held out his fiddle to Marise. "Here angel, why don't you show me what you've got?"

Marise hesitated only for a second before taking the fiddle from him. I shook my head and waited in anticipation. Marise took her time tuning the fiddle, and Pascal got dragged into a conversation with one of our other relatives, a distant cousin I recognized but didn't really know. Marise, meanwhile, took a deep breath and launched directly into Mendelssohn's violin concerto in Em Op. 64.

At the first passionate note, Pascal started as though he'd taken an arrow to the heart. Slowly he turned, gawping at her. So did pretty much everyone else in the vicinity. All nearby chatter ceased. Fortunately, Marise only hit the highlights of the piece or we would have been there for awhile. Even without the orchestra, it was plenty impressive.

"Who did you say she was?" Pascal asked me under his breath.

"Marise Gaudet," I murmured, trying not to laugh, "principal violinist of the Champlain Summer Music Festival."

"Does she play traditional music, too? I'm in love," Pascal blurted out devotedly. It was particularly well timed, though not on purpose. Marise had just lifted her bow to start another movement. Laughter broke out all around and she seemed to make a snap decision to end her impromptu concert right there. She handed the fiddle back to Pascal who took it reverently, as though it had been blessed.

"Marry me," he implored.

"I would never date a smoker," Marise pointed out.

"I quit," Pascal insisted. "Because of you. See? You're already making me a better man."

"Anyway," Marise said lightly, "I'm spoken for." The pleased smile on her lips made my cousin scowl.

"You can't be!" he countered, a note of desperation in his voice. Then his eyes narrowed as though he suddenly suspected her of playing hard to get. "By who?"

Marise ignored the question, but I discreetly pointed to Auggie, who, looking twice as big as usual, was laughing with Addy about something. His long, shiny, black hair hung loosely over impossibly broad shoulders, and he towered over Addy. While I watched, the big man gave my daughter a congratulatory hug, and then bashfully patted her on the shoulder with one large hand, totally engulfing it and knocking her slightly off balance. Pascal swallowed hard.

"Why don't you come around and play with us sometime?" I suggested to ease the blow. "We've got a little band. We jam together and play contras and concerts sometimes."

"Do you?" Pascal's surprise and undeniable interest showed on his face. "How come I never heard about that? I'd love it! Can I really come? I haven't played for a contra in donkey's years."

"No," Marise said.

"Yes," I said. I narrowed my eyes at her. "We can always use another fiddler," I argued stubbornly. "You say so yourself all the time. You said it would give us a fuller sound."

Marise sighed in exasperation. "Fine. Come if you want. But there's no smoking," she said sternly.

Pascal crossed his heart solemnly. "I told you. I already quit."

Marise stalked off as best she could, and Pascal never took his eyes off her. "She's wonderful. I can't believe she's existed in the world all this time, and I didn't know it."

I suppressed a smile. My cousin was a notorious charmer, a rather innocent one, but a charmer nonetheless. Unfortunately, he hadn't had much luck with women, having been scorched by two rather acrimonious divorces already.

He gave me a serious, plaintive look. "You'll call me for the next jam?"

I laughed. "If you insist."

"Oh, I do, I absolutely do."

I didn't think my mother had invited Seán, so I was surprised to see him weaving his way through the guests headed straight in my direction. His brilliant blue eyes were locked on me as he approached. He looked agitated or excited or scared. I wasn't sure which.

"Emerson," he said urgently.

I felt my throat go dry. Had he gotten some bad news? He'd been doing so well. "Yes?" I managed to croak. "What's wrong?"

"Nothing! I mean, hopefully nothing. Hopefully everything will be all right finally." He stopped, flustered. "I just, I need to talk to you."

"Right this minute?" I asked in surprise. Somewhere behind me I could hear my mother trying to gather everyone together so Addy could cut her cake.

"Yes!" He looked around skeptically, seeming to realize quite suddenly just where he was. He had the look of a man emerging from a dream. "Uh . . . I guess it can wait," he admitted reluctantly.

"You sure?"

He smiled, but it was clearly forced. "Absolutely. I shouldn't have come. It can wait."

He gave me an encouraging push toward the table where everyone was gathering around Addy as she prepared to dole out slices of cake and then open her presents and cards.

"Come find me after," I said. He nodded. "Promise?"

He nodded again. But later, as people drifted off back home and things wound down, I couldn't find him. I felt a sinking feeling of disappointment that he'd gone and wondered what it was he'd wanted that had prompted him to crash my daughter's graduation party.

An unsettled feeling of unease dogged me as I walked home through the balmy night air. I hoped he hadn't had bad news. I couldn't stop in and ask him though. His place was dark as I walked past. Sighing, I wondered how long I would have to wait to find out.

Chapter Twenty-Two

I was plucking a new tune out on the Whyte Laydie and the dogs were dozing at my feet, when a sudden knock on the door hurtled them into the air, barking like Tasmanian devils. Addy was out with her friends. They planned to camp out on the beach and watch the sun come up on their first day of "freedom." I remembered doing the same thing with my friends on graduation night. It was kind of a tradition. So Gyp and Dash's explosive barking echoed into the empty house as they leapt eagerly at the door. I set the banjo down reverently and made sure it was secure in its stand before I got up to open it.

"Seán!" He was the last person I had expected.

He had such a look of desperation on his face that when he staggered toward me, I backed away from him. "Emerson, will you," he paused as if he needed to gather courage, "will you marry me?" Before I could answer he continued in a rush. "I'm cancer free, clean bill of health from my doctor. Not a cancer cell left. I just got confirmation a few hours ago. Of course, there are no guarantees. It could come back . . ."

"You're not dying?" I blurted out, stunned. "It's . . . gone? You said it was incurable." In a bizarre way I was almost angry with him, as though he'd tricked me, purloined sympathy he had no right to if he planned to go on living. My mind struggled to grasp the meaning of what he was saying.

"Inoperable," he corrected gently. "I said it was inoperable. And it was." He must have comprehended the magnitude of my shock because he led me to a chair and guided me until I was sitting shakily on the edge, staring at him, tears threatening to stream down my face at any moment. Perhaps to prevent them, he hastily explained, finally answering all the questions I had been burning to ask him since the day we met, and he'd announced he was dying.

"I have . . . I had . . . a high-grade astrocytoma. It was inoperable because it was inaccessible. One of my colleagues, Jean-Philippe Bertrand, had developed a new drug, efluximustine that, in combination with stereotactic radiosurgery, was proving highly effective in some mid-grade astrocytomas." Seán glanced at me to see if I was following, and I nodded numbly. I caught the gist. He took a breath and plunged on. "The treatment was in trial phase, and I had been helping her with it. Some of my own patients entered the clinical trials. Then, shortly after I received my diagnosis, Jean-Philippe was able to end the trials early because they showed statistically positive results—

in trials the treatment cured 90 percent of the cases. They released it to the public much sooner than anticipated, and I became Jean-Philippe's patient in order to receive treatment. She . . . she told me this morning that it's gone. There isn't a trace left."

"But why?" I wailed. "Why didn't you tell me about the treatment? Why did you put me through that agony? I thought you were going to die."

He chuckled ruefully. "Emerson, I hate to break it to you, but we're all going to die."

For a second I almost punched him as if he were Marcel. And the momentary anger sparked another memory. "What about Trudy?" I asked, feeling suddenly as though someone had dumped a bucket of cold water on me.

Seán face went blank. "Trudy? What about her?"

"You've been *dating* her," I reminded him icily.

"Me? No, I haven't."

"Yes," I insisted, "you have. I saw you. Remember? I dropped by that time, and she came to your house. The two of you were going out. She was all dressed up. Around here that constitutes a date. And there were many other times."

He shook his head. "Trudy and I are cousins," he said, emphasizing the word "cousins" so hard he hissed a little at the end. "First cousins," he added significantly, raising an eyebrow and glowering at me. "I asked her to drive me to my treatments. She's been spending a lot of time in Montréal lately as it happens, and she was happy to do it. She's *dating*," he emphasized the word as I had, "Jean-Philippe's brother. He lives there."

I struggled with the implications of that. "So when you introduced us to begin with, why didn't you say something simple like, 'Emerson, this is my first cousin, Trudy, who I would never in a million years consider dating. She'll be driving me to the treatments that will save my life because I don't want to ask you to do it.' " He was already shaking his head.

"I never had the chance to introduce you," he pointed out. "Remember? You already knew Trudy. I assumed you knew our connection, too."

The first night I'd seen Trudy at Seán's house came crashing back to me in every detail. *"Oh, hello! Mrs. Giroux, isn't it? Adrienne's mother? We met at the . . ."* "Yeah, well . . . why didn't you ask me to drive you to your treatments? I would have been happy to."

Seán sighed heavily. "Impose on you when I barely knew you? And was attracted to you? I didn't even want you to know about them. Then, if things didn't go well, you wouldn't have to go through what I had to go through. The treatments were experimental, no guarantees. And going through them wasn't pretty. Besides," he glanced askance at me, "I wasn't really sure how you felt about me, aside from the fact that I might keel over at any minute. I put you off to protect you, but I was never sure how you felt. I was afraid the signal I was picking up could have been pity."

"It was pity," I said quietly and then added, to brace up the dejected slump of his shoulders, "self-pity."

Seán took both my hands in his own and knelt down on the kitchen floor in front of me. "Emerson, please, will you marry me?"

As I looked at him, so vulnerable, so hopeful, I couldn't even find the breath to speak. After all this time, after so many obstacles, with a path clear ahead and my most fervent prayer answered—alive and well and impossibly cured before me—I thought ahead. He was cured now, surely he'd be heading back to pick up where he left off in Montréal. The famous brain surgeon would go on saving lives, but what was there for me in Montréal? My life was here: my family, my farm, my friends. I couldn't leave everything. I couldn't discard them all. Not even for Seán.

His grip on my hands tightened as he watched my internal struggle. He seemed to know how much he was asking me to give up and worry clouded his eyes. "I can't . . ." I finally choked out. "Seán, I can't . . ." It felt like giant bands of steel were closing around my rib cage, and I struggled for air.

The pain that twisted his face made me feel as though I'd taken a kitchen knife and stabbed him through the heart. "I understand," he said quietly, quickly, as though he'd expected nothing better than a refusal. My hands felt suddenly cold, and I realized it was because he'd withdrawn his. He was across the floor and out the door before I even realized he'd moved.

By the time I stumbled through the front door and onto the porch he was halfway down my driveway and walking fast. "Seán!" The word wrenched itself from so deep inside me I think they must have heard my scream across the lake in Québec. He stopped as if I'd shot him. Turning slowly he made his way back, heavily climbed the three stairs of the porch, and stood silently for a moment. Then he tangled his fingers in my hair and drew me gently against his chest, cradling me there.

His murmured words were so soft I had to strain to hear them. "When Jean-Philippe gave me the results of the trials, when we realized how significant they were, what it could mean to me, I was numb. I was resigned to my fate at that point and working myself even harder trying to do as much good as I could before the end. I couldn't process the fact that I had this unexpected chance for life, that it was possible the treatment could cure me.

"I got in my car, and I drove. I ended up here, of course, tracing my roots, I suppose. I ran into you that day. Do you remember? At Angelique's. And then later we played music together, and that's when I knew I wanted to live so badly I'd do anything just for a chance." His soft chuckle was almost a sob; it nearly broke my heart. "I went back and told Jean-Philippe I wanted to have the treatment." He breathed one ragged breath into my hair, kissed me softly on the cheek, and said, "If you change your mind . . ." Then the shelter of his arms slipped away, and he was gone.

I stared into the darkness and finally found enough breath to finish my sentence. "I can't . . . live without you," I whispered into the night. I don't know how long I stood there with tears streaming down my face, but when I finally turned to go inside they were dry.

To say that I prayed about what I should do all night long would have been an exaggeration. I fell asleep by two o'clock at the latest, dragged under by exhaustion that made even my bones ache. When I woke up I was sitting at the kitchen table, my cheek glued to the open pages of my Bible.

Addy sat across from me, sipping her morning tea and eying me curiously. She looked tired from staying up all night, and I suspected she'd soon crawl into bed and sleep all day. "He asked you to marry him, didn't he?" It wasn't so much a question as a statement of fact.

"How did you know?"

"Mom!" Addy rolled her eyes at me. "Give me a little credit. What I can't understand is why you're out here . . ." she waved a hand to encompass the fact that I'd obviously slept in my clothes, at the table, head cradled on my Bible, " . . . like this."

I shook my head sorrowfully, tears threatening again, unable to speak.

"You didn't say no!" Addy's mug slammed down on the table so hard the tea sloshed out. "Why?"

"I didn't say yes!" I wailed. I wanted Marise desperately. I wanted a shoulder to cry on. I looked at Addy's bristling figure and knew I'd find no sympathy there. It was unreasonable, too. After all, she was one of the main people I didn't want to leave.

"How could I leave you?" I demanded. "How could I traipse off to Montréal and live in the city and leave everything and everyone I know and love? How?"

"He asked you to move to Montréal?" she asked, eyes narrowing to accusing slits, and I had the uncomfortable feeling that she'd known all along that Seán was going to propose.

"Did you know?" I gasped. "Did he tell you he was going to ask me to marry him?"

"Did he ask you to move to Montréal?" she repeated, ignoring my question.

"What? No, I just assumed."

She nodded, smug with satisfaction. "I knew it."

"Adrienne, he's a brain surgeon, a very famous one, he's not going to be content to live in a little backwater town like this one doing what? Farming? Bagging groceries down at the store? What kind of life is there for him here? There's nothing for me in Montréal except him and there's nothing here for him except me. I can't hold him back like that. I . . . I couldn't bear to think of all those people dying without him," I finished quietly. Not, I added silently to myself, when I know exactly how it feels to lose someone you love.

Addy reached across the table and grasped my cold hands in her warm ones. I knew it was the greatest gesture of sympathy I could expect from my undemonstrative daughter. "Mom, we have hospitals here. And even if he did want to keep working in Montréal, so? It's an hour away. He'd have to drive that far to work at a big hospital in Vermont." She tossed her hair over one slim shoulder. "It's no big deal; lots of people do it."

Could she be right? Could Seán truly have intended to stay here? Was it possible he could remain here and continue to do what he loved, what God clearly had called him to do? I looked across the table into Addy's shining eyes, and I knew suddenly, felt it throughout my entire being like one of those ringing truths, that it didn't matter. It would be wonderful if I did not have to uproot myself from the life I had made for myself and Addy but that life would never have any meaning for me without Seán. If being with him meant following him to the ends of the earth I was willing to do it. Nothing else mattered.

Addy saw the certainty dawn in my eyes, and she squeezed my hands. "Go tell him," she urged. "Right now."

Sobbing and laughing at the same time I gave her a quick hug and sprinted out the door. Somewhere off in the distance I heard a loon call. At the crest of the hill the lake opened out in front of me. The clouds were piled up steel gray, solid as mountains on the horizon, the waves violent, their caps frothing. I breathed deeply. The air was cool and smelled of seaweed and moisture. The wind whipped my hair around my face. Bobbing on the waves, like sentinels, I could see the pair of loons silhouetted against the waves.

Seán's Explorer was not parked in the driveway and the house had a deserted feel. I knew I couldn't change that no matter how long I pounded on the door. He'd already left, packed up, was probably waking up in Montréal right this moment. Did he feel the same pain that wrenched me, threatening to tear me in two? I felt nauseous and for a moment I thought I might vomit all over Mrs. McCarty's tidy front steps.

Staggering around the side of the house I willed myself, stumbling, toward the lake. The coastline was rocky here and a geyser of water shot up as a particularly strong wave crashed on the shore. I clambered onto a large platform of a rock near the edge of the beach. Sinking down I pulled my legs in close to me, huddling into the smallest possible form I could manage, as if I was trying to hold myself together, I thought bitterly. I stared out at the water and tried to think about what to do next. I was almost paralyzed with disappointment.

All the months of hope, longing, misunderstanding, frustration, and now regret culminated in a feeling of pain so intense it felt as though the waves crashing onto the rocks below were battering me down physically. I had not cried, really cried, since Danny's funeral but now I cried great, wracking sobs that shook my whole body. I cried so hard I couldn't catch my breath, and my body shuddered with trying to find a way to release the overwhelming pain that felt like it was strangling me.

Snippets of conversations we'd had, and ones I wished we'd had, streamed through my head. How? How could you go? I wanted to scream. Why didn't you wait for me? Don't you know how much I love you? Don't you know how much I want you? How much I need you? Can't you see it? I could hear him tell me again, If you change your mind . . . My mind hadn't needed changing; it had only needed making up. It had only needed me finding the strength to follow my heart. I could hear Seán's voice as though he was in the distance calling me. Emerson! Em!

"Emerson?"

Suddenly his voice was not in my head; it was directly behind me, but I was sobbing so violently it didn't immediately sink in.

"Em, what's wrong? Are you okay? What is it?"

When I turned slowly around to confirm that he was indeed standing there, I saw the most perfect sight I'd ever laid eyes on. Seán stood uncertainly, dressed in wrinkled khaki shorts, a rumpled T-shirt, and he was barefoot. He looked as though he'd been woken unexpectedly from a nap by a crazy woman wailing on the beach behind his cottage. The wind ruffled his hair, and his face seemed to have aged since I'd seen it last only hours before; there were new lines of sadness etched on it. "Seán?"

Springing off the rock I launched myself at him. I heard a strangled cry, like a wounded animal being let out of a trap, and knew I had made it, and it did not stop as he wrapped me in his arms and held me tightly to his chest.

"Shhh," he soothed. "Shhh, it's okay; everything is going to be okay." Eventually I became aware of his hand stroking my hair and felt his chest heave as though he was trying to contain some great emotion. Slowly, slowly I came back to myself feeling as though I'd released an awful burden. Without a word, Seán reached into his pocket and brought out some tissues, which he offered me. Realizing why he had a pocket full of tissues almost made me start crying again.

"You're still here," I said, stating the obvious. "Your car was gone . . ."

"There was a problem with the steering. I dropped it off at the shop last night. *Marcel* gave me a ride home." He pointedly emphasized my brother's name. "Em, is everything okay?" Seán's face had always been an open book to me, and now I read that he couldn't believe I'd come back for the reason he hoped I was there. I could tell he was afraid I'd just come running to him to give him a definite no, maybe try to explain.

"Seán, I love you. I love you and I can't live without you. I . . ." I never made it any further because Seán crushed me to his chest and then in the next minute his lips found mine and we kissed hungrily, as though it was the only thing on earth that could save us. When he finally released me enough that I could lean back in his arms and look up into his face I saw many things written there. Love. Relief. And desire. The last one made my knees feel weak, and I was grateful for his arms.

"Seán, please marry me."

He hesitated for a moment, and I felt my stomach flip. Then he reached into the other pocket, and pulled out a small blue box. Grinning he sank onto one knee on the rock, which made me laugh. He opened the box to show me the ring but I didn't see it; I was looking into his eyes.

"Emerson," he said, a catch in his voice. "I love you with all my heart. Will you be my wife?"

"Yes!" I shouted, laughing. "Yes!" I flung myself at him again, and he toppled over, using the opportunity to roll me onto my back on the rock. Cradling the back of my head in his hand, he leaned over me, kissed me softly, and then rolled onto his back next to me so that we could both look up into the sky. Gray clouds scudded past, but I was so happy the heavens could have opened and drenched us, and it wouldn't have made a difference.

Seán was holding my left hand, and I felt him slip the engagement ring onto my finger. He jacked himself up on one elbow so he could look at me. I reached up and touched his beautiful face, tracing the line of his lips with my thumb.

"I love you," I said. "That first night you came over, and we played music . . . I didn't want it to end. I felt my soul connecting to yours. You've come to mean so much to me. I can't imagine my life without you."

"I wanted to share a future with you more than anything," Seán admitted huskily. "I just didn't know if I would have one to offer you. I thank God every moment that I do." Seán studied my face. Below, the waves crashed against the rocks, but now they seemed to caress them instead of battering them. Above Seán's head the clouds had disappeared, the sky a brilliant June blue that matched his eyes. I was so happy I could have stayed there forever. "Em? Will you marry me?"

I could tell by the tone of his voice that he wasn't joking around, but asking me something very important. "Yes, Seán, I will."

"Right now? Marise and Addy have agreed to be witnesses."

Marise . . . so *that's* what she'd been hiding, but Addy, too? The knowledge that he'd sought Addy's approval before approaching me, meant a great deal. I pulled his face close to mine and kissed him with all the pent-up feeling I'd been warring with for so many months. "Yes, Seán, I will."

Honestly, I didn't see how I could wait another minute to belong to this man who had so suddenly and completely claimed my heart. As he wrapped his arms around me I felt as though I had finally, finally come home.

The End (of The Beginning)

Acknowledgments and Apologies

It would be impossible to acknowledge all of the people, particularly musicians, who influenced the writing of this book because of the music I heard them play, or the music they taught me to play, but without traditional music this book would have died a lonely death as an unfinished file on my computer. However, I would be remiss not to thank my first fiddle teacher, Brendan Taaffe, who introduced me (or maybe it's more accurate to say, reintroduced me) to the music of my roots and taught me how to play traditional music by ear (something I never thought I could do.) And Pete Sutherland, a legend in his own time, who picked up where Brendan left off.

It is thanks to my friend Brad Krueger who asked questions that helped me to realize I should focus on traditional music rather than classical that resuscitated this story and gave it life. That one point was holding up the story and once it changed the rest practically wrote itself. (You know, eventually.)

Everyone with access to a computer and Google Earth can discover that there really is a town so close to Lake Champlain and Québec that if it moved one step closer to either, it would fall in or need to change citizenship. That town is not Toussaint, but it is where I grew up. Toussaint does not reflect the town as much in reality as it does in imagination, particularly my imagination, where it resides in a pristine state. I drop by to visit whenever I'm feeling nostalgic. In other words, the way I depicted the people and the town is not based on any kind of tangible reality. But some of its elements *are* based on fact.

The Home Demonstration Clubs in Vermont began in 1917. By 1939, there were more than 8,500 women enrolled in 308 community home demonstration groups. Home demonstration agents arranged meetings to demonstrate labor-saving devices and instruct homemakers on good household management, food preservation techniques, sanitation, and many other skills. In the early years, the agents traveled to the meetings and gave talks. My mother and mémère (and probably at least some of my aunts as well) were both in a Home Dem club at one time, and I remember my mother saying that there was often a speaker at the meetings, but whether this was an official agent by this time (the 1970s) or the members just took turns, I don't know. I do remember that they were always learning new things, and I wish now that I'd gotten involved.

The food Marise cooks is all traditional French Canadian food. Some of it I've eaten, or variations of it at least, and I have had some of the vegetarian counterparts and like them just fine. (Don't tell Emerson's mother though.) And I often make "cinnamon snails" with leftover pie crust. For recipes, consult the upcoming Farenorth Press Community Cookbook Project. The recipe introductions are good for a laugh, and some of the food is, too.

I'm sorry to say that I invented the drug efluximustine that cured Seán. But I give blanket permission to use the name if you would like to go out and invent a drug to cure brain cancer. The rest of Seán's medical history is plausible and medically accurate, but without a drug like efluximustine—or a miracle—he would not have survived.

I borrowed the syntax and pronunciation for Nicolette LaPierre's speech from my own mémère, Alberta Gagné, who spoke French all of her life and a heavily accented English when speaking to us kids. I loved to hear her and my mom, sitting in the kitchen speaking Franglais, slipping back and forth from French to English as easily as changing dance partners, throwing in anglicized French words like "le sweater". If I had a time machine I'd go back and listen to them again for a very long time.

People always wonder if authors put themselves in their books. People who know the author wonder, with even more interest, if they are in the book. I am sorry to say that no one I know personally appears in this book although for the first time I make a brief appearance in one of my books, a cameo really, Hitchcock-like. Only people who know me well, and have known me for a very long time, will recognize me. But I will offer two hints for those curious enough to puzzle it out: I appear as a teenager. And I didn't give myself any speaking lines. (I was a shy kid.) Oh, and to Brendan Krueger, who is the only person who might understand the French horn reference, I am truly, abjectly sorry. Still.

Lake Champlain, I apologize for writing bad things about you. I love you, and I miss you.

How to pronounce the names in this book:

Alphonse LaMotte: Al-fons La-mot
Agnès: Ahn-YES, if you're pronouncing it the French way, or Ag-ness if you're pronouncing it the English way.
Angelique: Ahn-zhah-LEEK
Armand Brouillard: Ar-man-d Brool-yah
Etienne (Stephen): e-TEA-yen (e - as in 'e' in 'pet', yen - rhymes with pen)
Gadbois: Gad-bwah
Giroux: Jir-oo
Jean-Guy: Jhawn-ghee
Louis-Philippe: Loo-ee-Fill-eep
Marise: Mah-rih-se
Marquette: Mar-ket
Mémère LaPierre: Meh-may La-pea-air
Nicolette: Nick-o-LET
Pacifique: Pas-ih-feek
Seán Bachand: Shawn Bah-shan
St. Croix: Sahnt Crwah

French translations:

Absolument: absolutely
Bienvenue: welcome
Brune: brown
Ça va mal: I'm not doing well; I'm terrible/bad.
Chéri/e: dear, darling
Comment ça va? Or Ça va? (more informal): how are you?
J'ai besoin vous: I need you
Ma chère: my dear
Misère: misery
Misère de chein: Literally: dog misery; figuratively an expression of exasperation or dismay. Also an expression my mother always used to indicate exasperation.
Pauvre: poor
Pauvre petite chouette: Poor little cabbage (a term of endearment)
Pièce de résistance: crowning achievement
Pet de soeur: (Nun's farts—don't ask) A type of pastry made by spreading pie dough with butter, cinnamon, and sugar, rolling it up and cutting it in thin slices and then baking it.
Poutine (poo-tsin): A dish that originated in Québec, Canada. French fries topped with brown gravy and cheese curds.
Quel dommage: What a shame.
Qu-est que tu fait?: What are you doing?
Salut: Hello
Tant pis: too bad, tough
Tête-à-tête: face-to-face
Tête dure: hard head
Tout de suite: Immediately
Très bien/Très bon: very well/very good
Un petit peu: A little bit.
Viens vite: come quick
Vite: quick, hurry, colloquially "Get a move on."

Bible verses used or referred to in this book:

"Jesus said to him, 'I am the way, the truth, and the life. No one comes to the Father except through Me'" (John 14:6, NKJV).

"Heal me, O Lord, and I shall be healed; save me, and I shall be saved, for You are my praise" (Jeremiah 17:14, NKJV).

"Then, because you belong to Christ Jesus, God will bless you with peace that no one can completely understand. And this peace will control the way you think and feel" (Philippians 4:7, CEV).

"Be strong and courageous. Do not be afraid; do not be discouraged, for the Lord your God will be with you wherever you go" (Joshua 1:9, NIV).

If you enjoyed this book, you may also like other books by this author. They include:

Digital and Print:
Life & Death
Salome's Charger (with Glen Robinson)
The Shaking
The Disciples
Prayer Warriors
Guardians
Prayer Warriors: The Final Chapter
Playing God
Making Sabbath Special

Digital Only:
Eleventh Hour (with Eric Stoffle, updated version)
Midnight Hour (with Eric Stoffle, updated version)

Print Only:
The Third Coming
Eleventh Hour (with Eric Stoffle, original version)
Midnight Hour (with Eric Stoffle, original version)
Joy: The Secret of Being Content
I Call Him Abba
Adventist Family Traditions
Making Holidays Special
Banza's Incredible Journey (and other stories from ADRA)
Sunnyside Up (with Eric Stoffle)
Juventud y Alegria
The Shoebox Kids: Jenny's Cat-napped Cat
More Power to Ya
iChoose Life

For more information, visit the author's website: cperrinowalker.com. For updates on new releases and to be eligible for prize drawings, sign up for the Reader's Group. (Links on any page of the website.)